JUL 2 0 2022

WHERE DOGS BARK WITH THEIR TAILS

Where Dogs Bark with Their Tails

Estelle-Sarah Bulle

TRANSLATED FROM THE FRENCH BY
JULIA GRAWEMEYER

FARRAR, STRAUS AND GIROUX   NEW YORK

Farrar, Straus and Giroux
120 Broadway, New York 10271

Library of Congress Cataloging-in-Publication Data
Names: Bulle, Estelle-Sarah, 1974– author. | Grawemeyer, Julia, translator.
Title: Where dogs bark with their tails : a novel / Estelle-Sarah Bulle ; translated from the French by Julia Grawemeyer.
Other titles: Là où les chiens aboient par la queue. English
Description: First American edition. | New York : Farrar, Straus and Giroux, 2022.
Identifiers: LCCN 2022005439 | ISBN 9780374289096 (hardback)
Subjects: LCGFT: Novels.
Classification: LCC PQ2702.U53 L313 2022 | DDC 843/.92—dc23/eng/20220204
LC record available at https://lccn.loc.gov/2022005439

Designed by Abby Kagan

Our books may be purchased in bulk for promotional, educational, or business use. Please contact your local bookseller or the Macmillan Corporate and Premium Sales Department at 1-800-221-7945, extension 5442, or by email at MacmillanSpecialMarkets@macmillan.com.

www.fsgbooks.com
www.twitter.com/fsgbooks • www.facebook.com/fsgbooks

10 9 8 7 6 5 4 3 2 1

To my parents
To my children

WHERE DOGS BARK WITH THEIR TAILS

I LEFT MORNE-GALANT AT DAWN. It was the only way to avoid baking in the sun. Morne-Galant is nowhere, that is to say, a womb from which I freed myself the way a calf extracts itself from its mother: legs first, willing to risk its life in order to tear itself away from the loins holding it back. I had witnessed it dozens of times before I turned seven, the threat of a bad end looming as a calf was being born. Papa always allowed it to happen that way; nature deciding who lives and who dies.

And yet, Papa loved his livestock. He had five or six head of cattle by the time I left. They lived around the outskirts of the property, and their prolonged lowing grew hoarse as they insisted we take them out to the corrugated iron trough in the middle of the field. One by one, Papa would unhook the chains from the stakes and they would run to the trough. On scorching days, they'd strangle themselves if he didn't move quickly enough. He would settle them with a sharp cry, *"Là!"* and slap the nervous bulls with the butt end of his machete. He left the little ones unchained for their first three months so they could stay close to their mothers.

Back then, Hilaire treated his children like he treated his animals: a glassful of tenderness, a bucketful of authority, and a barrelful of "*débrouyé zòt*'"—best figure it out yourselves. At the sparsely populated edge of the town—half an hour on foot down the main path, which even by our standards then you couldn't call a road—there was only us and the cattle. In those days, Morne-Galant dozed, curled tight into itself. Guadeloupeans still say this about Morne-Galant: "*Cé la chyen ka japé pa ké*." Your father never spoke to you in Créole, so I'll translate it for you: Morne-Galant is where dogs' bark with their tails.

I did see some strange dogs and other apparitions late at night. Hilaire would often leave us at the house by ourselves and I would wait for him by the window. As soon as the sun set, we would close the shutters, and the hens would climb one by one to perch high atop the mango tree. The soft sound of the crickets muffled all other noises around the house. We children played around the table, naked. We fought over a doll made of grass or a frightened *souda* hermit crab. Night would settle in with its gold-enameled moon against the dark sky and the light from the kerosene lamp would flicker. We'd fumble around in the dark as we unfolded our beds. I'd often have a hard time sleeping and would open the shutters, looking out for Hilaire on the horizon.

At sixteen, I waited for the right moment, braved the spirits of the night, and, as soon as I heard the song of the pipiri that morning, hit the road, never to return. There may be more important departures in my life—all the way up to my departure from this Earth when the Virgin Mother will open her arms to me and say with her beautiful soft voice, "This is the end"—but the only two that truly counted were when I left Morne-Galant in 1947 and when I left Pointe-à-Pitre twenty years later, the afternoon when I took my first flight to Paris, leaving behind everything that I had built.

Though it's been an eternity since I arrived in Paris, I still haven't quite found a place that feels like home. Sometimes I run into other Antilleans, but they live out in the suburbs—that no-man's-land where buildings have sprouted like sick flowers in the middle of muddy fields. I see so few Antilleans in the capital: only the unhappiest and the most tenacious of them are still hanging on here, all the rest are just spineless.

I have known Algerians—too thin, still working at the factory. Taciturn Chinese vendors who sell us the soursop fruit that grew so easily behind our house back home. If I ever fight with the Senegalese who collect my trash and yell at them to go back to their country, they glare at me and call me a slave sold off by their ancestors. But *they* are all foreigners. Whereas I am just as French as these Whites who mistake me for an African.

I am comforted by the sisters of Sacré-Coeur who give me saint medals and encourage me when I mess up the canticles with my shrill voice. They love to hear me talk, especially the new ones; fragile, pale girls arriving from Indonesia or someplace, speechless Congolese women who after a few months become too chatty. I never went to school past junior high, but I know how to tell a story, especially about the angels who come to visit me.

I've held gold in my hands. I am talking about real nuggets, those heavy, beautiful little things. I have never had a boss and I'll never have one. I'm not one of those women who sit bored behind the glass of some welcome window of an administrative building or who walk up and down empty hallways at night between desks with a mop in their hands. I don't worry about having a fatherless son going astray while I'm breaking my back at work. But I was like them all for a long time, stiffening each time a White French person joked about my accent or my hair, scheming for months in advance to buy the cheapest ticket possible out of Morne-Galant.

So now, *petite*, you've come here to see me, and you're wondering where our place is, the place for those of us who come from between two worlds. Your father will surely tell you a different story. I raised him as well as I could, my brother. Siblings can still love each other even though they act like strangers toward one another.

You tell me that there's no solidarity among Antilleans. But if you throw any ten people in a waiting room, do you think they're going to end up as one big happy family? Guadeloupe is like a waiting room where they've randomly thrown together *Nègres* who have nothing to do with each other. These *Nègres* don't know what they are doing there—either they are waiting for a White person to show up or they are looking for the exit.

Take a seat over there. I'll do your hair since it needs a good untangling. But first, show me your hands. Ah, you see, that's why we get along so well. We have a magnetic energy, a *fluence*, a witchy kind of connection. There, I can feel it in the tips of your fingers. Do you feel it? Like a protective wave of electricity. Don't laugh, one day you might need it.

You're thirty years old and I'm seventy-five. Even though I'm sitting right here in front of you, it's like there's a whole century standing between you and me, along with seven thousand kilometers and an ocean. You could never imagine the journey I've taken, even though you've been before. You grew up with the orderly streets of that soulless Parisian suburb where you were born. Your father drove you to school every day in a car. Well, when I was little, I woke up to the rooster crowing under the window and I went to school on foot, if I went at all.

1947-1948

The Niece

AND THAT'S HOW my conversations with my aunt Antoine started. I walked up rue Poulet for the first time with my mind full of questions, not having told her I was coming to her store, hoping to surprise her. When I rang the bell, two dogs started barking asthmatically. Antoine opened the door, scolding them gently, routinely. I saw her in the doorway: a tall woman wearing the same confident smile that I hadn't seen in years. Her eyes sparkled beneath her thick white hair, hastily pulled back as though she had started a sensible coif and then abandoned it halfway through. She placed her long fingers on my shoulders and kissed my cheeks familiarly, as though we had seen each other just the night before. Her face smelled like jojoba oil and Miss Antilles hair lotion. Her face was full, radiant, barely wrinkled.

My last memory of Antoine was of her hunched silhouette as she stood on a metro platform after one of her rare visits to our house. I was a teenager. My father and I had driven her to the Créteil-Préfecture metro station. I had liked her strange allure, a mixture of outdated elegance and anarchy. At that point, I had heard so much about her that I would have been disappointed with anything less. She wore a dark green rain-coat that weighed down her shoulders and she had not taken it off the entire day. She wore old men's shoes and held a delicate, faux-leather handbag. When she stood up from the kitchen table where we had gossiped over tea until dusk, she adjusted the classic veiled fascinator on top of her head. I laughed inwardly at my father's seriousness, his face stony all afternoon, later in the car and then again on the metro platform. He was annoyed and distracted, his gaze floating a bit above her, his demeanor betraying impatience and the haste with which he would have liked to rush her into the metro car.

Few people other than Antoine, his older sister, had this effect on him. It was comical and mysterious to watch. He was usually open and smiling, offering an empathy and warmth toward others that earned their trust easily, even strangers. But with Antoine, I could see that the effort he made in order to hold back his rage—and protect himself— was written all over his face. Each word she spoke, no matter how harmless, was an attack against all that was important to him: moderation, serenity, a rational and analytical approach to the world. I saw in him a child struggling silently against powers at once loving and terrifying. One day he told me very proudly that he had never fought with his sisters, not once. He preferred running from them.

Fifteen years after that day in the metro, I entered the old building that had once been Antoine's store, nestled below the Sacré-Coeur Basilica. Now that I was an adult, I wanted to speak with Antoine alone. I wanted her to tell me about the past—about Guadeloupe, about her family—in her own words.

When I saw her, she still looked a little bit like a friendly witch that the British are fond of, Mary Poppins–style or *Bedknobs and Broomsticks*. I didn't need to pass any kind of test to get her talking, though; she opened up right away. I think she was happy I'd recognized that she was the link from the past to the present, from Guadeloupe to Paris, like an underground root, full of life.

For our next visits, she insisted on coming to my house. I lived in the eighteenth arrondissement on boulevard Ornano. She wanted to see what my apartment was like and how I lived, and to cuddle my three-month-old daughter. She was happy to have a reason to stride across the neighborhood she knew so well. On the way over, she would stop in front of the Chinese grocer's stall and inhale the scent of citronella stems to gauge how fresh they were. She would bring me infusions of aloe vera that she had steeped in plastic bottles or a lumpy dessert sprinkled with bits of egg swimming in cloudy milk. I would swallow it all down so as not to hurt her feelings. When she left, I would watch her for a long time from the window as she walked away. She was a whole head taller than the other pedestrians, who seemed tiny in comparison, and only after she had passed would they seem to be of normal height.

In our family, everyone calls my father Petit-Frère, Little Brother, as though he had never been anything other than the fragile being my aunts shepherded, more or less, through childhood, back when they weren't totally lacking in tenderness. There had been tenderness, certainly, but measured out, like salt or bread.

I was born into what looks like a typical French family, but without clearly defined relationships. For example, a childhood friend at our house can also be considered a cousin and referred to as such. We see our real cousins rarely and then they are forgotten. Others—illegitimate children swept in with the rain and whose paternity is never really known—become cherished brothers, even more than brothers by blood.

My family fills an entire street in Morne-Galant, all of them Ezechiels, which quickly drives any new postman crazy. A sister can be the godmother of her own brother, who will call her *"marraine"* as opposed to her official first name. That's how it works with Antoine and my father. When he calls her *"marraine,"* I hear only *"ma reine,"* my queen. And now I know that she has all the makings of a sovereign, proud and independent.

When I was a teenager, prone to leaving my clothes all over the floor, I'd shrug as my parents lectured me for the hundredth time to reconsider my outfit or stand up straight. When I was being disrespectful, Antoine's name would always surface: "There you go, acting just like your aunt Antoine!" or, "Well you certainly get *that* from Antoine!" For a while, my parents were slightly worried about the size of my feet. They would declare with resignation: "The same feet as her aunt!" Upon first glance, the comparison wasn't very complimentary. But a tiny part of me was flattered because even though people said my aunt had a lot of character flaws, I could sense a certain admiration for her, the woman who was accountable to nothing but her own desires throughout her life, with no regrets whatsoever, all while cultivating an art of catastrophe.

UNTIL I WAS THIRTEEN, my parents, brother, and I lived in Créteil, on the ninth floor of a rectangular black-and-white tower at the intersection of rue Lepaire and rue Marie-Curie. I liked to sit at the window, my back to the sky and flirting with the danger of falling thirty meters backward to the ground. As a little girl, I was a good student and kept a low profile, not wanting to stand out. I would imagine myself becoming invisible, melting into the view that stretched out around me. I liked becoming as neutral as the big, straight roads, and the succession of buildings laid out according to the social standing of the people living there: the lower the rent, the narrower the building's windows.

From my lookout spot, I would puzzle over the countless little details about our family that, in my opinion, made us unlike other families. Why did we tend to widen the circle of our extended family until you could no longer discern its boundaries? And why did my father's friends and neighbors tease him about his noticeable lilting accent, his dropped *r*'s, as he, a French citizen, tortured the French while trying to speak it? Why did my grandfather exist as only a gruff voice most of the time, ghostlike after traveling the seven thousand kilometers of telephone lines stretched across the ocean?

Our neighborhood on the outskirts of Paris was the giant maelstrom of the middle class, where diverse lifestyles were swept up in the current of uniformity that characterizes the French Republican model of *"vivre-ensemble,"* the peaceful co-existence of those willing to embrace French ideals. In the midst of this heap of offshore debris on the suburban outskirts of the city, Antilleans were one minority among others and *métis*, mixed-race children, were a rarity. The term *métis* was rarely used. I felt like I was somehow breaking the rules on the rare occasions that I declared myself *métisse* at school, with my friends, or in the street. To be mixed-race is to be caught in between—in that space that resists categorization. Our French neighbors, newly arrived from the department of Sarthe or from Deux-Sèvres, our second- or third-generation Portuguese neighbors, and even the poorer Parisians didn't know what to call me. They had my father figured out more easily. After five minutes of talking with him, they would say,

"Oh! Réunion Island! We've been meaning to go there on vacation!"*

My father would politely correct them, but for most people, the Antilles, a bit like Africa, was a single entity too complicated to separate into precise geographic areas, which included the ensemble of French overseas departments and territories, all the way out into the Pacific Ocean, into the Indian Ocean. And for most people, French Guiana is an island and Guadeloupe and Martinique are interchangeable! But we couldn't be too mad at our neighbors, since we had a hard time locating Croatia on a map, where our building's janitor was from, or the Algerian port city of Béjaïa, where my brother's best friend returned every summer, or the coasts of the Algarve, which were on posters in the living room of my first babysitter, a Portuguese woman who cooked me the most delicious buttered rice.

All during the late seventies until the end of the eighties, my parents saved up so that every two years they could buy tickets to Guadeloupe on Air France. My mother was always thrilled to go. I was of two minds and I wondered why she was so enthusiastic. What was so exciting about burying herself deep in the countryside, far from what she knew—my mother, who grew up going to festivals in Borinage near the French border in Belgium, who was accustomed to early mornings with hot espresso and the blooming cherry trees in summer? Why would she be excited to find herself in this mysterious place, where the day falls upside down, where people live without running water or electricity, where rats and toads eye you suspiciously, where you get caught under a sweltering sun that is tempered only by the shade of a sizzling-hot piece of sheet metal?

---

* Réunion is in the Indian Ocean; Guadeloupe is in the Caribbean Sea. —Trans.

During my first days in Morne-Galant, I was pretty bored and I missed the orderly streets of the city. And then little by little, I was sucked into the beauty of the vegetation, so strong that it enters you from every angle and seizes all of your senses: a violent red of petals against dark green leaves, the scent of rotting almonds, the salty breath of the sea, the sting of fire ants. I saw my father become the pillar of support for his own father, who would hide his tears when we climbed into the car to return to the airport after a monthlong visit.

Once back at home, I wondered why Papa and those like him—people with the same skin color and the same lilting accent that was as ever-present as the bandage *Tintin*'s Captain Haddock never managed to shake off—had such a warm demeanor compared to the rest of the world, a demeanor that barely masked a deep fragility. He spoke openly to me about his childhood, and throughout all of mine, I listened happily.

I never said anything about this constant feeling of confusion, of being out of step, since there were certainly more complicated family situations than my own. I should have considered myself lucky to have a stable family environment and two working parents. Some of my friends moved constantly between living with their families and foster homes. Some fathers spent entire days at the bar. Others didn't speak French and never left the house. For most of the adults, situations were so complicated that it was clear that we, their children, were the future.

One year, I decided to ask my father and his sisters about their past and how they each ended up leaving their island. I asked all three of them, but separately. My grandfather, Hilaire, had just died at the age of 105, and shortly thereafter, I'd given birth to my daughter. As I held my baby's small, smooth hand in my own, I thought of the touch of Hilaire's old hand—rough but gentle, with wide nails—as he had held me at four years old, then nine, then eleven, his grip becoming less and less sure as the years went on. I wanted to hear stories about Guadeloupe, stories from back in Hilaire's time and stories about what came after, to connect the threads of these stories with the ones that I had already heard. One by one, Antoine, Lucinde, and Petit-Frère offered me their memories. I took notes and didn't show them to anyone.

Years passed; my own family grew older, and I became increasingly caught up in busy adult life. Then, ten years later, during a particularly harsh winter, I practically fled to visit Guadeloupe, which made me think back to those conversations and to my notes. The voices had all tightened into a chaos inside of me, one that I needed to untangle and piece apart. When I returned to Paris, I dug out my notebooks from the bottom of a drawer. The words, expressions, and snippets of conversations hastily scrawled returned to me like a conversation that I'd only just had. More and more, I wanted to put it on the page. I balked and waited some more. One day, Antoine, Lucinde, and even Petit-Frère would be gone. So I set to work at last, trying to recount as accurately as possible the narratives they had entrusted to me. I tried to preserve the scenes and conversations that they had re-created for me in our exchanges. I hoped to understand, by looking backward, the contours of my own existence.

Antoine: Childhood in Morne-Galant

PAPA AND MAMAN WOULD LEAVE EARLY in the morning to take care of the animals and open the store that you could see as you entered the village of Morne-Galant. Your aunt Lucinde and I would eat in silence, a bit of fraxinella mixed with hot water. When Maman went into town, Lucinde and I would go to school. It was five kilometers on foot to the middle of the town. I could have easily stayed all day, wandering through the big woods next to the house, but Maman could see from her spot inside the store, her elbows resting on the countertop, whether or not we walked by. If she could have supervised Papa the way she supervised us, maybe things would have turned out better.

The other kids didn't talk to us much and I pretended it didn't bother me. We lived too far away from the other houses, and having a mother like ours did not help. Because of her, they ignored us. Despite the fact that each family stocked up on goods from Maman's *lolo*, more than a few adults talked about her behind her back, and you know that children guzzle down gossip like coconut water. First there was the color of her skin, a sort of off-white color. And then there was the mahogany trunk that she brought to her wedding, which was the only thing of value in our house. That alone was enough to make people wonder about the money we had.

I must say that she dazzled me and Lucinde as well, turning even her own daughters' heads. We loved to watch her closely at night: her thin, pale arms and long hair that dropped down to her waist, her two lovely headscarves with fringe that she would fold carefully away in the trunk. It made us feel superior to the other children. I was her daughter, but deep down, even I would observe her as though I had not been born of her myself. It seemed impossible, the incredible difference between her and us; Maman so slight and small, me so tall with my big feet, long neck, with my dark cocoa skin and my kinky hair. Lucinde inherited her tiny waist. In every other respect, we looked like Hilaire, your grandfather.

I couldn't see myself in her and maybe that's why we were never close. She always preferred Lucinde. She'd call out, "*Minette*, honey, come here!" and Lucinde would run to her and jump into her arms. I wasn't jealous of all that. I found my sister weak and manipulative. Everything she did was for one reason only: to prove her superiority to our parents. She tried to steal more than her fair share of the attention. She obeyed them like a trembling little calf, and after Maman died, she transferred her need for approval onto the town's gossiping matriarchs until she found a way out. Lucinde is a two-way mirror; that's her survival strategy.

The other thing that made Maman seem strange in the eyes of the hillbillies in Morne-Galant was how she arrived from Grands Fonds—just like that, on the back of Hilaire's horse, Hilaire sitting up straight under his dark hat, a bloody wound at his temple, clutching the reins in his huge hands. The fair-skinned beauty was sitting behind one of the darkest *Nègres* in the region, who was also one of the most *brigand*, like we say at home, one of the best bandits—it was a slap in the face to both of their worlds.

I told you that we lived in the poorest part of Morne-Galant, which, at that time, had only one road and just ten houses. Even though we were isolated, we still belonged to the town; we constituted a part of it. Any visitor could stop by our house on the way back from Port James or come in and negotiate a day's pay for work in the sugarcane fields. But farther from us, back deep in the woods, there was a dirt path that turned left, then right, then right again, snaking beneath the green shoulders of the hills.

Back there you would find another world. The route to get there wasn't too difficult. Maybe eight or ten kilometers of hairpin turns squeezed between two cliffs covered over in roots getting larger and larger, ferns dripping with rain, and mist condensation. The deeper in you went, the lighter the skin of the people living there. At the heart of this mille feuille, this ever-growing foliage, lived the people everyone called the Blancs-Matignon—difficult people to approach. We were afraid of them. And that's where Maman came from.

Maman's family, the Lebecqs, were Bretons who had come to Guadeloupe as poor and desolate as Job, two or three hundred years before. They fought to make it, there on the slopes that were never bathed in sunlight, but where the earth was soft, rich, and as black as coffee grounds. They prospered quietly thanks to their cultivation of coffee and cocoa, and then they attempted to grow cotton. They were hardworking, protective of their earnings, not rich enough to afford slaves, but they would never allow any *Nègres* to move in and settle into the hollows and folds of their land, where they would have ended up mixing.

From what I gather, over the centuries, crises would sweep

over them like storms that they would endure, backs curved against them. The price of cocoa and coffee tanked, the cotton never took. They started breeding horses and would hike up from time to time to sell vegetables to poor Blacks and White sugarcane plantation owners alike. They wouldn't associate with either group. They had complicated alliances with the families that looked like them, stuffed away as they were in the furrows of earth that they had learned to love with all their hearts and souls.

Little by little, the patois of Brittany, Normandy, and Franche-Comté disappeared. When I was young, they spoke only Créole and it baffled me, these blue-eyed White people speaking the language forbidden to us children—if we ever spoke it, we would get our mouths washed out with soap. To be honest, in some ways the Blancs-Matignon lived more like former slaves than the former slave masters. But they insisted on keeping their blood as untainted as possible.

It would take Papa returning with Maman on that mare of his that never left his side—Papa, who was afraid of nothing and was as arrogant as a fighting rooster. He must have met Eulalie at a village dance or maybe while buying a kilo of rice in the tiny store where she worked. Can you imagine the earthquake their relationship must have caused in that little green gully protected from every kind of intrusion? So then Eulalie's two brothers assumed the role of cowboys from the Old West, willing to take a knife to Hilaire to protect the pretty, delicate flower that was their sister, Eulalie.

One night with scarves masking their faces, they ambushed Hilaire on a dark path as he was passing through on his way to the dance where he was to meet Eulalie. Hilaire's mind was full of plans for the evening when the two brothers stepped out in front of him like ghosts in the night. His mare lurched quickly to the side, snorting wildly, and the frogs fell quiet. At first, he thought they were *soukounians*, the devil's wicked servants—monsters who had come to drain him of his vitality and spit him out like an empty shell. But as they drew nearer, knives in hand, Hilaire recognized the feverish eyes behind their scarves.

Before Hilaire had set eyes on their younger sister, he and the Lebecq brothers had been longtime friends. They had played dominoes until two in the morning, shared recipes of concoctions to make their fighting roosters stronger, even coating them in an ointment that would poison the opponent's bird. They had shared the same rum around a slaughtered pig, its throat slit to celebrate a wedding. The truth was, the Lebecq brothers had always loved Hilaire for his constant good mood, his lack of malice, and his endless stories, rattled off in Créole.

At the dances, Hilaire dove into a mazurka or a fistfight with the same enthusiasm. The Lebecq brothers, who weren't ordinarily daredevil types, followed his lead and would have died at his side in a brawl. On our little island where everyone knew everything, Hilaire and the Lebecq brothers shared an entire life, a boyhood. The only things that the brothers would never share with Hilaire was their blood or their future.

That's why the brothers waited for him there in the middle of the night, spurred on by their mother. Man Lebecq, your great-grandmother, who never left Grands Fonds unless a hurricane came and drove her out. But she was the most vindictive of them all, and her sons adored her.

So there at the bottom of the ravine, Hilaire had two choices: gallop off and try to dodge the blades of their knives, or face certain death. He didn't wait long to decide: he knew the two brothers well and he must have noticed the hesitation in their feet, the barely perceptible trembling of their hands holding the knives. They were huddled too close together, waiting, not knowing who should strike first. So he stopped his horse and called down to them from the saddle, first in a friendly tone, then more firmly.

The brothers came closer and demanded he dismount. Hilaire allowed his beloved mare to take a few steps back, afraid that they would try to slice the backs of her legs. He loved the mare with all his heart and never would have allowed anyone to hurt her. He raised his voice even more and, at that time of night, it must have resonated throughout the countryside, startling a few souls out of sleep, making the dogs bark. The Lebecq brothers must have attempted to snag the reins from him, but Hilaire wouldn't let them slip in behind him. He kept talking.

As the minutes ticked by, the brothers thought about the police, since they would have to kill Hilaire to accomplish their mission, and then bury him deep in the hillside where the crabs would slowly pick his skeleton clean. They'd have to slaughter the mare, too. It occurred to them that the whole endeavor was much more complicated than they'd envisioned that morning, sitting next to Man Lebecq as she restlessly rocked in her chair.

Deep in the gully, the three of them slowly circled one another in some kind of macabre dance. The two brothers realized that if they didn't speed things along and make a move, someone would surely take notice and come to investigate.

At that moment, the good Lord decided enough was enough. Just as one of the brothers was about to attack the mare, an otherworldly light began to materialize, falling noiselessly upon them from high above. The luminous blue veil of silent sparks chased the dark of the night away. They froze in the blinding light, as though angels had come to sit without a sound on the branches around them. All the nearby plants started to quiver, the leaves and trees speaking to one another. The men were too terrified to fight each other. The Lebecq brothers stepped back. The blue streams of light converged to form a shining cloud that hung still, just above their heads. After a few seconds, the cloud drifted to the left, gathered speed, and took off into the night, its trail disappearing in the dark. Everything was calm again. The stars shone, all-knowing, in the clear sky. The Lebecqs retreated, kissing their holy Communion medals. Papa calmed his mare and continued on his way.

OH, YOU DON'T BELIEVE ME? You think that this is another one of my visions and that I'm turning a simple rainstorm into a divine manifestation? And why not believe me? The night is not a liar like the day is. It's during nighttime that you can read inside yourself just like a book, and see others as they truly are. What I know is that Hilaire was courageous that night and that the Lebecqs, in a way, accepted him. Maybe your grandfather's formidable reputation was enough to deter them.

During World War I, he fought an officer on the boat that was taking them to Lebanon. There, he developed a reputation of being a fighter, which he maintained that whole time—so much so that they started calling him *Gros-Vaisseau*. That's how people knew him, Big Ship, equally ready for trouble and for a party, from Morne-Galant all the way to the other end of Guadeloupe. And maybe also the Lebecqs didn't actually want to target him. But that didn't mean that he was out of the woods.

When the Lebecq brothers came back to their homes and told their version of the story, Eulalie must have had a good cry about it, then decided that she would choose her own destiny. Hilaire went to see her a few weeks later. By the end of the visit, his smooth talk had her falling in love with him. He had paid his dues to the Lebecqs with that small cut on his forehead. That cut was really from Man Lebecq, your great-grandmother. And it must be said that I am not entirely absent from this part of the story, either, where the Lebecqs give up their fight, because on the day that Hilaire made his triumphant return to Morne-Galant with that blood on his forehead, I was already in Eulalie's womb.

THE LAND OF MORNE-GALANT where we settled is the land of the Ezechiel family: Papa's side. I'm not saying "our" family because the other Ezechiels considered us separate from them. We were, after all, Hilaire's children and half-Lebecq. There are five sisters and four brothers on the Ezechiel side, and Papa is the oldest. Each sibling spread out to try their luck across the island. In Morne-Galant, only Papa stayed behind to work the sugarcane. Hilaire's grandmother had been born on a plantation and had borne witness to the scars from the whip on the backs of her parents. As an adult, she was smart enough to buy a bit of land to ensure a future for herself, and to marry a man who had the same ambitions she did: she was the first Ezechiel to no longer be a slave and also the first officially registered to her last name. She was so smart that, fifty years after abolition, after years of patience and toiling, the family finally possessed twelve acres and only Hilaire knew the exact map of it—one border defined by a lone gum tree, the other marked by a collapsed bridge over-taken by purslane roots.

Sugarcane is the hardest work there is, the most painful in all of Grande-Terre. Therefore, Papa's brothers and sisters nearly all left to seek out a future elsewhere. But they considered Hilaire head of the family and guardian of the land where the wind plays in the furry tufts topping the pale blond cane—tender green, or dry and white, depending on the season. They always treated Hilaire like he was crazy for living with us in this remote corner of the island without running water or electricity, but they were indeed pleased that he took on the role of guarding the farm, because although it was grueling to work it, land was land.

Papa loved being loved so much that he couldn't turn down the role of patriarch of the Ezechiel clan. Once his brothers and sisters nudged him forward, he didn't resist. Perhaps he also thought that in doing so he would impress the Lebecqs. He made a point of paying taxes in the name of the entire family each time the administration remembered his tiny bit of Guadeloupe, unfindable on the map. He would show up at the tax collector's office with his worn-out fedora, his cleanest shirt, and his pointy dress shoes, a red handkerchief in his hand, and sit down to emphatically sign a three-figure check.

I never saw a single Ezechiel accompany Papa. Not one uncle or aunt offered to pay for any of it—even after the pack of fatherless boys and girls living next to us expanded, children adopted or begotten by Hilaire's sisters, when a temporary husband moved in with one or two rejects and then left them behind. They figured that Papa should be the one to pay. Papa's absurd pride about his land would be our downfall.

Little by little, because life was harsh, the Ezechiels

returned to Morne-Galant. I would see them coming up the dusty road. One year, it was an aunt with a giant clubfoot who would scowl at me and wait until evening to talk with Hilaire. Another was the daughter of the third sister who had lost one hand in a distillery accident and was looking to settle here, expecting Hilaire to buy her four steers. Then it was a cousin who was half *dek-dek*, a little crazy, and who may not have even had anything to do with our family at all. Having forgotten where he lived, he'd shown up on the advice of a neighbor simply because Ezechiel was one of his two last names.

Papa distributed plots of land to them as if they were the dominoes he dealt on Friday nights to his friends. Money and material possessions didn't mean much to him. But on the other hand, he loved deciding where each person's plot of land would be. He drove a stake into the soil to announce his decision while a relative looked on with respect and showered him with kind words. Papa, that idiot, was full of pride and continued to buy everyone's animals and pay their taxes, and front the money for the wedding of a cousin or the tuition of his youngest brother, who wanted to become a customs officer. I never understood how his heart could swing so wildly between two modes: it was always *yes* for them and *no* for us, his children. So much so that we would go hungry while he traveled into town to buy a pair of shoes for one of his nephews.

YOU TELL ME I'M OBSESSED with all these stories about money, but because of him, all we have now by way of an inheritance is words. It was Mother's blood that we lost, drop by drop, in all his business deals. If the sugarcane rotted before the harvest, or if it didn't bring in any money because of the war, or if there wasn't any livestock to sell, Hilaire took money from her. To think that on top of all that, there were also the cock-fights, the specialty of Morne-Galant. Imagine Hilaire, valiantly pulling from his pocket the fattest pack of bills that the island's bank had ever seen, and you would have an idea of where Eulalie's savings went. She tolerated it for our sake, even though the Ezechiels secretly wished that the new *lolo* she opened in town would fail. All of that meanness, based only on the fact that her braid swung too conspicuously down her back, that her light eyes had an unnerving quality to them, that she could read and count, that she kept two scarves in her mahogany trunk. And because they thought she had mountains of gold since she was a Blanc-Matignon.

At first, her husband's behavior put Mother in an awful, angry state. But she never said a thing because she knew she was being watched and that people were waiting for the moment when they could say that her failure was a foregone conclusion. Especially the Lebecqs, who were still bitter. She couldn't admit that her husband was stealing from her while he played the benevolent feudal lord to the detriment of his own family. So for a time she persisted. She worked for all six of us; in the morning with the animals, during the day with her *lolo* where she could sell a pair of glasses to a blind person, and in the evenings digging in the garden that she and Hilaire had at the top of the hill.

Antoine: One Bad Jolt and Then I Was Gone

SO I WAS BORN FIRST, and for my legal name, they chose Apollone. But for my *nom de savane*, they chose Antoine, the name that you know me by. In Guadeloupe, we give every baby a baptismal name, but we use a *nom de savane* to confuse the evil spirits—everyone calls me Antoine, and very few people know my real name. After me came Lucinde, and then a baby who died prematurely, and then your father, whom we call Petit-Frère. By the time she fell to pieces because she was so angry and so full of shame, Eulalie was pregnant again.

And the kind of illness she had did not make things any easier given her already having left her family, her isolation, and so on. The doctor said she couldn't eat salt, and he talked about eclampsia—seizures during a pregnancy—as a serious condition that required her to get a lot of rest. But I don't see how she could have ever rested. Her days began before dawn and finished after dark.

One day when I was six or seven years old, I saw her go pale midsentence and fall suddenly to the floor like a panic-stricken lizard. I was alone with her at the house, and when I saw her collapse, the best thing I could think to do was slip some grains of salt on her tongue to wake her up; that's how we did it back then. She was so pale and so still that I was terrified. After a moment, she felt the salt on her tongue and it woke her up. She looked at me, her eyes regaining their focus, and said, angrily: "You know very well that I can't eat salt!" It felt like an electric shock. From that moment on, I tried to spend as much time away from the house as I could, to separate myself from that constant state of worry.

The doctor wasn't happy; he said that this pregnancy would kill her. And then the doctor stopped coming because the war started and made everything more difficult. I remember her waddling around, her enormous belly preventing her from walking upright. To see her like that threw me into an inexpressible, inexplicable rage. She miscarried, and recovered from it very slowly.

So the war danced around us like a goat in heat. The governor who had been sent by Pétain put requisitions in place that sucked the island dry of its wealth. Everyone worked their own plot of land to scrape by, but half of what we grew was claimed by the government. The animals disappeared. We began to go hungry. A few neighbors hid a pig in their home for months at the risk of being thrown in jail if they were discovered. The pig's throat was slit in secret at the bottom of a gully under the cover of night. It fed two or three families for months.

Mother went back to work somehow after her miscarriage, but returning during wartime was difficult. Then she became pregnant with your father, which threw us back into feeling anxious about her health. But, as though the baby understood that he shouldn't ask for too much, he arrived early. He was premature and small at seven months, yet he had the will to live. I was twelve and Lucinde was ten.

One morning, we were watching the baby and Maman had gone to her store. When she arrived, she saw that instead of customers there waiting for her, there were two men in linen blazers and a dozen onlookers. She understood immediately that something was awry. The men called out to her angrily and accused her of being late on her payments. She didn't understand right away, but then she recalled that she always handed over the money from the store to Papa, who was then supposed to take it to the bank. It turned out he had never taken it there. He spent it as he pleased. He spent so much without paying that her suppliers sent over these bailiffs to collect on what she owed.

She had to surrender all of her inventory that morning. When they left, she ignored the bystanders who were still there taking in the scene and whispering among themselves: *"Mi bab mi, fanm la lèd aprezan . . ."*—"Boy, she's angry now . . ." She pulled down the wooden shutter of the store, adjusted the padlock above the heavy doorknob, and walked home.

We saw her coming as we played in the shade of the hill where our vegetables grew. She went into the house and laid down facing the wall. She stayed like that for hours, without saying anything but never falling asleep. Lucinde came in from time to time to stroke her forehead. Mother didn't move. And your father, who was only two years old then, sat and watched her, his eyes calm, one finger in his mouth. I didn't go near her. It seemed like if I touched her, she would pull me into her darkness. Papa came home at lunchtime and, when he saw her, sent us to play outside.

In the months that followed, she slept more and more during the day. She said she was sick, but it was a fatigue much deeper than an illness; it was a kind of despondency. She got up around four in the afternoon and then began to walk aimlessly around the outside of the house. One night she didn't come home, so Papa went off to look and found her wandering under the moonlight in a sugarcane field. He went to her, crying out tenderly, "Eulalie, *oh*! Where are you headed off to like that?" Without turning around, she answered that she had to leave, but offered nothing about where she was going. He took her gently by the wrist, brought her home, had her drink a bit of broth, and scrubbed her whole body with leaves from an avocado tree.

Sometimes during the day, instead of going to school, I would secretly follow her to be sure that she wouldn't wade into a marsh or fall into a hole. I hid in the tall grass. I would not have let her see me for anything in this world. If she had looked over her shoulder, she would have turned me into stone with her gray eyes. My heart hammered in my chest; my legs trembled. She walked quickly. One day when I was prowling carefully and quietly behind her like an iguana, I didn't see a piece of sheet metal half-buried in the grass. I stepped on it and cut my foot so deeply that in just a few seconds it was covered in warm, sticky blood. I stopped dead in my tracks. She continued walking straight out in front of me. It was as though she was warning me. I turned to hobble home and never followed her again.

The war was over, but business had dried up. And you would think that awful Hilaire would have left her alone, but he most certainly did not! She was expecting another baby. Petit-Frère was three years old. I was fifteen and had storms of ideas churning in my head. I wanted to break free from our house, our sugarcane fields, our unhappiness. It felt as though my ribs were being squeezed tighter and tighter in a straitjacket that would eventually suffocate me. I felt strong and willful, but death was all around me, like water rising. And then I would see your father playing in the dust, and felt the last thing I wanted was to take care of him. Hilaire continued his errant life, always going off in one direction or the other, with us never knowing when he would be back. Most of the time, I left Lucinde in charge playing house to please Papa, and I would go off into the countryside, to secret places where the angels would talk to me.

The memory of Eulalie's store—that place where she spent years, that hub of town life—followed me. You could find anything in that store: lard, soap, fine-tooth combs, shoe polish, and even, at the height of its success, lovely plaid fabric of madras decorated with lace and an entire collection of men's suits. She had reigned like a queen behind her counter. After her *lolo* closed, the store that replaced it was run by a chatty Syrian who sold bags of rice and flour. Unlike Eulalie, he didn't have an eye for items that were hard to find in a tiny hole like Morne-Galant. I dreamed of owning a store myself one day—better than Eulalie's and far better than the Syrian's.

MOTHER DIED IN JANUARY OF 1947. She had fallen again a few days prior. The doctor was no longer making house calls, so Papa had taken her to Pointe-à-Pitre by bus. It was a "*bus forfaitaire*," an alternative bus, as he called it: sometimes it came by, other times it didn't. You had to wait a long time beneath the noonday sun. Maman couldn't stand up on her own. I remember Hilaire lifting her up like a sack and throwing her over his shoulder. Her head lolled from side to side as he walked down the path. He continued on like that, with Maman on his back, until the bus arrived, sputtering to a stop so they could get in. They came back that night the same way. She could no longer keep her eyes open.

Our aunts and the neighbor ladies came to watch over her. We children kept out of the way. Lucinde wept silently. Papa had stuffed a *doucelette** into Petit-Frère's mouth, who was running around the bed. When Maman died, I saw her belly lift twice, as though the baby were trying to get out. I remained frozen against the wall, my hands behind my back, legs stiff. I couldn't take my eyes off of Maman's belly. I was petrified, as though I had left my body and was floating up above the entire scene. One of my aunts on the Ezechiel side showed me some rare mercy and took my head in her hands, and turned my face away from the scene. I stared at the stars for a long time. I didn't hear the singing or the people coming and going from the house. I didn't hear anything.

And then we were alone—me, Lucinde, and Petit-Frère, who didn't understand where his mother had gone. After the three-day wake and the burial at the Morne-Galant cemetery—during which Papa was in the fields—the rest of the Ezechiels arrived. They acted as though we children weren't even there.

One of my aunts opened the mahogany trunk, grabbed the two scarves, and looked disappointed not to find much else. Another aunt dragged her finger across the rings and a cousin took her earrings, declaring they were for his sweetheart. They told us, "You don't need this," and, "We'll keep these until you are older." They even hauled off two big pans that Eulalie used on the rare days when we would cook fish in broth that would stink up the house for the whole afternoon.

---

* *doucelette*: a cinnamon lime coconut candy typical of the Antilles. —Trans.

They didn't hesitate to pocket her money. They were stripping away everything we had left of her.

When two of them started carrying the mahogany trunk toward the door, I couldn't just watch it happen. I stood up and shouted, "Don't touch that! That's Maman's!" I threw myself on the trunk that they were taking away as casually as if they had bought it at a consignment store. I laid down on top of it. I was already taller than most girls my age, and I had Papa's loud voice. The trunk fell heavily to the floor and it would have taken four men to pull me off it.

I shouted again, "Papa won't let you rob us like this!" I gave them an earful! The Ezechiels reacted as though they had just been insulted by the devil himself. They were so swollen with self-importance, these people who always acted so modest in front of Hilaire in order to get what they needed out of him. Honorette, the one who had a clubfoot and who always scared us, caught me by the hair: "Who do you think you are, talking like that to adults? Just because your mother is dead, you think you get to make the rules around here now?" One of her sons grabbed me by the arm: "And who gave you permission to insult my mother like that? Where are your manners?"

While I struggled, a cousin tried to sneak in and pry my fingers off of the trunk one by one. But I kicked and screamed. "To think you'd do this in the house of a dead woman! You should be ashamed! Maman's ghost will come right back and pull on your feet tonight!"* Lucinde had fled with Petit-Frère

* The dead are shown a lot of respect in the Antilles, and the worlds of the living and the dead intermingle. The notion that both live side by side is so strong that a person who feels they have been hurt by someone can threaten to come back after their death to torment the person still living. This plays out especially in families: parents threaten to come back after their deaths to torment their children. —Trans.

to the back of the house. At one point, Honorette's nails slid from my hair to my neck. With all my strength, I reared back and pushed her away, and she rolled like a heavy metal tub to the other end of the room. I sat on the trunk and started windmilling my feet and kicking away at one aunt's chest, getting another in the head. I tore the shirt of one of my cousins and left bloody marks of my teeth on his chest, so many that he ran outside screaming. I inhabited my anger like a night train careening at full speed down the tracks. They couldn't get near me. They ended up leaving, threatening me with their fists in the air. The one who told me to go wash out my mouth also called me a floozy and a *bougresse*, a country woman. And as they were leaving, they put on a concert of furious *tchip*ing* like you've never seen.

THAT NIGHT, HILAIRE CAME IN carrying the full weight of his bad days. He called out to me: "Antoine! *Vin' ti brin!*" I wanted to tell him everything that had happened, but his sisters had reached him first, said that I disrespected the entire family, that I was a bad example for my brother and sister, that I was a lost cause, and that they were ashamed of me. Papa listened to his sisters and, as usual, took their side. It didn't matter to him that Eulalie's things had been taken since he didn't need them. The trunk might as well disappear too—which is what happened, incidentally, a while later, after I had left Morne-Galant, and I never did find out where it ended up. But it was inexcusable that I had insulted the adults, that I had even offered an opinion, especially as a young girl. Papa never dared raise a hand to me. He knew

* A *tchip* is an expression of disdain throughout the African diaspora involving a prolonged sucking of the teeth. —Trans.

what I was capable of and he didn't like beating his children. But his order was clear: "Tomorrow morning you will go and apologize to Honorette," and then he changed his shirt and left.

I hissed through clenched teeth: "*À pa menm jou fèy tonbé an dlo i ka pouri*"—one day my aunts would pay for what they had done. The next morning, Papa looked everywhere for me, but I never did show up to apologize to Aunt Honorette, choosing instead to forgo meals for the whole day. I slipped away into the tall grass to find juicy yellow mombins whose pits I would spit out as far as I could, and to talk to myself without anyone bothering me. But I wasn't really talking to myself. I had already discovered I had the *fluide* to talk to invisible beings. I can teach it to you, but you'll have to listen to God a little closer. If you had seen all the angels that stretched their arms out to me, whispering secrets. Every time that I felt a little tingle in my fingertips, I knew they were there. To this day, they give me advice. That's what they did that whole day.

I was stretched out at the top of the hill, where you can just make out the sea in the distance, like a low cloud that is blue, a little denser blue than the sky, and I let the wind talk to me. For a long time, I chatted with the leaf-cutting ants and the earth enveloped my whole body. I sat there until I realized that above my head, the branches were taking the shape of words. So I decoded the long sentences exhaled by Gabriel and by the most beautiful of all the angels, Michael, who watches over me with special care, right there alongside Victor Schoelcher, he who the Blacks in Guadeloupe always voted for and who ended slavery once and for all, as you know—and if you don't, well then you don't know a single thing about the French Republic.

When night fell, I went home and tapped on the shutters on the side of the house where Lucinde was sleeping and called out to her quietly. I had startled her, but she opened the window and I was finally able to crawl through. I went to bed but did not sleep. I stayed up thinking about the best way to leave.

Lucinde

I WAS KIND OF LIKE NOBILITY. I don't know, it's just been like that since I was a child. I wasn't like the others. In my mind, I in no way belonged in Morne-Galant, that tiny place in the middle of nowhere. For starters, my mother was a *béké*.* Which was really something, you know. A stunning woman with white skin. Of all her children, I was her favorite. She called me Minette. I coveted her thin ankles; I wanted mine to be just like hers and she assured me that I had the shapely legs of a barefoot little vagabond. Your father is the one who inherited her thin nose—and that was hard for me to accept. And to think that I was the one who darned the seats of all of his pants, that little brat. It was his fault that I couldn't go and do the things I wanted back then. Oh, if only I hadn't had to take care of him!

As for Antoine, you couldn't count on her; she couldn't even take care of herself. One day when we were little, she stole the underwear that I had sewn out of an old canvas bag. I found them, dirty, balled up in the corner. Not only had she stolen them, but she had worn them first one way and then again, inside out, instead of washing them. When Maman

* *béké*: the White Créole descendants of slaveholding colonizers in the French Caribbean. —Trans.

scolded her, she ran off to the top of the hill and picked up a big rock and threw it at us with all her might. Well, guess who got the rock right in the leg! Maman. She was pregnant at the time, and she crumpled to the ground in pain. Looking at Antoine, who had frozen at the top of the hill, she took a deep breath and told her: "You will regret that when I'm dead and gone."

Antoine had already gone *dek-dek*. And that incident probably didn't help things.

Petit-Frère

BE CAREFUL, GIRL. Your aunt Antoine is exhausting. She'll talk your ear off with her stories and take up all your time. She will want to coat your baby with a potion to keep evil spirits away and have you swallow Deschiens syrup for strength. Don't go over to that dump of hers just because she tells you fascinating things. She's dirty and could get you sick. Does she at least still have heat in her store? One day we'll have to clear all that stuff out, arrange for the dogs to be taken care of, and manage the paperwork at city hall. Lucinde is kidding herself if she thinks she is going to take care of Antoine like she did Hilaire. You know how it will go. I'll be the one to do it all.

You wouldn't believe what Antoine looked like back then—as beautiful as the sun, radiating even more beauty in her irrational behavior. She's not the only one who can tell you about Guadeloupe: a few marvels and then nothing but pain. But oh! How I drank my fill of freedom once I arrived in mainland France! Like I had been dying of thirst. I didn't speak Créole to you because there was no reason to. I wanted you to get a good education and climb the social ladder. But our world isn't meant for *Nègres*—that's just how it is. I wouldn't have wanted you to marry some hillbilly from Morne-Galant or even an Antillean. I know how they are and that would have made me worry. I did everything I could to avoid turning out like them. And Hilaire—who stayed faithful to the memory of Eulalie even sixty years after her death, who was the most *sacré vié nèg'** that the world had ever seen—wasn't quite like the other Antilleans either.

And no, I'm not turning my back on where I came from. Love does not mean you cannot be severe. I am fed up with Guadeloupe. And besides, all Antilleans criticize each other.

---

* *sacré vié nèg'*: a hillbilly, one hell of an old *Nègre*. —Trans.

Antoine: Leaving for Pointe-à-Pitre

AT FIVE IN THE MORNING, the dark of night covers all of Guadeloupe like the heaviest lid of all the kettles you own. It's not like here in Paris, where you see all kinds of subtleties in the gradients of light before the day breaks. Last week, I woke up terribly hungry in the middle of the night. I looked at the clock and it was about to strike one. I got up and decided to cook the beautiful chicken that I had bought the day before at the market.

The chicken had called to me from the moment I put him in my basket, and the whole time I was walking up the road, he had been telling me I had to cook him up respectfully. From inside the refrigerator, he made it clear he was in a hurry. So I was barely out of bed and still in my nightdress when I took him out and began to butcher him up next to the window in the kitchen. Every once in a while, I would watch how the night was slipping away from the Earth, getting chased off by the honking of passing buses. You know the lovely kind of deep black that changes very slowly to blue? It's the kind that you see right before dawn, and I was happy because the liver of my chicken was a deep red that complemented the blue of the stained-glass windows of Notre-Dame perfectly. I started singing a canticle. The first early car horns were like *Alleluias!* punctuating my song in the background. And then the sky faded and the color drained from it as if the water of the clouds had diluted it all, and I had in front of me the lovely blue of the beginning of the world, primitive and stunning. I pulled back the yellow skin from the shiny flesh of my chicken. All naked and gleaming, it looked like the inside of a conch shell. As I went to put the pieces into my pot that I'd filled with garlic and hot oil, the sky was milky. Then the sky silvered itself as the sun rose; you couldn't see it just yet, but it was still there, brewing under the plume of the cumulus clouds, made to shine by the cold winter air. And then everything sped up. The air turned the color of a beige moth and the pale day set in. My chicken had just started to sizzle and sing beneath the chives where he sat in the pot when the rain mixed all the colors of the sky together.

In Guadeloupe, at five thirty in the morning, a giant hand lifts up the lid to the kettle and *tchoup!* The dazzling day is there. On the morning I left Morne-Galant without a sound, I had to be sure not to let the daylight catch me since all the residents, except for those who were sick in bed, would have seen me walking by and would have asked questions from their doorways.

At four in the morning, I was in our house, jumping at the tiniest sigh from Papa. I carefully grabbed a few items and slipped away from the house. By the time the turtledoves had started to gather in the leaves, I was already headed down the road that led to Pointe-à-Pitre.

I walked for an hour or two. From time to time, a car would come up behind me. Without turning around to look, I would wave my handkerchief, continuing along the berm with my umbrella under one arm and my men's shoes held tight under the other.

AT LAST, A PICKUP truck stopped a bit ahead of me. The truck was blue beneath a thin layer of dust. I walked toward it, not speeding up, and when I reached the door, I acted very self-assured even though my stomach was in knots. I spoke in the same way I heard the brave women proclaim on market days: "What's the big idea, bothering a hardworking woman who's been walking all morning on her way to make a living!"

In the time it took the driver to answer, I had sized him up and I decided I could climb in. He was thin with a serious face and he seemed to be on a schedule. "Well, monsieur," I told him, "it's nice of you to give me a ride! How are you doing? Wait here and I'll put my things in the back. No need to help, I'll just climb in back. I like to take in the fresh air on a fast drive!" I hoisted myself to the top of the truck bed where I sat on an empty crate. I had on my sturdiest dress made of white muslin and carried a red umbrella for some shade. I was quite happy to be in the back, worry-free, and I watched the sun rise out of the steamy dawn.

NOW LET ME TELL YOU a bit about what a sight I was back then. You know that frills and *makakri de donzelle* are not my style—all those girly antics. As long as I've got clothing on my back that fits, that's enough for me. But I have to say, I always picked up on how people looked at me and what was behind it: desire in the eyes of men and envy in the eyes of women. Look at me now, me with my white hair—but I'm still kicking. And you're thinking to yourself, Why, what smooth skin she has despite all those years she's carrying around on her back. So imagine how I must have looked at sixteen! At the time, my only reference for beauty was Eulalie. I didn't look like her. I never would have considered myself a pretty girl. And yet, I was starting to hear that I was *on bel ti fanm'*, a pretty little lady. Even my aunts on the Ezechiel side would say it to Papa. For a while, on Sundays after mass, there was a swarm of boys that would buzz around me like bees around a sugar apple growing ripe. I knew better than to talk to them or else I would have Hilaire on my back, and let me tell you, I was not interested in getting an earful from Hilaire. I kept my eye on Lucinde and reprimanded her often because she enjoyed the attention from those cocky young men all too much.

People would always size up my body like it was prized merchandise, but I was wise not to smile at anyone I didn't know. I learned quickly that reality always has two sides. Any Antillean knows that. Some examples? Well, beneath Maman's facade like a satin doll, she was very strong. And the Créole dialect that we were commanded to hate was so delectable that the adults always used it when telling their stories. You had to respect the fat White priest in our parish, lower your eyes in front of him, but everyone knew that he had impregnated more than one *Négresse*. The devil was supposed to be black like sin, but I had never seen as much of the devil as I did in Governor Sorin, who starved all of us during the war—and whom we chased out later. A double reality, I am telling you. That's why the real name your mother gives you, you keep hidden. Your *nom de savane* can soak up all of the bad things in this life. It's like a secret treasure that protects you.

So, as I was saying, I inherited all my features from Hilaire: his height, his sculpted shoulders, thin waist, strong arms, and muscled legs, all covered in supple skin that's soft to the touch. Add to all of that my bust, which filled in quickly when I was around fourteen or fifteen, and my pleasant face thanks to my heart-shaped lips and high cheekbones that you'd have thought I stole off an Apache Indian. As for Lucinde, she was sorry she didn't have my thin nose or my glossy black eyebrows. And yet, she had the advantage of being lighter-skinned than me: they say that with that caramel-colored skin, she was "*née sauvée*," born spared.

All of this to say that the truck driver had been drawn to my appealing shoulders and long torso in that tight white dress. It was not charity that had made him stop to pick me up but rather curiosity about whether my front side was as promising as my rear. So I was content to sit alone in the back and to only have to close my eyes to lose myself in the wind as we sped along. I had even forgotten to ask him if he was going all the way to Pointe-à-Pitre, but I was sure that that day was a lucky one because my fingertips were tingling.

As a child, I had been to Pointe-à-Pitre only two or three times. I loved walking around, especially in the narrow streets lined with shops around the port. The town seemed enormous and full of promise to me, even as Maman held me close to her and warned me about the dangers of the neighborhoods we were walking through. I eagerly scanned the scene. I had always known that my future was in the city. La Pointe was only twenty-five kilometers from Morne-Galant. But in 1947, to travel to the capital from way out in the country, you had to wake up very early and muster up the courage to do it. On the morning of my departure, I hadn't wanted to waste my time waiting for a bus. I wanted to arrive in town before the noon heat. I had already decided I wouldn't return.

My idea was to go knock on the door of Éléanore, a cousin who was only five years older than I was and whom I saw from time to time on Christmas Eve in Grands Fonds when the Lebecqs agreed to have us over. Éléanore was the daughter of my mother's favorite sister. The year before, we had been invited to her wedding to a man much older than her, a mulatto who had made a fortune in the funeral business. Despite how young she was, out of respect for her, I called Éléanore "Man Nonore." She wasn't expecting me, but I had no other place to go.

AFTER HALF AN HOUR on the road, the truck stopped in the middle of a deserted crossroads. The driver got out of the truck without looking at me and headed toward a tiny sheet-metal house that stood lopsided against the side of the ravine. I stayed under my red umbrella and I watched him call out a loud hello. There was a soft movement behind the door attached to the wall on two bent nails. It was a store, and right away I guessed what the driver had come for. I figured he must stop here every time he passed through and I was sure that he had started coming even during the Occupation under the control of that damned Governor Sorin, when rum was drunk only among trusted friends. Those who hadn't been careful enough were picked up by the police and could have been deported to other islands for simply having hidden a bottle.

After the war, the *békés*, descendants of the White *grands propriétaires*—big landowners from before abolition—were still saying that alcohol watered down the stamina of the French *Nègre*'s race too much, and the same went for music, festivals, and local gatherings. That's what those people making a nice living for themselves off of our backs were saying. Even when I was very young, it made me want to throw a bottle in their faces because I saw how the men, women, and children slaved away in the sugarcane fields during the harvest so that the rum could flow: that clear liquid that allowed them to send their sons to better schools in France. If we Blacks had let the landowners do what they wanted and keep their giant fields and their distilleries, they would have shaken the Nazis' hands, who were nothing other than modern slave traders. At that time, just like it is now, all of Guadeloupe and Martinique belonged to a few *béké* families, not to us. During the war, those who disagreed and who shouted *"Vive la République!"* ended up in jails in Cayenne or Fort-de-France, unless they were able to sneak away by boat at night to go live among the English.

So as I was saying, the truck driver stopped there like he probably always did. A kid opened the door of the shack and I still remember, as I watched impatiently, the clear little rectangle of green light behind him. The man said a few words, the kid disappeared and came back with the bottle, the bill went from his thick hand to the child's small one, and at last we were able to continue on our way. The driver didn't even look back at me, angry as he was that I had sat in the back. Luckily, that was the only stop before Pointe-à-Pitre.

WE ARRIVED around nine o'clock. You are used to the large gridded cities of France, so you can't understand the effect that arriving had on me, to have found myself in this magnificent heap of slums and palaces. My heart beat quicker as the roads became more clearly defined and the lightweight wooden houses accumulated in the twisted streets. More and more bleached-wood facades appeared, more and more enclosed yards and lopsided coconut trees popped up from tiny inner courtyards and exploded high above the red roofs.

Children ran in tight packs, about twenty bare feet disappearing around the side of a two-story house or down a hallway overrun with grass. I lifted my head and saw balconies full of people—women breastfeeding newborns, doing laundry, or using gray water to clean the floors that formed the roofs of the galleries of covered shops along the roadside, lined with pots in tight rows, fabrics, sacks filled with bread, jars of lard.

The truck struggled to maneuver through the road, where squatting women had spread out their merchandise on the ground in front of walls of straw hats that vendors could erect for their displays and then disassemble in just minutes. Blood sausages smoked in giant blackened pots. Picnic baskets rested at the feet of the women selling them. I saw children heavy with boredom sitting out in front of the shanties, spending the day selling *sik a coco* candy, trying to entertain themselves by arranging their displays in extravagant towers. I remember the scents of the town, how they changed as we moved through neighborhoods—sweet, then bitter ones that signaled a pyramid of trash at the end of a courtyard full of crates stacked one on top of another, creating a *case créole** housing three generations.

A bit farther away, we stopped by a calmer alley where I could smell the salty breeze from the sea mixed with the aroma of a peacock tree and bougainvillea. The workers who

---

* *Cases créoles* refer to the small, brightly colored living spaces seen in Guadeloupe and other former colonies with a history of slavery. —Trans.

had arrived at dawn carted around their wares. I remember a horse-drawn wagon driven by a shirtless driver. It stopped at every door to pick up cans full of filth carried on women's heads. It was the filth produced by what looked like a hundred stomachs, probably thirty of which had been sick with dysentery or malaria. I saw the *marais* of waste that appeared beneath the improvised shacks. In Morne-Galant, we never would have slept in places like that, where the mosquitoes devour you as soon as the sun goes down. But I also saw impressive homes with painted wood, wrought iron, situated around a square with archways and a fountain at the center. I had never seen a fountain like that, with water constantly flowing. It attracted a whole galaxy of laundrywomen in cotton dresses and naked children in hats. It was so pleasant that I could have stayed the whole day there amid the joyful chatter, laughter bubbling all around.

It was a varied crowd, gathered there around the fountain: the skin of some was a deep red clay color, others a velvety cocoa, or the light bronze of the Chinese, the darker bronze of the Syrians, the grilled-coffee-bean color of the Indians. There were also white faces exuding authority but also sometimes reflecting the same general misfortune as the others. Some men dressed casually; others wore stuffy suits. There were factory workers coming out of the big Darboussier refinery, office clerks, schoolteachers. I saw all of this from up in the truck as it hiccuped and spat out suffocating black smoke.

I learned that day that there were two ways of being that did not exist in Morne-Galant, that quiet, sleepy town. In Pointe-à-Pitre, there was a poverty crueler than that of Morne-Galant, but also a possibility, modest as it was, for success and freedom. I didn't know if I was going to be rich like, say, Eulalie had been in her heyday, or poorer than an Ezechiel who rejected working the plot of land that he begged off Papa. Either way, I was excited. I was sixteen, after all.

AFTER NEARLY AN HOUR of driving through the convoluted streets, I thanked the driver and hopped off next to the square where the largest covered market was, decorated with cast-iron pillars. At that hour, the square was almost deserted. I sat near the market, at the corner of rue Duplessis and rue Gatine. I had packed a bit of bread brushed with oil and a little salted codfish wrapped in a cloth. I ate with it spread across my lap. I was thirsty. That's when I approached a fish vendor washing bloody cutting boards under a water pump.

"Can I drink this water?"

The woman looked me up and down.

"If you want to get sick, that's a good way to do it. Drink that and I guarantee in two weeks you'll still have the runs even in your sleep."

"So where can I find water to drink?" When she didn't answer, I offered that I had just arrived from Morne-Galant. Just like everyone else, she asked the next logical question: "Which family?"

"Ezechiel."

"I knew an Ezechiel near Trois-Rivières."

"I'm from Morne-Galant."

She had finished scrubbing her boards and was wiping her hands on her apron. To be sure she wouldn't just leave me there, I added, "Wait a minute . . . yes, we do have a cousin in Trois-Rivières. He's an older man, right?"

"Hmm," she said as she dried the board, which could have meant either yes or no.

"His name's Hector, isn't it?"

"Mmm, I don't think so. Don't remember."

"Is it Fabien?"

I was dragging the conversation out, see, just to give her some time to size me up. Then she stood up, thought a minute, and I knew that I could keep talking because as she put away her board, she said, "It's a lady Ezechiel."

"Oh yeah, maybe that's it," I said. "I remember an Aunt Ezechiel in Trois-Rivières."

"That guy, he married a Madame Ezechiel. She is the one from Trois-Rivières. He is originally from Bouillante."

"Yes, that sounds familiar! I will have to ask Gros-Vaisseau. Do you know that name?"

"Gros-Vaisseau . . ." Her frown disappeared. "Yes, I know a Gros-Vaisseau from Morne-Galant."

"That's my father."

"Ah," she said. Her tone was impenetrable. I tried that angle because sometimes for us, Papa's children, his name worked to our advantage. Other times it worked against us.

"You said you just got here?"

"Just this morning. It's hot today."

"And what have you come to do? You're so young. Shouldn't hang around alone here. Did you come to get work?"

"I'm seventeen," I lied brazenly.

And I casually mentioned that I was headed to my cousin's house in the neighborhood near the cemetery, that I knew exactly where it was, and that I just needed a little fresh water to continue on. The truth was that I had been to her house only one time when I was little and the house still belonged to one of Eulalie's great-aunts. All I remembered was the front of the house and the cemetery beside it because Maman had let Lucinde and me spend some time there, and we had been reprimanded by one of the town matrons for playing around on the graves.

"Dédé!" the fish vendor called out as she laid her boards down in the sun. "Dédé, where are you!"

"*Oh!* I'm over here!" A young man hoisted himself up from somewhere below where he was unwrapping their equipment.

He was of average height, chubby, smiled widely, mouth open like a coin purse. When he came closer, I guessed that he was around twenty-five years old, but I found out later that he was thirty. At first he barely looked at me, but once his mother had ordered him to accompany me to Nonore's, I saw that he was studying my face a little too long, like he was imagining what kind of family I came from just based on how I looked. I also noticed that he seemed pleased to walk with me down the hot sidewalks.

Though I acted as though it was not a big deal, I was impressed when he handed me a tin bottle of cold water; it meant they had an ice chest inside. The first time I ever saw ice I thought that it was salt. It was at the Lebecqs' house; my grandmother gave us sorbet that she had just made with condensed milk and fresh papayas. Lucinde, Petit-Frère, and I had been dumbstruck with delight sitting on the small, hard bench where we held our cups.

SO THERE I WAS, walking with Dédé down one of the roads in Pointe-à-Pitre. Delighted, I opened my umbrella and pretended that I wasn't surprised by the sights we encountered: men wearing suits on a day other than Sunday, the head-spinning stench that took us by surprise coming from the latrines, the twangy music that floated out balcony windows.

Dédé chatted, though I would have preferred to walk in silence so I could take it all in. So he and I talked while we walked, which I never could do in Morne-Galant without being grilled by Papa or the neighbors.

"So where does your cousin live?"

"In the neighborhood by the cemetery."

"Do you know the name of the street?"

"No, but I'll recognize it."

The whole way there, Dédé was keen on making himself seem important by telling me his whole life's story, emphasizing that he knew the town like the back of his hand and that where he lived, in the north neighborhood, he had plenty of friends. This was probably because he and his mother were part of an organization called Cuistot Mutuel, for those who cooked and organized parties and dances for the neighborhood from time to time. Back then, there were all kinds of organizations like that. I had seen them also in the country, where the cane harvesters and distillery workers would come together to help one another. I figured out quickly what he was talking about and his neighborhood wasn't, in my opinion, really in *l'en-ville*;* it was a part of the slumping and wobbly *cases* that made up the dripping gray landscape that stretched from the wooded hillsides all the way to the port.

"So you don't actually live in town, then," I said, raising my eyebrows.

He insisted: "Well of course I do! Our neighborhood is definitely a part of Pointe-à-Pitre. You'll see when I have you over. Really, it's a peaceful spot where we throw the best par-

---

* *l'en-ville*: a term from the Créole "*an-vil*," indicating the town's center, which has been used in the Martinican writer and scholar Dominique Aurélia's postcolonial discourse and also appears in Patrick Chamoiseau's novel *Texaco*. —Trans.

ties on Saturday nights. We get a smoked chicken going and pass it around. The best in all of the Pointe. My cousin makes it. If you stay, you may want to see it. Or maybe you're just here visiting?"

"I've come to work at my cousin's house. I'm going to take care of the house and help out with her baby until I find something else."

"I could help you. I know a lot of people."

"People who could give me a job in a store?"

"Do you want to work in a store? That would be easy, looking the way you do. You won't have any trouble. I'll take you where you need to go."

"I'd like to work in a store, right next to a church."

"Is the church part important?"

"Yes, so that I can get there easily."

"I remember seeing a parade for the Virgin Mother last year, I followed it for a bit, all the way to the mangrove."

"I was there too with my sister when the procession passed through Morne-Galant. There were a lot of people but I was the only one the Virgin Mary smiled at. There were lots of people there, but I was the only one she was looking at."

"The wooden Virgin Mary?"

"She wasn't made of wood, she was alive with soft cheeks. But I was the only one who saw her smiling."

So that's more or less what we talked about until the moment I recognized Man Nonore's road.

I stopped at the entrance of the road. I didn't want them to see me the same day I arrived prattling on with a stranger. But this Dédé wasn't in any hurry to part ways.

"So we'll see each other again soon, and talk more about those people I know," he said.

"The people who would hire me?"

"Sure, for a spot in a store."

"Oh, yes!"

"I'll come find you when I've found something."

"That sounds good." I closed my umbrella quickly to encourage him to get going. He did not look like he was going anywhere.

"So will you have to stay at your cousin's house all the time?"

"I suppose so."

"Maybe you could come take a walk in the evenings once in a while."

"Maybe."

I didn't say anything to encourage him, but I wasn't impolite about it. Then he had a brilliant idea.

"I will show you all the best churches," he declared.

"The best?"

"The ones where you can hear a good mass."

"Alright," I said as I walked away.

How naïve I was back then. If I had been paying a bit more attention to both of them that day, I would have noticed that Dédé's mother had been delighted to send her son off to accompany Gros-Vaisseau's daughter wherever she needed to go. Because her little Dédé, with his round face and shy way of talking, was thirty years old and still hadn't found a *doudou*. She could tell that his life as a bachelor was no longer enough for him. Not a single *donzelle* had come around generating any kind of scandal with her son; she hadn't even heard of a single neighbor lady with a growing belly anywhere in the square—and it worried her. Someone lighter-skinned like me would please her.

Man Nonore's house was just up rue Frébault, the busiest artery of Pointe-à-Pitre. Rue du Cimetière, away from the town center, seemed peaceful. Like I had seen elsewhere, there were several shacks standing in a crooked line either built directly on the ground or propped up on stones, then a vacant lot burned by the sun. Then the road went uphill slightly and I saw the cemetery spread out in the sun on a steep hill, with a large crucifix watching over the most striking tombs. The city of marble tombstones was more organized than the real city below.

I waited for Dédé to disappear around the bend in the road and then I walked on, examining each house carefully. Right away I recognized the one I was looking for.

Antoine: Koté Lebecq, the Lebecq Side

NONORE'S HOUSE WAS BEAUTIFULLY BUILT, constructed with raw timber that had a bleached color to it, with a second story and a balcony—not wrought iron, but it wrapped around the building all the same. It was the largest house on the little cemetery road.

I thought about what I was going to say and then knocked on the door. I stood up as straight as possible, pressing my umbrella against my leg. After a moment, I heard footsteps and a child crying. After another long moment the door opened; at last I saw my cousin's pale, tired face in the doorway. Back then, Éléanore was a young woman with narrow shoulders. She had long, frizzy red hair that she pulled back in a braid crowning her head, and her eyes were a shade of gray that flirted with green. Her face was thin, a bit angular like the other Lebecqs', a cream color that would have quickly turned to white in a winter on the mainland, her mouth large with supple lips that rarely smiled. She seemed older than twenty-one.

When she opened the door and saw me, she jumped a little, and hesitated before saying hello. "Oh, it's you." She glanced quickly over my shoulder to see if the neighbors were watching and then invited me in. My goal was to spend the night there and I didn't know how hard it would be to convince her. "How are you?" she asked as she turned her back and strode down the dark hallway. She had a dragging tone to her voice, as though it cost her quite a bit of energy just to open her mouth. She walked the same way; you'd think that her feet were stuck in buckets of molasses. I strode behind her confidently. She turned around and I saw her nervously pull a shawl around her shoulders, but she had no other option than to welcome me down the narrow hallway, dark and cool.

"Hello, Man Nonore. How are you doing?"

"I'm fine. And your father?"

"He is well, thank you."

I set down my umbrella against a wall covered in pale green wallpaper. I looked her straight in the eye like a friend would. I could read on her face that she thought I was being cheeky. Like all the Lebecqs, her attitude was to merely put up with the Ezechiels, including me—the tall, slightly strange girl I had become, who looked nothing at all like Eulalie, with my clay complexion, barely lighter than Hilaire's.

"And your brother? Your sister?"

"Everyone is fine. And cousin René?"

"He's well, thank you. He isn't here."

Of course he wasn't there, I thought. René, Man Nonore's husband, had built a flourishing funeral business from scratch in Petit-Camp, a nearby village on the coast a few kilometers from Morne-Galant. He had married late, to my young cousin, once his financial success had allowed him to claim a girl with good marriage potential despite his caramel coloring, and only after taking full advantage of being young and unattached. Although Nonore was only fifteen when they were engaged, her future husband had promised to move them to Pointe-à-Pitre as soon as they married. That is how she left Grands Fonds, on her eighteenth birthday, betrothed to this forty-year-old man who was balding prematurely and sported two gold teeth.

Annie was born a year later, and Nonore languished by herself, in charge of the house, while René spent all his time outside of it—some of it at his business, but most of it at different women's homes or traveling to other islands.

The young girl started whimpering and trying to climb out of her bassinet. I rushed over to help her despite her shrieks of terror at my approach, and declared to Nonore:

"I'm here to help you out."

I held out a little present that I had brought with me—a coconut cake, slightly crushed from the journey. She gave it to the child to quiet her. And then I delivered my second lie of the day:

"The last time that I went to Grands Fonds, your mother told me you were very tired. She said that you needed someone to take care of you. And your little girl. She's gotten big, hasn't she? But you . . . you're so thin!"

The child whined as she crumbled the cake at her feet, so I took out the cloth from my pocket that had held my codfish and wiped her nose with it. Nonore looked disgusted but she said nothing.

I walked through the house and complimented everything I saw: the furniture, the room with a mosquito net around the bed, the indoor kitchen—where I came from, we cooked in a circle of stones out in the yard because the risk of fire inside was too high. What I liked best was the loft. But they were renting it to another family, so I couldn't take in the panorama from the balcony. Man Nonore followed me, still wordless, carrying Annie in her arms.

After the tour of her house, I didn't know what else to do,

and Nonore still wasn't saying anything other than "Hmm" from time to time in response to my running commentary. I announced that I was going to heat up some water for the vegetables for the evening meal. She let me go back toward the little kitchen, so I grew even bolder and opened a cupboard. From the kitchen door that led to the rear courtyard, I caught sight of the trunk of a soursop tree. I kept talking.

"Be careful about the trunk of that soursop—they attract rats, you know. Just for Annie's sake, be careful. You don't want to let her get bitten. I hate rats; they terrify me. Do you have any poison?"

She didn't answer. Annie, nestled in her arms, had calmed down. The two watched me with the same green eyes, wary, as though I were a chili pepper that was going to sting their eyes. Nonore hadn't even offered me a *ti verre* of water before I set out to cook, but I was intent on making a good impression. I examined the room:

"Do you have any root vegetables? Or a breadfruit?"

"There, in the box." She pointed to a shelf above the sink, hidden behind a curtain.

I set to work. As I told you, I am very good at filling the air with words. I spoke without even catching my breath as I leaned over the pans. I chose a big ripe breadfruit and sat on a little bench low to the ground, a bowl of water between my legs. I looked past it to watch Éléanore. Behind her condescension, her face was truly sad and tired. A long time after, I would come to understand that she was wondering what René was going to say when he discovered I had moved in with them out of nowhere.

I hadn't noticed a single trace of a man living there: no shirts hanging on a nail, no hat, no razor sunk at the bottom of an emptied gourd filled with water. It was as though my cousin lived there alone with her daughter. But even though René wasn't physically present, I learned that he weighed on her, imposing a haze of solitude. And as hard to imagine as it was, in the moment, this frail woman, closed-off and taciturn, truly did love her husband.

That first evening in Pointe-à-Pitre, we ate under the blue light of a lantern sitting at the center of the table. Then Nonore showed me the little room where she had decided I could stay: a corner in the back of the house that was used as a laundry room, dirty clothing piled up all around. It almost felt as though I was out in the yard, the way the scent of the trees wafted in through the window. I loved being in there, except for the fact that it was just beside the latrines. In the night I often woke up hearing people come and go.

THREE MONTHS PASSED. That's how long it took for me to earn Nonore's trust. Her loneliness was a doorway for me to slip inside. And maybe it was also a sort of curiosity that she felt toward me. In our family, people speak badly about Hilaire—that scoundrel—who had let his wife, Eulalie, die of sadness. Her uncles Paul and Guillaume, the famous Lebecq brothers, adored their sister; and so she felt somewhat obligated to Eulalie's family. As for me, I tried as hard as I could to be sweet and patient with little Annie, even when she threw tantrums and filled the house with earsplitting screams.

I must say that at the beginning, Nonore was on guard and almost surly. Then she started to observe me. I could feel her sizing me up as I went about my day, never asking her for anything, making decisions on my own, whether it had to do with dinner or Annie's baths. She was always there, quick to deliver a curt reproach if she thought I hadn't swept the living room well enough or if I had washed her daughter's hair poorly.

I was aware of my strengths and my weaknesses. Clearly, I wasn't great at housework. As for cooking, I was okay, but I could by no means whip up a full menu of meals. I tended to cook the same thing over and over. She never complained, but the look on her face—her eyes that wouldn't meet mine, her stony expression—told me I had overcooked the *madères* or let the pigs' tails burn. That's how I realized that Éléanore badly needed company. And here I was, a family member who had arrived out of nowhere and asked only for a place to stay. Someone she could scold a little. All in all, it was a good deal for her.

On the other hand, I did know how to make soursop infusions to make Annie sleep through the night, how to sing song after song and tell her stories about *bêtes longues*, snakes that could talk. I would resurrect stories from the recesses of Éléanore's memory, stories that she hadn't heard anyone tell except her grandmother's mother, back in the ravines of Grands Fonds. In those moments, she didn't argue with me about having used the same dirty chiffon for days to dust the furniture, dry the plates, and wipe Annie's snotty nose.

SHE AND I STAYED UP TALKING later and later once Annie went to sleep. The days were very quiet and I was surprised that Nonore seldom left the house. Since I had arrived, we hadn't gone out a single time. I was itching to wander around Pointe-à-Pitre—even just on a Sunday—but I didn't dare ask her for permission to go by myself, and I also didn't have any money.

One night, she told me about a traffic accident that had

happened that morning. The neighborhood had been buzzing about it all day: a child had been struck and killed by a bus. She was pleased with herself for avoiding dangerous situations altogether by never leaving the house. I jumped at my chance.

"What do you mean, you never go into town?"

"I went at the beginning of this year, with Maman, to buy furniture."

"And after that?"

She shrugged.

"You never go and see people? You stay here like a hermit?"

She thought for a moment and then responded, slightly irritated: "I don't have a lot of friends here."

"I have a friend," I said, and regretted it immediately.

"You have a friend in town?" She was half-offended and half-amused. "How can that be? You've only been here for what, three months? I haven't let you go anywhere except for the haberdasher at the end of the road! What, are you slipping out the window while I'm asleep?"

I explained that I had met Dédé the day I had arrived. That perked her ears up right away.

"How old is he?"

"I don't know. Around twenty-five."

She gasped in mock surprise and covered her mouth like a child caught doing something naughty.

"But that's too old for you!"

"Too old for what?" I asked defensively.

I didn't want any rumors getting back to Hilaire; the few kilometers between us would certainly not be enough to protect my reputation.

"Well then, what does he want from you? You say he's a friend. What do you mean?"

"I don't mean anything! He was going to take me to church."

"To church!" She guffawed. "Are you going to get married?"

"Of course not!" I was angry.

"So he's a priest?" She rolled her eyes, amused. "Be careful of young priests, you know what they say—beneath all that piety, they're usually hypocrites!"

I was shocked by what Éléanore had said. She seemed so anemic and ordinary, a little girl so sad and weak you could jerk her around like a dangling wooden puppet—and she had, for the first time, shown her complicit side. I figured that if it took some boy talk to finally see her smile, then so be it.

"He's not a priest. He has a stall at the market where he sells fish and food his mother makes."

"*Pouah!*" Nonore said, serious and disgusted. "Now don't go hanging around with just anybody!"

"He and his mother aren't just anybody. They live in *l'en-ville*. Well, almost. His mother seems responsible and hardworking. She is in the Cuistot Mutuel," I added knowingly.

She *pffff*ed again and then her voice turned smooth and authoritative and she frowned disapprovingly.

"Now tell me, do you know what happens sooner or later when you talk to a man?"

"For now, I don't have anything to worry about. I haven't gotten my period yet."

Back then, we weren't smart like the girls are today. We were stupid. You had to be, or pretend to be, to keep your reputation. Any talk related to sex was drunk men's talk you heard at night at dances and shouldn't ever repeat. When Lucinde got her period, a neighbor told her, wagging her finger in her face, "From now on, if you even talk to a man, you will get pregnant!" At first Lucinde was terrified. She ran like a rabbit the minute she saw a man appearing on the horizon. Eventually we realized that we had been told lies—*tout bitin an kouyonad*".* But we still had to pretend to be afraid, and we truly *were* afraid of being punished if we were caught alone with a boy trying to kiss us. That's how adults tried to control us, inside those nets of fear. But I felt very safe. I explained to Nonore that every month, I made a sign over my belly with my hands that would protect me from all that. Her eyes went wide.

Once again she listed off my desirable features in the eyes of men: my firm breasts, my skinny waist, my round hips. She devoured the fotonovelas that René brought back from Trinidad that were full of young women. She couldn't believe that I hadn't gotten my monthly yet.

"So you've never bled?"

"No, and I am in no hurry for that dirty stuff! I saw what it did to Maman. So men, no thank you!"

"But your mother was sick. I remember hearing some kind of complicated name for her illness at one point."

"Yes, she was sick, but far too often she was in the family way. All those babies—*that* is what killed her."

And then I told her how Maman's belly rose and fell like a bellows the day that she died, and how the doctor had come that evening only to declare that we needed to get the death certificate in order. I confided to her that at that moment, in my head, I had already given the baby a name. Even though it never had the opportunity to come into this world. No one knows that it had a name but me. I still think about it even sixty years later, and I see that baby, with its soft skin and

* *tout bitin an kouyonad*: nonsense. —Trans.

blind eyes, who never had the chance to be born. Ever since that awful day, I've been scared of pregnant women. When I see one in the street, I cross to the other side.

Other times it was Éléanore who confided in me, about the early days of her marriage or about Annie's birth.

"It happened at my parents' house in Grands Fonds," she told me. "I had to stay in bed for a month. It's always like that for women who have just given birth, you know."

"And did you get a leaf bath every day?"

"Every day! I wanted to get up because I couldn't feel my legs anymore from lying down so long. When I saw my mother coming with her basin and her leaves, I wanted to run away! I was bored just lying there in my bed, except when I had Annie in my arms. But even with her I was uneasy; there was always someone giving me advice about my sore breasts, someone telling me not to do this, not to do that. I wanted to keep Annie and have her sleep in my bed, but they wouldn't let me. René's former *da*, an older woman, came every night to check on me and bring Annie in for me to breastfeed. The rest of the night, that woman snored so loudly it kept me awake, but I told her that it was Annie's crying that bothered me, just so I wouldn't offend her. So of course, then she suggested staying longer than the month she had planned, and I didn't know how to get out of it. And that broth every day—it made me have to go to the bathroom all the time!"

AFTER SIX MONTHS at Nonore's house, we were finally smiling at one another. We were two young women laughing together. Even though Éléanore was older and fully immersed in married life, it sometimes seemed like I had more life experience than she did.

One day, she noticed that my dress was stained, the same one I had shown up wearing. She lamented my lack of style, my unfashionable thick braided hair parted into a checkerboard pattern, neat and efficient, that made me look older. Nonore decided to give me the dresses she no longer wore, but I was much taller than she was. She declared, "We are going to leave Annie with the neighbor and go to rue Frébault to see what we might find to dress you. And then we will buy some red snapper and you can point out that Dédé you mentioned—but don't you dare wave at him!"

From then on, every so often we would go out for the afternoon. Sometimes we would walk in front of Dédé, who would wave at me but I never waved back. Still, I knew it made him happy to see me, even from a distance.

On our second outing, Éléanore bought me a long pink dress with thin straps from an old seamstress whose hands were nearly paralyzed. The dress had originally been made for a customer who had returned it after discovering that the old woman's fingers had messed up the stitching around the collar. So Nonore bought it for a song. The dress showed off my shapely shoulders and highlighted my long arms, so long that they could have easily fit around one of our metal rainwater barrels.

From that point forward, I became known in the neighborhood as the young cousin who had come to help Man Nonore. Back in Morne-Galant, Hilaire had accepted my departure, glad that I'd at least stayed within the family. He never asked if they were paying me for my work. My status there was just above that of a runaway and just below that of an employee. But it was better than the life I had known before. Everything was going well. And then René came back.

Petit-Frère

WHEN MY SISTERS LEFT Morne-Galant—first Antoine, then
Lucinde—I was left alone with your grandfather. They did
come back regularly for extended visits. Antoine, who was
always ready to bare her teeth and even use them, did just
about whatever she wanted. Papa looked on, proud that she
was making her own way. I have to hand it to her: from sixteen on, Antoine never asked him for a single thing. Only
once did he intervene in her business; I'll tell you about that
someday.

As for Lucinde, it was more complicated. Although she
seemed obedient, she would always go to great lengths to get
what she wanted. I once watched her quibble with the woman
who sold us bread—a Chinese woman who lived alone with
her half-blind father—so that Lucinde would get the biggest
banneton at a discount, but then she announced that the
woman who sold the bread to her was poisoning people in
town with her undercooked flour. The bread vendor never said
anything, but from then on I felt ashamed whenever I went to
buy bread. Another time, when we were adults, I heard Lucinde complain about a stack of cinder blocks that Hilaire had
given to Antoine when she had the idea to build herself a

house on the hillside. We knew that she would never build it, but the very sight of the stack of cinder blocks set aside for Antoine unleashed waves of jealousy in Lucinde. Lucinde always claimed to have our mother's noble heart, but in reality, her own had turned petty. Hilaire was no fool and wasn't easily manipulated by people's questionable intentions. He was aloof, liked to brag, and had no thought for the future, but he never raised a hand to his children. At least, it was rare that he would hit me. My sisters would tell you a different story, but it isn't true. You think he was more severe with me because I was a boy? Maybe. But looking at the facts objectively, I think he treated all three of us the same.

When I was left alone with him, it was our neighbor, Madame Zamuy—who had both Black and Indian features—who took pity on me and took me under her wing. I spent long afternoons on her tiny patio, set a bit back from the house like ours was, just a few hundred meters from our house. I was a small child and didn't say much. She would take me in her arms and stroke my hair. Her looking after me worked well for Papa when he went off into the fields or out wandering. He often traveled to the other side of the island, or to the mountains where maybe a mistress was waiting for him, one whom I never saw but whom I would have liked to know. Knowing his mistress would have at least given me some kind of mother figure—even if she had been mean or strict—at least there would have been someone there to take care of me.

Madame Zamuy was the closest thing I had to a mother. Antoine and Lucinde will tell anyone who will listen that they were the ones who raised me. But I must say that early on, in Morne-Galant, they tormented me by pantomiming what they thought adults did. So when I caught up to them in

Pointe-à-Pitre, I knew better than to let myself get pushed around again.

Why am I mad at my sisters, you ask? The endless hours they made me sit in the back of the town church. Christmases in Grands Fonds that they spent dressing up and showing off at the Lebecqs' house while I wasn't allowed to move a muscle so I might keep my polished shoes clean. The pomade they put in my hair to smooth it down. The beating I took from Lucinde because people saw me holding a girl's hand after school let out—a double sin since it was the distillery supervisor's daughter. Every year, I had to muster the five francs on my own for the school cooperative fees. Hilaire always forgot to pay them. Lucinde didn't care. Antoine might give me half of the money and then announce that Papa would have to hand over the rest. Not paying my fees meant I spent hours being punished, kneeling on a cheese grater with my hands behind my head. My primary school teacher—a wicked maniac whom no other adult ever questioned—had no problem inflicting pain on children's bodies.

Even though for seventy years Antoine and Lucinde have been fighting and then making up and fighting again, they've always been able to agree on making the worst decisions where I was concerned. For example, despite how terribly my teachers treated me, I loved school and I worked hard. One day I brought home a stack of books that I had been given as a prize for being the top student in poetry, history, and geography. The whole way home, I squeezed the books tight under my arm, making sure out of the corner of my eye that people saw them. It was the start of school vacation. At the house, I never even had the chance to open those books before they disappeared. Which one of my sisters sold them to buy a pack of socks or a new pair of underwear? I never found out, but I

do know that they were the ones who did it and that confronting them would have been useless.

No, I didn't complain much back then and I'm not
complaining now. I'm just telling you my side of it. To start,
my mother was not a *béké*. Lucinde is always exaggerating.
Our mother's family lived in Grands Fonds with the Blancs-
Matignon, but I am not certain that they were Blancs-Matignon
themselves. Maybe they were *petits Blancs*, poor Whites that
History had left behind, some of them slaves just like the
Nègres had been. From the start, our family's roots were nestled deep where chimeras live, our legends and histories an
unknowable amalgam of fiction and half-told stories.

Antoine: "Mache!" Get the Hell Out of Here!

WHEN RENÉ CAME BACK, he was like a ghost for a few days. He had appeared one afternoon out of the blue. The sky was cloudy and it wasn't too hot, so all three of us were in the garden transplanting tomatoes. Annie was next to me rolling and unrolling the *congolios*, the millipedes that multiplied with each spade of soil we dug up. Out of the corner of my eye, I saw Annie look up, hiccup in surprise, and then crawl quickly toward the door where René was standing, unmoving, watching us. He stood tall, wearing white linen pants and a matching shirt with pockets and six wooden buttons descending in a line down his chest and across his round stomach. The gentle sun glinted off of his bald spot and I imagined that a tiny pool must collect there on rainy days.

Éléanore was the last to look up. When she saw him, she dropped her spade and strode toward him in measured steps, as though she were back in time walking down the aisle on their wedding day. He rewarded her with just a quick kiss on the forehead. She addressed him quickly while he looked me over. I stood up reluctantly and went over to him, my mouth already filling with polite questions and words of welcome. He barely looked at me. He was tired from his trip and went

straight inside to lie down. I didn't see him again until later
that night.

From that day forward and for as long as he was there,
Éléanore shifted back to being as taciturn as when I had arrived. I would make them coffee early in the morning while
they were still in their room. René always came out first in a
satin robe that swished against his pajamas. At first he said
nothing and I didn't like his perpetually half-closed eyes. So
I would go to look in on Annie until Éléanore came out. He
talked to her about his business, about the next store he
wanted to open in Saint Martin where people needed all sorts
of things, about a heroic struggle between a mongoose and a
snake that he had witnessed in Martinique.

Nonore nodded along to everything he said and served
him his steaming coffee. She adopted a submissive attitude
with him that irritated me. When he arrived, he had sized
me up silently. After two days, he'd accepted me. I understood that he loved to talk about himself before an audience
more than anything else. My being there gave him plenty of
opportunities to retell his stories. Day after day, especially in
the morning, he went into detail about the growing success of
his business, and then all sorts of other stories. And I must
admit that he was the most eloquent speaker that I'd ever met
in my life. It wasn't surprising that his businesses had been so
successful. Even though I was skeptical, he had an excellent
and convincing gift of gab. He certainly brightened up my
mornings. He would sit for hours in the kitchen making me
laugh. Sometimes, Nonore, having put Annie down for a nap,
would come in and watch us, uncomfortable. And then the
mood completely changed. So I felt bad about laughing along
with him while he paid no interest to his wife—Nonore, who

spent all of her time waiting for him. René would speak a little louder, addressing only me with wild facial expressions.

"So just imagine it—the two guys that I had at the depot to deliver the caskets were climbing into the truck. One sits in the driver's seat and the other gets in back with the casket to hold it in place during any turns. They head off to Petit-Camp on the road that winds along the sea. It has a lot of twists and turns and you have to be a great driver like I am to navigate them all. But my guys know what they're doing. And they know you can't deliver a damaged casket."

"Mm-hmm," I said, continuing my cooking as he went on excitedly, waving around a cigar with a stink that lingered long after.

"So then it starts raining. Luckily, my truck—a Citroën that I went myself to pick up in France—has good windshield wipers and great brakes. I wash it each week, piston by piston. So what does the guy in the back do in the pouring rain? Well, he's had enough. He doesn't know how long the rain will last. He doesn't want to get soaked like a baby goat out in the countryside—he has on his best shirt and doesn't want to ruin it. He thinks for a second, checks that the casket is tied securely to the bars of the truck, and gets the bright idea to slip inside it. He lays down between those four freshly sawn boards, ramrod straight like out of a portrait of Henry IV. The thing was, that box was as comfortable as his momma's womb. The casket was just his size, I am telling you, his exact size. He could even take a little nap inside. And, *Petite*, believe it or not, that's what he does. He stretches out on his back and to shield himself from the pouring rain he closes the lid of the casket, just a little bit. Not too much! He still wants to feel the light fall across his eyelids. So he lays there stiff as a board in my brand-new casket and he waits for the sky to clear up. Okay, so then my driver sees a man in a suit standing on the side of the road, waiting desperately for someone to stop and pick him up. He's soaked, and he would have just about melted if the rain were to go on like that, with his nice shoes and all. So the driver pulls over and suggests that he hop in the back of the truck. The man gladly agrees so he can get out of the mud on the side of the road, and they head off. He sits down next to the casket and just after he settles in, the rain slows and he's happy as a clam thinking that he's about to watch the scenery go by as he dries off in the sun. The rain stops. The water is glistening in front of him in puddles stretching out behind them as they race by. The man is happy, so he takes off his nice shoes to dry out his feet"—here René used his whole body to act out the scene, a real Marcel Marceau—"he takes off his jacket and spreads it out over the wood. He looks up at the sky as he unbuttons the collar of his shirt. He's about to wring out his hat. And that's when my other guy, the one laying in the casket, who also wants to enjoy the sunshine, sticks out his hand to be sure it's stopped raining. *Boom!* goes the heart of the man in the suit. He jumps off the truck and doesn't dare stick around to see what was coming out of that box next. I swear it! The man jumped out of the moving truck! Bare feet, no jacket! He jumped out and fell right into a puddle!"

And René laughed so long and so loud that it woke up little Annie. Éléanore hurried off to her cradle and I looked down into my pans, still smiling, and then René asked me about my life in Morne-Galant, about Hilaire, and gently made fun of the men's shoes I wore, saying that for a scarecrow, I wasn't half bad. He said that I looked older than I was, that he thought I could easily be twenty. He talked about the trinkets he would buy for Annie on his next trip. When he stopped talking, though, I was happy to no longer see his gold tooth shining.

ONE DAY, he and I were alone because Éléanore had left very early to go to the doctor with Annie. He was sitting in the kitchen, as usual. On the sly, I threw a pinch of salt over my shoulder—it makes unwelcome visitors leave your house. I had promised Nonore that lunch would be ready by the time she came back. The kidney beans were rinsed and I was preparing the dough for the *dombrés*. All of a sudden, René stood up and pressed himself behind me and whispered, "*Ma belle, ma douce*, I won't hurt you," and started pushing himself harder and harder against me as he let out sharp little cries. The bowl full of flour fell to the floor.

Since I had been expecting him to pull this kind of thing on me eventually, I had left a kitchen knife out on the table. Even though René was heavy, I was able to turn myself around and wave the knife at him. I remember he smelled like cologne. At that moment, I employed the strategy Hilaire used whenever he was angry; I shouted as loudly as I could, cursing him with words that I must have heard in the fields or passing in front of the *grain dé* bar in Morne-Galant where fights constantly broke out when the men played dominoes.

Uncle René was shocked and pulled away. But he was getting ready to close in again. I didn't really want to hurt him. I acted so quickly that I still don't know how I did it. In the blink of an eye, all the buttons of his linen shirt, the one with all the front pockets, were rolling on the ground into every corner of the room. I kept yelling and swinging the knife around. He looked worriedly toward the loft in the house because of the knife and the noise I was making and retreated toward the door.

I picked up each button from the floor. They were proof, you see. I could tell Nonore what had happened and show her the buttons in the event he ever dared try anything again.

When Nonore came home with Annie, the meal was ready. René stayed out the entire day. I didn't say anything, but women can sense these things. Nonore looked at me as she walked around the kitchen, her gray eyes troubled and mysterious, and was particularly cold to me that afternoon. I knew then that my days in that house were numbered.

NOT LONG BEFORE, I had celebrated my seventeenth birthday alone in my room. While I was doing my hair, I found a single white hair in my thick black mane. I swelled with pride. What I wanted more than anything was to be an adult. That white hair dignified me. I figured out a way to part my hair on the diagonal to show it off. It was my birthday present and so I thanked Saint Michael; there was no one else around to celebrate with me.

From that day on, the chitchat in the kitchen with René ended. He was looking for a way to get rid of me. He began to manufacture all kinds of grievances against me. At first, Éléanore made excuses for me when he said the yams weren't peeled correctly or the laundry had been poorly ironed. And so you know, back then, we used a heavy iron, almost like an anvil, that you had to heat over embers. Not easy work! Once a week, the neighbor lady upstairs borrowed the iron to straighten her hair. It smelled like burned pig through the whole house. Back to my story.

Sometimes, I would give little Annie a mamoncillo fruit

to chew on and she loved it. René shot me a dark look and told Nonore before he left, "Watch and make sure she doesn't let the baby choke on a pit." Nonore kept turning to look at her daughter worriedly, who right at that moment spat out the pink pit, nice and clean. What a joke! All the *ti-moun*** on the island ran around with mamoncillo branches in hand—it's the fruit of childhood.

ONE NIGHT I SAT ALONE in my room on the straw mattress, braiding my hair by candlelight as I rested my tired feet. I heard René call out to Nonore, furious:

"Éléanore! Get over here and look at this!" She was putting Annie to bed.

"What is it?" she asked from the hallway. I stopped braiding my hair to listen.

"I said, get over here and come look at this!"

I heard Éléanore head toward the front door. I slid up behind her. René was standing at the door looking at something in the road. He wasn't alone; the neighbor lady from upstairs was with him.

"*Mi bab mi*, would you look at that," I heard her say judgmentally. She turned to me. "Haven't I told you before not to do your nasty habits in the street?" She continued, "It was Antoine, I see her doing it at night! And even in the mornings! Soon they'll be so used to it that they'll come right into your kitchen! And one of these days, they'll make it all the way upstairs to where I am!"

She was talking about *les chiens créoles*, créole mutts. Sometimes I would throw them the leftovers before I did the dishes

---

* *ti-moun*: children. —Trans.

in front of the house. When it was pigs' tails, even if there were only tiny ends of cartilage wrapped in sauce, all the dogs in a ten-kilometer radius would come running. It was fun to watch them snap at each other. Those mutts eat everything; even the skins of avocados. They all look the same, there's just the brown of their fur that varies in intensity from one to the other—and the glint in their eyes.

You can pick out the *tèbè* ones and the wily ones easily, the alphas and the cowards. Their ribs jut out of their nearly hairless bodies. For the most part, they are the smartest mutts you'll ever meet. People kick them just as much as they pet them. They look at you with their eyes shining beneath the very short hair on their heads. Sometimes they jump around, dancing on the beaches. You can yell out *"Mache!"*—get the hell out of here—and they run away with their heads down. But they always come back when night falls to sneak a little breadfruit, which makes the teeth in their long snout nice and white. And like us, they never protest.

I had gotten into the habit of letting them enjoy our leftovers. They waited for me beneath the moon every night. But once René started watching me, I did it less often. After several days, those smarties began to protest my neglect. A dozen of them had shown up here, at our door, standing in a perfect line. Some had only one eye, others had infected paws, or tails thrumming with flies. Attentive and quiet, they all cocked their heads to the same side, collectively inquiring about their meal.

Éléanore's mouth hung open in surprise looking at them. The neighbor lady looked disgusted. She loathed those dogs. René had taken off his leather belt and snapped the air yelling out meanly, *"Mache!"* The dogs retreated but not very far. Each time René moved toward them, they backed up only the bare minimum to avoid being hit with the belt, eyeing the house as though they expected me to intervene. The neighbor *tchip*ed and turned on her heels. Éléanore told René to come inside, promising the neighbor that we wouldn't give them any more scraps. I silently returned to my room and resumed my braiding while René called me incompetent and uncivilized.

The next day, Nonore suggested awkwardly that I go back to Morne-Galant, for my own good.

I took my bag and my umbrella and I left without a word. I felt a bit sorry for her since I knew that as soon as René left again, her loneliness would sting, harsh like a dozen centipedes. And then I thought, "Too bad for her! *Pffff*, I don't even care!" and I was back in the rue du Cimetière just like on my first day in town, only I was wearing a pink dress instead of a white one.

The Niece

CRÉTEIL IS ONLY TEN YEARS OLDER than I am. Why was I born there—that paradise of no history, no rituals, no traditions, no one looking over your shoulder all the time like in Morne-Galant—instead of somewhere else? Why there, in that poor, drab suburb that had engendered its own way of life? Did my parents choose it deliberately or was this just inevitable, a consequence of needing work in French society in the 1970s?

In 1974, my father is thirty-one years old. He is pushing my stroller in Créteil, the idealized city of the future, down the street that will become avenue du Général-Billotte. Général Billotte was a Gaullist who served as mayor from 1965 to 1977 and dreamed of modernity for Créteil during his tenure as minister of the DOM-TOM, the overseas departments and territories. Billotte said that at a moment when "men are walking and dancing on the moon," he wanted to build a modern city for children who would learn to be "clean and French." France was suffused with a certain pride and optimism during those years, as well as a deeply rooted paternalism vis-à-vis a whole rainbow of populations, from foreigners to poor people, or toward Antilleans, whom the minister knew well—*les immigrés de l'intérieur*, immigrants from within France itself.

Brasilia, Louvain-la-Neuve, Chandigarh, Ciudad Caribia, Créteil . . . each city designed on a map, preplanned and artificial, to house the war generation's children or those born during the Trente Glorieuses,* the glorious thirty years of France's postwar economic growth. These new cities were a poetic consequence of the war and an important demonstration of the power of the French state—more visible than the baby boom itself, the American dream, or decolonization.

I AM TWO YEARS OLD. I am learning to walk in this city that was conceived of as a test run for the future; I am a little girl, clean and French.

I am four years old. I am in the pink bathroom in the apartment designed for one couple with two children. I open the striped tube of toothpaste. I have just watched the cartoons and puppets of *Récré A2* on television. There is short orange carpet in the living room that skins my knees when my brother and I play and make a racket. In the street, people always want to touch my hair.

I am eight years old. Just like every Saturday morning, I am rollerskating in front of the café next to our building. The café is noisy, dark, and filled with men and smoke. The front window is tinted glass, the ceiling lights are on even during the day.

A vaulted concrete arch connects the café to the wall of our building, creating a kind of sinister cave that reeks of urine. I have to walk through the dark passage to get to the square

---

* The Trente Glorieuses was a period of massive social, cultural, and economic change in France after World War II that lasted until 1975, and which led to social benefits integral to the modern state, such as holiday allocation, retirement payments, and social security. —Trans.

where I will play all afternoon. To avoid it, you have to go all the way around the other side of the building, which takes much longer. My instincts tell me that the café is not a place for children. I never look inside where a high copper counter-top snakes through the room. I have only a vague image of the faces that watch me as I pass by. It smells bad, the stench of tobacco, old cooking oil, and boozy perspiration spilling out from the open door. I skate as fast as I can, pumping my legs and chanting to myself with every stride, "The monster can't catch me!"

But that Saturday, the monster catches me. It's the café bar owner's dog. The mere sight of the giant German shepherd calms the more agitated café customers. The dog is irritated by the metallic clanging of my skates. The skates are cheap, each just a thin iron plate with four wheels screwed into it, the whole thing connected to my tennis shoes with leather straps. They don't go very fast. On the asphalt it sounds like a pack of screws being scraped angrily on the ground, *krring, krring, krring*. In two bounds, the guard dog is on me. His weight throws me off-balance. I collapse on concrete that is covered in spit and old gum. I kick at the air for a few seconds. The dog bites at the meatiest part of my body. Everything happens so quickly that I don't have time to even cry out. The café bar owner, who sees it all from behind the counter, leans out of the doorway and calls, "Rex! *Ici!*" The dog complies. The man and the dog go back into the café. I stay sprawled on the ground.

THE MEMORY OF THE GERMAN SHEPHERD and the intense feeling of shame I felt at that moment came flooding back to me during my visit with Antoine. "You have always lived on the mainland," she told me. "You don't really know what racism is." I didn't answer her because I wanted to keep listening. But the memory flitted around us, butterfly-like, as she said it.

When I was sure that the dog had left, I stood up onto my skates. The bite wasn't too painful, but I was very frightened. I made it to the elevator and then to the ninth floor to seek refuge in my parents' arms, who were watching television. The humiliation began to spread in my stomach and rose into my chest. I was relieved not to see anyone in the hallway. My mother opened the door. I hesitated a few seconds and then began to let the pain pour out. To speak about the incident was to confirm it had actually happened, so I paused, but then went on anyway: "The dog at the café bit me."

My mother hurried toward me, examined my body and found the two holes in my right buttock. My father went to get some cotton. I hadn't yet fully understood the heavy feeling that was weighing on my chest. I waited for my parents to explain it to me. My mother cursed the awful dog. My father cleaned my wound in silence. His movements were imbued simultaneously with rage and tenderness. Then he removed my skates, put on his jacket, and, holding my hand, took me back downstairs in the elevator.

That was the first and last time I went into the café. I felt minuscule. The smoke blinded me and the acrid smell burned my eyes. I was too little to see the man behind the counter who my father was talking to.

"Did you see what your dog did to my daughter?"

"He didn't do anything."

"What does that guy want?" asked a woman behind the counter.

My father went on: "He didn't do anything? Then what is this?"

My father turned me around and lifted up my skirt. For a second I was scared that he was going to pull down my underwear as well and that everyone would see my rear end. But the wound was clearly visible with just my skirt hiked up. I was ashamed; I wanted to run out. Above me, there was silence, then the man behind the counter announced coldly, "My dog isn't mean. The kids rile him up, making noise nonstop out there in the street."

We went to the police station. The owner of the café bar was summoned. The police simply wanted proof that his dog had been vaccinated. The owner came back to the police station with a certificate. Vaccinated! As though to say: "It's no big deal, she is just a *Négresse* after all!" Problem solved.

I went on passing by the café every day, walking with my back straight, never once looking inside, a slight pain in my stomach that dissipated once the dark passageway was behind me.

1948-1960

The Niece

THE SUMMER I TOOK MY FIRST STEPS, my mother had held my hand as we walked along a field dotted with poppies. A few months later, that field was replaced by a shopping mall and next to it was a supermarket, a parking lot, a hypermarket, and the exit to the metro station, at the very end of the metro line that traversed Paris uphill. The mall grew a little bigger each year as though it were the only solid, everlasting thing in the universe. When I was around twelve years old, I liked to explore the area with my friend Dominique, the only one of my friends who was Antillean. He lived with his mother in public housing, an HLM that had already blackened with time and cracked on the side where there used to be a school for girls. I don't think he ever saw his father, who had stayed behind in Martinique. No matter the temperature, Dominique wore the same synthetic electric-blue jacket. He was chubby and awkward, had a wavering voice, and was too tall for his age. He smiled readily but would avert his eyes whenever adults were present.

Dominique came over to my building to play on the giant asphalt area that sprouted into the market on Saturday mornings and was claimed by the children the rest of the time.

From inside the building, parents had a complete view from above down onto the games we played.

One day, Dominique was walking me back to my apartment and slid a photo out of his pocket of the Black American actor Mr. T, which he had carefully cut out of the TV guide. In the photo, which Dominique had smoothed between his chubby fingers, Mr. T stood in threatening profile, arms crossed in a jean jacket with the sleeves torn off to feature his giant shoulders.

"Look," Dominique said, "it's your dad." He held the precious photo out to me but wouldn't let me touch it. I peered at it, doubtful. Other than the color of Mr. T's skin, I saw no other resemblance between my father and the brute with the shaved head sporting a giant gold chain like some kind of guard dog.

We came out of the elevator and my father opened the door to our apartment. I showed him the photo Dominique held out: "Look at this, Dominique thinks you look like him!" I thought that Mr. T looked more how Dominique might eventually look one day, if he played a lot of sports and grew a few centimeters taller. Dominique tried to stuff the photo quickly back into his pocket but my father took it, examined it, and burst out laughing before he handed it back to Dominique, who was embarrassed. The comparison between the two amused me, but it both delighted and flattered my father.

That was back when we would watch *Dallas* on Saturday nights. There were practically no Black people on French television, and not a single Black woman. But sometimes we would catch sight of Sidney Poitier or Ray Charles, whom my mother loved—men brimming with talent and sure of themselves, classy and infinitely more glamorous than the

Antilleans we knew. They made us proud, even if our pride was misplaced.

Antilleans and Black Americans shared the same minority experience and held a part of history in common, but France and the United States did not mold individuals in the same ways. Undeniably, there was less violence in France against Black people, but on the other hand, we Antilleans had no real role models either.

What heroes could we have had? Gaston Monnerville, who led the French Senate for ten years and almost became president but was absent from France's national memory? Louis Delgrès, a stark reminder that the French Revolution quickly betrayed the very values that shaped it? Camille Mortenol, who was relegated to the dust of centuries past despite his strength and courage? Gerty Archimède, too female and too communist ever to become famous? Black writers and athletes appeared from time to time on television, but only very few. No entrepreneurs, no bakers, no "Captains of Industry," no traders, no researchers, no university presidents, no organized-crime bosses, no bishops, and no directors of prestigious cultural institutions—none of these people were ever Black. Nonetheless, we stayed on the lookout; we made a habit of it. When we actually saw a *Noir* on French television, we would call out, laughing, "Well what in the world is he doing, lost all by himself up there on TV?" France reflected the White version of itself on television back to its citizens as a uniform group without any ethnic distinction. Throughout the 1980s, people were losing faith in the notion of equal opportunity more and more, especially given the experiences of the first-generation children of immigrants: born in France, graduates, out of work. My father marched from Place de la Nation to Place de la République in protest against the privatization of banks, automobile factories, and telephone and television companies. Everywhere, the State was pulling back like a wave retreating from the beach. Fortunately, Yannick Noah had won the French Open, which lifted our spirits. Antilleans continued to want to integrate themselves into the national landscape and even enthusiastically celebrated the values of *la patrie*, of France, but we definitely felt that something was not quite right about the promises the French Republic had made.

The older I got, the more I noticed this gulf. During my schooling in prestigious universities throughout the 1990s, I stopped spending time with students from overseas France. Those whom I used to know in Créteil had mostly given up on college. None of my cousins or second cousins had undertaken lengthy degree programs. In the best of cases, like their parents before them, they were preparing to get jobs in public service or in factories. It was not with the same insouciance and optimism that Petit-Frère and Lucinde had conveyed when I asked them about arriving in Paris in the 1960s. Thirty years later, the atmosphere had completely changed. Young Antilleans, whether they were born in Sarcelles, La Courneuve, Villeurbanne, or in overseas towns like Pointe-à-Pitre and Fort-de-France, were at the same time better protected than their parents—they were French citizens with rights like any other French person—but also up against the same obstacles that immigrants from Africa or the Maghreb were facing—they were treated like foreigners.

Because they had none of their own, they chose role models from across the Atlantic: they preferred the sparkling American dream, which was harder to achieve but at least those obstacles were more concrete. In France the difficulties were ambiguous, and obscured by the country's insistence on *l'universalisme*. They identified as much with magnificent gangsters as they did with rich businessmen, rappers from ghettos, and Black New York supercops. And yet, they sensed that it was indeed an illusion: the French Antilles, although so close geographically to the United States, were fundamentally different. And the America they saw in the movies had nothing to do with the real United States. France was still their homeland, where economic success glimmered before them, but was ultimately unattainable.

Antoine: In Pointe-à-Pitre

AFTER I LEFT ÉLÉANORE'S HOUSE, I spent the next three years living with Dédé and his mother in the hills of Pointe-à-Pitre. Not in the center of town, but just about. When I left Éléanore's house, I headed toward the market and declared right away to Dédé that I was going to come and live with them. He looked at me as though I were some kind of apparition—I have never seen anyone look as happy as he did that day. We climbed the footpaths all the way to their *case*, which was set up on four concrete blocks. From there, we had a view of all of La Pointe, which spread out across the two main branches of the island, the spot where the butterfly wings connect.

Before me rolled the bluish hillsides of Basse-Terre. Behind me, Grande-Terre stretched out its plains in the sunlight like an iguana. At my feet, the ocean knocked on the door of the Pointe-à-Pitre harbor. Every morning, I looked out and devoured the compact, energetic body of the Pointe. The Pointe was small, curled tight like a shell in the fist of the ocean. To the south, the Darboussier refinery continuously spat out black smoke as cane was transformed into sugar. The factory marked the entrance to the port with its warehouses and long commercial ships packed tightly together. It was the nerve center of the town, the point of reference for all the inhabitants, much more than the Saint-Pierre-Saint-Paul cathedral, which sat a few hundred meters away. Between the two was the older grid-like part of the city with its lovely old houses and wobbly *cases* and the animated streets whose businesses I had visited with Éléanore.

Behind the refinery stretched the shantytowns of the Carénage district. All of it was mixed together, you see, and that's what I loved so much. It wasn't like in Paris where almost every neighborhood is all one color—except for here in my beloved eighteenth arrondissement. Pointe-à-Pitre was a city made up of all the strangeness and variety of every skin color; you'd go from seeing the bizarrely rich to the mundanely poor as you went from one door to the next. Everyone dumped their shit into the same gutter. And this gutter really existed—right there in the middle of the city, back when it was just a little current flowing on boards joined shoddily together that ran through our filthy neighborhoods. People living in the shantytowns went either uphill or downhill every day toward the center of town to work.

I also went downhill to work. I had to help Dédé and his mother pay a small fortune to the Black grifter who rented them the tiny square of bare ground where they had set up their house. Every week, he waved his finger under our noses and threatened to evict us. I still don't know who gave him the rights to that tiny strip of land. He must certainly have earned it through some swing of his knife.

Local authorities allowed this kind of embezzlement and racketeering outside of the city. It kept the mayor from having to build housing for the poor people. The Whites and the mulattoes who owned the city center also let it happen. That way, they always had a teeming labor force available nearby without ever having to build a single wall of housing for them.

The residents would collect sheet metal and boards near the port to build a window or a fence, and after every big storm, they would start over again. They did this so often that one little house would take on a hundred different shapes over the span of two years.

Sometimes I would go with Dédé to pick over the debris near the harbor. That's how we ended up building a little room not much bigger than a closet, out of the way from the main room where his mother slept.

More than ever, I had the idea to open a store. It was the spirit of my mother's, Eulalie's, that I was striving to re-create. Nothing less than what she had. Maybe more than that, one day, if I did things right. Dédé introduced me to a shopkeeper in town, a woman named Man Pilote, a coolie* who carefully selected and sold clothing she would buy in Martinique.

Man Pilote was older, reserved, and mostly quiet. Her children had left to live in mainland France. Every month she would send them money, but she never heard any news in return. She wore several heavy gold necklaces that weighed down her dress. She wore her Indian hair pulled back tight without a single gray strand to be seen. Her face, however, was wrinkled like the skin of a blood sausage sucked dry. Her piercing eyes sat deep in their sockets and were crowned by the red ink dot that coolie women wore on their foreheads. She looked me over from head to toe. After a moment of not saying anything, she asked me:

"Your name is Antoine? Like the saint, the hermit?"

"Yes—the hermit Antoine talks to me often. He comes to see me. Maybe because of my name."

"And what does he say?"

---

* coolie: in both French and English, a pejorative term for an unskilled native laborer in India, China, and some other Asian countries. —Trans.

"He talks about his difficult journey and encourages me on mine."

"And what do you know about business?"

"I know everything there is to know: sell more tomorrow than you did today."

"I'll see you tomorrow then. And get here early so I can explain everything to you."

AND THAT'S HOW I STARTED OFF. Dédé knew I would get along well with Madame Pilote. She was eager to sit way in the back of her store, far away from the blinding noonday sun and haggling customers. Back there, sitting still, she would think about her sons and tend to her aching lower back. I quickly understood that her pain would not go away as long as she didn't hear news from her children. That was fine by me; I basically had the entire store to myself, with no one looking over my shoulder. And for the first time, I had a salary. I was hoping that her sons wouldn't show up out of the blue and decide to close her store; I needed to get my training in. During my first days there, I was an excellent salesperson.

As I got older, I grew even more beautiful. At nineteen, I was a ripe fruit at the height of the season, firm and sweet. I drew men and women to me with my smooth talk and my sweet smile. I willingly spent entire days on my feet at the store's entrance greeting passersby. I'd arrange and rearrange the wooden hangers that held the sheets, dresses, and blouses for sale ten times over. When a customer came inside the store, I became their hands, their eyes, and their ears. With my talk, I spun stories that made every item seem precious, even the dish towels that were just squares sewn out of flour bags. As for the men, they were eager to linger for five minutes to listen to my sales pitches, provided that they could check me out and ask me—always in vain—out on dates.

AT NOON, Man Pilote and I would close the store until two o'clock and I would stay and eat a delicious goat Colombo curry that she had prepared the night before. We talked mostly about religion. I showed her the lovely glittered illustrated cards that the Sisters of Charity had given to me at the Saint-Pierre-Saint-Paul Catholic church. I only had to wave my hand over it to feel jolts from head to toe. I shared the message of the cards with her. She was intrigued—sometimes she laughed, sometimes she looked at me worriedly, but she was entertained all the same. I confided to her that I wanted one day to go on a pilgrimage to Lourdes to honor Bernadette. She told me about the respect that we owed to our ancestors and to our reincarnations, blending together the Catholic saints with Indian gods. I had never been to any Hindu ceremonies, but I had seen one of their temples near Morne-Galant painted in bright colors with silk flags flying overhead.

Man Pilote gently teased me about how young I was.

"You don't know anything about life, girl," she said, "and yet you spout off your advice about living right all day long."

Hanging the new dresses on hangers I would retort, "But I saw a vision in our field back home."

"Sure," she would say skeptically. "Save your fancy talk for the customers."

"No, but I did! It happened one night when I was waiting for my mother. I was alone and I was puttering around near the front of the house. No one was around, the neighbor wasn't home. Not a sound. You know how it is in the country, Man Pilote, at that time of the year. The sugarcane had been cut for some time so things were quiet and I could see far away from the house, and I stayed outside because the moon made it brighter outside than inside. I wanted to see my parents as they came home. So I opened my eyes wide and thought I heard something right in front of me."

"Right in front of you? Well that was no doubt your stomach growling."

"No, I am telling you, it was right in front of me, but I couldn't see anything; it was pitch black, but I heard it getting closer."

"What did the noise sound like?"

"Well, like heavy feet stamping. And breathing."

"Was it your parents?"

"Oh no, Man Pilote, it wasn't my parents, but I didn't want to be scared, so I walked out into the field where it was coming from. I didn't have a light, but I could see pretty clearly with the round moon just over my head, and I wanted to see what it was."

"And did you see it?"

"Yes! All of a sudden, I saw it! It was a steer, a beautiful white steer that was lying on the ground."

"So it was nothing, then."

"Well sure it was, Man Pilote! Because this steer had two brilliant rays of light coming out of his eyes! They shone! *Shone!*"

"Like the headlights of a truck?"

"Oh, brighter than that! Like two suns spinning! They shone like the entire sky was there in its two eyes! And the steer watched me and didn't move. With those two whirls of light in the middle of his face. He was laying down, calm, beautiful, and white. It wasn't one of Hilaire's cattle—I knew all of them."

"And its horns, what were they like?"

"Big. Also white. Very sharp."

"So what did you do?"

"Well, what else do you do when you come across a steer lying in the field? I left him there and watched him as I walked back to the house. But I will never forget those eyes."

WHILE MAN PILOTE LISTENED to my stories, she would laugh and clap her hands. In the evenings after I had pulled down the metal curtain to the store, I would walk back up toward Dédé and his mother's house. You had to know the neighborhood well and grope around in the dark in the labyrinth of narrow streets because there weren't any city lights on that side of town. The kerosene lamps that glowed red in the open windows of the little houses—we called them *chalumeaux*—lit my way. Some houses were as dark as caves because the kerosene cost so much, but I could hear lively discussions happening inside. The women cooked outside in barrels sawed in half, with a brood of hungry, whining children around them. The prostitutes came out around that time of night and would murmur hello. I undressed and went to swim in the little river that flowed just behind our home, where everyone washed up and threw out their trash.

I kept my eye on the neighbor who lived closest to our house who had lived alone ever since his wife had left him and taken their children. Camouflaged in the dark, he would lean his tall, skinny frame near the corner of our place. He was always ogling me. He was perfectly quiet, but I could feel his presence. Everyone in the neighborhood called him Bilar because one day a doctor decreed that his house was "full of bilharzia." At first, not understanding, he was very proud of the designation. But then he started pissing blood and they tried to make him take a bunch of medicine. He didn't have a job and lived off soup brought by the neighbors.

Even though our neighborhood was a mosquito-infested hole and a haven for disease, I liked it. During the day, bloody old Bilar was not a total oaf. He'd split coconuts and pour me the refreshing coconut water. Madame Gouyolle, who wove between her thick, smooth legs the most beautiful baskets in the market, popped out one bright-eyed baby after another like clockwork. There was Phaëton, the shoemaker, a skilled craftsman who worked hard to feed his six children. They were the first in the neighborhood to go to *lycée*. Even the youngest one with the twisted-up foot went to school, and Phaëton made a magnificent pair of shoes especially formed to his foot. In addition to having a good head on his shoulders, Phaëton also had a kind heart and cared a lot about children. He would make them thick-soled sandals out of strips of tire, explaining that they would protect them from illnesses. But most of the children preferred to play barefoot in the puddles, so they caught worms that later broke through their skin. All those filthy children would run between the houses with kites, hurtle down slopes in wagons they'd made themselves, and play *palet* throwing their iron disks onto the board and yelling out, "*Y ké, y pa ké!*"—don't make it, don't make it!—joyfully up and down the streets.

LIFE WITH DÉDÉ WAS DECENT even though his mother didn't particularly care for me. Oftentimes when I would refuse to help her in the kitchen, she would mutter, "*Bèl pa ka tchuit an* *kannari*"*—which meant that I was lovely but useless. I would shrug with contempt. She mellowed when she saw Dédé come out of the small space that served as our room with a blissful smile on his face. It seems I was good in bed, so she tolerated me, hoping that I would give her a whole brood of grandchildren.

In our *case*, the only thing that was remotely attractive was a newspaper photo of General de Gaulle and his wife, Yvonne. Man Dédé had cut it out and put it in a gold frame that she set on top of the wooden trunk where she kept her two dresses. She wore the blue dress from Monday to Saturday, washed it on Sunday, and then put on the yellow dress for the following week. On the Lord's day, she would wear a simple long shirt. Before she fell asleep on top of the iron bedspring that she folded up during the day, she would take one last look at Yvonne.

"Why do you like Yvonne so much?" I asked her one day.

"I just adore her! Yvonne is the mother of all of France. She looks after the general, which can't be easy—I too know what it's like to have responsibilities."

"But why exactly do you like her so much? God is the only one we are supposed to truly adore."

"Because she was born on the same day and in the same year as I was."

"So?"

"So she's like my sister. I know that she and I would get along very well. She is a strong woman. She has lived through many incredible hardships, but she is very brave!"

"What incredible hardships has she gone through?"

* *Bèl pa ka tchuit an kannari*: a common Créole expression that means "beauty is not cooked in a pot": beauty cannot be eaten; it is therefore useless. —Trans.

"Apparently she has a daughter who is ill. Very sick. So ill that she doesn't go out in public."

"So what, we aren't brave? Just because she wears big hats and has a big fancy automobile that follows her everywhere, even to the market?"

I *tchip*ed and muttered like Hilaire used to do: *"Ka ou pé comprend!"*—that's nonsense!

*

DON'T THINK THAT I WAS NAÏVE. I knew who de Gaulle was. During the war, people would resist with both provocation and discretion at once, murmuring his name discreetly, right under the nose of Governor Sorin and his police. Some painted de Gaulle's name in black letters on the walls next to Valentino's name. Valentino—our district representative who was openly opposed to the Vichy agents and had called for Guadeloupe to rally with Free France before he was eventually sent off to a labor camp. On June 18, many had tried to tune in to the BBC broadcast on a radio hidden in the meadow to hear de Gaulle's speech. For three years, Guadeloupeans had fought with no support against the Vichy French racists, who, with the support of the *békés*, held the French islands under the heel of their boot and violated freedoms they would have never dared to breach in unoccupied France. We still remembered when Napoleon had reinstated slavery. So the women and men had taken up arms, distributed food and supplies, and kept up our relationships with British islands nearby.

It was the same in Martinique. We had our heroes, young people, both women and men who fell to police gunfire, and we ended up blocking ships carrying France's gold in our ports, ships that the Germans and Americans wanted badly.

In 1943, the entire Antillean population chased out Governor Sorin and Admiral Robert. But in the end, where de Gaulle fell short was after all that, when he arrived on the Champs-Élysées with his tanks and his flags, he uttered not a single word about the Resistance in the Antilles. When he created his National Council of the Resistance,* did you see a single *Nègre* invited to participate? Not a one—it was as though crossing by boat on a windy night from Guadeloupe to Dominica under Vichy naval fire wasn't worth as much as the sabotage of a train between Valence and Grenoble.†

So, Yvonne de Gaulle, in her little golden frame on Man Dédé's trunk, seemed to be looking down her nose at me. And I just wanted to slap Man Dédé and her idiotic devotion to that woman. Her lack of ambition for herself, for her son, for us, infuriated me.

At sunrise, I would watch the town. I felt like one of the boats down below, ready to sail the Caribbean Sea. Dédé and his mother tended to leave very early for the port to buy fish they would resell at the market. In the afternoons, she would cook the dasheens and crabs in our back courtyard that she would sell the next day. This suited them. The only thing that scared Man Dédé was the idea that her son would leave to grow bananas in Basse-Terre like his uncles and cousins. She would declare with urgency:

---

* National Council of the Resistance: the body that directed and coordinated the different movements of the French Resistance, including the press, trade unions, and members of political parties that were hostile to the Vichy regime, starting in 1943. —Trans.

† The French Resistance coordinated explosions of trains run by the Germans via the Vichy government. At the same time, the Antillean Resistance in Guadeloupe and Martinique, *la dissidence*, orchestrated reconnaissance missions by boat, which involved the same level of danger and impact but were never acknowledged. —Trans.

"I didn't raise you to go and break your back working for the Whites!"

Dédé would answer, "When I have enough money, I'll buy a nice piece of land over there and plant hectares of banana trees."

"And who will sell you the land?" I'd ask. Because I agreed with his mother on this point. Man Dédé retorted, pounding her fist on her thigh:

"Grande-Terre and banana trees are for the *békés*. Who do you think you are, going over there, going up against them like that? You'll end up working for them, oh yes you will. Is the life of a slave what you want? Take your cousin's boss— what he likes most of all is patrolling the rows of banana trees, his gun on his back, checking to see if the *Nègres* are working like they should. I did not leave Basse-Terre so that my son could go right back there and get himself killed. The future is in *l'en-ville*. This is where you should be, no matter what it costs you."

And I'd nod enthusiastically. So Dédé would give in for a while. But the dream of bananas continued to hold him captive.

On Sundays, we would walk around the Place de la Victoire and then observe the never-ending activity on the port. Dédé would point out the boats one by one:

"That one is coming from Port-au-Prince. That one's coming in from Martinique."

"And where does the prettiest fabric come in from?"

"I don't know. But I know which cargo ships take the bananas to the mainland—I dream of getting on board one of them sometime, to go see what France is like."

"Why France?"

"Well first, because it's our homeland. Second, because I

don't speak any other languages. And also because that's where the bananas are going."

"But what about the rest? Where are the other goods going?"

"You see those boats over there?"

"Sure I do. Is everything stored in the hull?"

"In the hold, yes, in the shipping containers."

"That one comes from Venezuela, doesn't it? Man Pilote is always telling me that that's where you can get the finest cotton."

"Don't you worry. Your wedding dress will be the most beautiful dress you've ever seen," Dédé whispered, wrapping his arms around me. I just shrugged.

They say me perpetually dodging a marriage with Dédé drove him to despair. But I left him because he never really knew where his own boat was headed.

Lucinde

I MOVED IN TO ÉLÉANORE'S HOUSE after Antoine left. Éléanore was proud and snobbish and wanted to be able to get by on her own, but even with her husband's business going well, she couldn't manage by herself. She came to Papa's house to pick me up one day when I was playing on the patio with your father. You better believe I jumped at the chance to go with her!

So now it was my turn to leave for Pointe-à-Pitre. When I went to see Antoine at Dédé's house, she warned me about Uncle René. I was scared, but in the end I was spared by Nonore's second pregnancy: she wanted another maid. They could afford it and there was certainly enough work for both of us while she played at *mater dolorosa*, the martyr. As a result, René must have thought that it would be less risky to go after the other one, a skinny dark girl, who didn't say much and had no family to complain to. So I was fine on that front, and when René disappeared into his room with her, I looked the other way or set myself up in the yard to work on sewing.

Then, after a few months, I'd had enough. First of all, I could sense that Nonore wasn't getting along with me as well as she had with Antoine. And yet, I took much better care of the house. René even said so. Whether it was the children who exhausted her or her lashing out at me instead of René, she was quick to strike out and would often hit me with one of her slippers.

One day, I worked up the courage to tell her as respectfully as I could:

"Man Nonore, I would like to work. What I mean is that I want to work outside this house. I would give you half of what I earn."

She looked at me as though I had uttered an obscenity and set her arms akimbo on her misshapen hips.

"Half of what you earn? So remind me, who's feeding you here? You want me to put a roof over your head while you do nothing around the house, and then you want to go out and earn even more money, taking full advantage of how generous I've been?"

"Alright then, I'll give you all of what I earn. But I have to learn a trade. For later."

"I know that better than anyone. You are my family and I'm supposed to help you, and I'm not going to let you sit there yawning on the bench in the backyard any longer. I have to do something—the neighbors are watching after all. I'll help you for your father's sake, and for the sake of our dearly departed Eulalie, who everyone loved, from what I can remember. I was so young, after all."

Everyone loved to bring up the story of how everyone loved my mother. So how in the world did Eulalie end up struggling all by herself? Why did no one from the Lebecq side come to help her when she lost the store? They knew very well she couldn't count on Hilaire. I listened to Nonore patiently, and, at the end, she told me about a baker who was looking for help. That's how I got my start in the bakery two streets over.

I was happy even though she made me come home as soon as my workday was over, as well as cook meals and do the dishes for the whole family on Sundays. "Don't ever let anyone say that I left you to wander out on the streets!" Nonore would huff, slumping into her favorite chair.

In the evenings I would race home, both wanting to spare myself Nonore's ire and fearing the street corners where the most dangerous *Nègres* lived. But what did Man Nonore think, that I wasn't going to meet any boys at the bakery? Well, quickly enough, there was one boy who stopped by almost every day, supposedly to buy a croissant, but really he came to check me out. He had very light-brown skin, almost white, and wavy hair, clean shoes, and a smile like a crooner. He would stand there shuffling his feet and floating in a shirt too big for his body, scratching his head as he tried to figure out what to say. One afternoon, when I was putting the warm loaves into the display baskets, he felt confident enough to come over.

He strode across the street and stood in front of the counter. I had just begun wrapping a First Communion cake with flowers on it, all white with a cross made of sugar pearls on the top. I can still see him once he arrived, carefully inching toward me, one foot on the blue-tiled entryway of the store, the other still in the dusty street, his hand on his hip, thinking he was striking a cool, relaxed pose. He leaned his forearm on the counter, revealing a gold bracelet on his wrist. He let a blue-and-white checkered handkerchief dangle from his fingertips.

"*Mademoiselle?*"

"Yes?"

"Would you please wash this handkerchief?"

"*Non, monsieur.*"

"And why not?"

"Because I don't even know you."

"But you've seen me around."

"I have seen you around, but I don't know you. And I don't have time to wash your handkerchief."

The conversation was never about the handkerchief, but I was happy and he was too. From then on, we'd always exchange a few words and joke around. His name was Charlemagne Tarsis. Everyone called him Tatar.

The adults jumped on our case right away. Éléanore started:

"Alright, so who is that dandy who thinks he can chat you up while you're at work? You should be ashamed!"

"But he wasn't saying anything!"

"What do you mean, not saying anything? Why was he flapping his gums, then?"

"But he wasn't!"

"Uh-huh! And so you were just flapping your gums too for no reason, then? Wait till your father finds out about this!"

Not long after, a family meeting was held with Hilaire, Man Nonore, and Antoine, who was, ridiculously enough, considered a respectable family elder at that point. During the whole conversation, I stayed seated with my head down. But I felt I was on the verge of adulthood and wanted them to know it.

"I know his mother," Man Nonore began. "She limps so badly that you'd think she was a ship pitching back and forth out at sea. She works ironing clothes. No father in sight. But"—she sighed—"he's a hardworking boy from what I have heard. He works at Darboussier."

"Well they should just get married, then," Antoine who didn't want to spend all day discussing the matter, declared.

"How long should the engagement last?" Éléanore asked,

as if she were checking on how long a cake should bake in the oven.

"Six months," Papa said.

"Six months? That takes us right to Christmas. Come on now, they can't get married at Christmas."

"In that case, ask him for a three-month engagement," I suggested shyly.

Each face turned in my direction, furious and dumb-struck.

"Mind your own business!" Nonore hissed.

When I think back on it, I wonder why they were watching me like a hawk while, at the same time, Antoine was living with Dédé and wasn't even married. She never had to answer to anyone. She's lucky because on more than one occasion, Dédé could have gone and complained to the police. Instead, he came to the house. When it got really heated between him and Antoine, she became ferocious. Once he lifted up his shirt and I saw two nasty scars on his back. Antoine had attacked him with scissors. That's just like Antoine.

Antoine: The Shipping Container Life

IF WE WERE BACK IN GUADELOUPE, I would have prepared a leaf bath for your baby. We would put the leaves in a big tub and let it heat up in the sun. All the kids were rubbed down like that to help them sleep soundly or to cure a cold. Or calm itchiness. And what do you use here, hmm? Creams and powders, without knowing what any of them are made of! I also believed in France's medicine, up until a White person told me one day that she was treating her daughter's throat by rubbing her chest with Jamaican black castor oil and bay rum oil. Can you imagine? That's exactly what our grandmothers used! And if a White person does it, you can be sure that it's quality stuff and that it works. So where did we leave off last time? Oh yes! *L'en-ville!* Living in town!

I was beginning to grow tired of the landlord who showed up at our door every weekend demanding rent for the muddy square he was renting us. How long was this going to last? Were we going to keep paying him all that money until our dying day for a hole with no water or electricity, where the firemen wouldn't have even come to put out a fire or send help in an emergency?

After three years working for Madame Pilote, I had

amassed a small sum of money that would allow me, at last, to take charge of my own life. Dédé agreed to move with me to the city center, but Man Dédé didn't want to follow us there. She was smart; she understood that life with me in the city would be no picnic for her.

"I'll stay here," she said, settling onto her stool. "Go on and live your life in *l'en-ville* if you want to."

I took one last look at the room with its four windows that let the trade winds blow in, the floor and the walls of boards crammed together, bleached from the rain, the red sheet-metal roof hanging on fat nails. It sat on six big cinder blocks to keep it out of the mud, which made the whole thing look fragile. But actually, the winds had often blown in beneath the ceiling but never succeeded in carrying the house off, and it was left intact even after the harsh winds of the rainy season.

So we left our *case* and Man Dédé was fine staying behind, on the condition that she could come see us whenever she wanted, and that Dédé would help her pay the weekly rent. I was still thinking about Éléanore's pretty house on rue du Cimetière, and I didn't want to go on living like a rat.

Dédé found a place with an apartment for rent on rue Schoelcher. It wasn't as good as rue Frébault, which was the best road for businesses, but it was a good spot. It was near the harbor and had a similar kind of excitement to it. It was the former house of some well-to-do notary or doctor that had been divided into three small apartments. Ours was in the center of the house, laid out over two stories. Two stories, just like at Éléanore's house! The pinnacle of elegance. We moved in joyfully. I'd had the idea to use the ground floor for my future business. We would live above it with a kitchen, a bedroom, and a living room. Man Pilote helped us out with the first installment of rent and the deposit; she had complete faith in my business skills. She gave up her trip to the mainland in order to invest some money in my business. Dédé became a kind of all-purpose employee. He kept busy clearing out our new place, cleaned it, installed furniture, and bought a cash register.

I knew rue Frébault inside and out. I knew all the little shops that opened out into the street and everything that was sold in each one. I knew who stocked up in good locations and who knew more than one way to get around paying import duties, who was working with and dependent on the *békés*, and who would try to go it alone.

My first idea was to set myself apart from the other stores by selling goods that you couldn't find anywhere else, which I would choose myself, item by item. To this end, I learned all the schedules of the boats that left the port in Pointe-à-Pitre. On the twenty-first of every month, it was Roseau, the capital of Dominica, Sainte-Lucie, and the Grenadines. The fifteenth was Port of Spain, Dutch Guiana,* and Cayenne. In April, a boat arrived from Marseille. September brought in the highwinds as well as the uncertainty about arrivals and departures. I also learned to arrange things with the customs officers on board: they didn't need to know about every single thing I was buying. It was easy to hide gold in my blouse or in my underwear.

MY FIRST TRIP was on the *Magellan*, which left for Caracas at eight in the morning. I sat on the deck with my ticket in my

---

* Suriname.

hand. The men were watching me because of my tall, hour-glass frame, my green dress embroidered with lace (a gift from Dédé), and my men's shoes. I remember that morning a sailor tried to get a bull to cross from the front deck to the rear one. Try as he might, that bull was paralyzed. When the sailor tried to get behind it to push, he lost his balance and grabbed the railing at the last minute. Then he rolled under the animal's feet. In the end, it took five of them to free him from the desperate animal, who was mooing as loud as the horns of the boats leaving the port.

Watching the boats come and go, I imagined my future store with its organized window display, crowds gathering to press their foreheads against the glass and gaze inside. I was very excited. The boat finally left the port. I saw the detailed contours of the coast of Guadeloupe in front of me stretching farther and farther out, with its coconut trees that looked like flowers and the mangrove like a gray carpet spotted with white birds. Then it all grew smaller and smaller until it was just a dot on the ocean where the boat was leaving a frothy trail.

Caracas wasn't very different from Pointe-à-Pitre. It was much larger, with giant mountains all around it and a few large roadways. I found some Antilleans there who worked in construction or in oil refineries. I quickly began speaking Créole mixed with Spanish. People in the market understood me well enough to launch into endless dealmaking chatter, and I had sufficient vocabulary to buy decent quantities of fabric and a bit of gold jewelry. We hadn't seen gold in Guadeloupe since the time of rations in World War II and it was starting to reappear little by little, like stars in the night. The women went crazy for it. On that first trip, I also bought a few kitchen utensils that you could find only very rarely at the market in Pointe-à-Pitre.

When I came back, I sold my merchandise at Man Pilote's store and split the profits with her. For the next trip, she gave me a sum to invest in items I thought were the most interesting. That's how I built up my stock, little by little, for my own store.

My real passion was business. It wasn't the profits that interested me so much as the ability to move items from one place to another, to possess one day what I would abandon the next with no regrets. I was focused on trinkets and fabric. My merchandise was like water that needed to flow steadily, like a strong river. I nourished my supply with wholesalers on the British islands and the South American coast, and I knew how to please my clients—just like a bee making its nectar and feeding its larvae. I returned to Guadeloupe charged with bundles and packages that were as important to me as the blood in my own veins.

During all my trips to and from the port, I watched Guadeloupe change. At the beginning of the 1950s, our population lived off the rhythms of the boats arriving in the port. We surrendered to the whims of the biggest businesses that were colluding with elected officials, the elected officials themselves colluding with the mainland. For ages, not a grain of rice had grown on the archipelago, but sacks arrived every day from Pondicherry or China. Even the hardiest wheat wouldn't have been able to sprout in our humid, salty earth. But now, French bread was preferred to the flat, gray, old-fashioned galette we made from local manioc, and bakers stocked up on wheat flour from France on credit. Guadeloupeans paid for codfish caught in the cold water of Newfoundland, then dried and salted. The fresh fish sold by Man Dédé at the market was too expensive for most people.

The trade of the shipping containers forced an entirely new

identity onto those of us who lived there. It was an identity forged by ripping away our old, local culture, and cobbling together the shreds of an odd assortment of histories: curry from the Indies, codfish from the boats, French baguettes—all against a backdrop of Caribbean and African cuisine. In exchange for all this, we had only rum and bananas to export. Little by little, local cultures disappeared. Importers headquartered in Le Havre and Paris reigned. And I was changing too. I got by as well as I could in the free-for-all environment where customs officers and police always sided with the most powerful.

ON MY THIRD TRIP to Caracas, as I was waiting in a café on the port for the boat to leave, a man came and sat down across from me. He was quite tan and seemed like a White man who had lived his entire life out in the sun. He wore a worn-out gray linen suit and a hat that swallowed half of his face, but I could still make out his long, hooked nose underneath. He began his overture with a refrain that I knew well, speaking in French but with a funny accent:

"*Mignonne*, you are the flower of this garden."

"Instead of a garden, I see only boats, rats, and smoke," I told him, on edge.

"You're right. I prefer to toast the end of a hard day of work with a glass of rum rather than the questionable water in this café."

He ordered a *ti punch* and offered me one. I declined. He smiled and dabbed at his forehead with a handkerchief. I was impressed that a White man I didn't know had just spoken to me that way. But I remained on the defensive.

"This isn't the first time I've seen you. You seem to me like you're a clever, resourceful person. Where are you from—Guadeloupe or Martinique?"

I didn't answer. He smiled behind his hat and guessed: "Guadeloupe." He began speaking to me in Créole with his strange, fascinating accent.

"Where are *you* from?" I asked.

"I was born on les Saintes.* I grew up in French Guiana but I live here in Caracas."

He smiled. His look, his accent, his attitude hypnotized me. So many new experienes at once, you understand. And all of it in some tiny café where I had ended up, tired after checking my merchandise, where I didn't dare order anything other than a small glass of guava juice.

The café owner, a casually dressed young man, was nowhere to be found. We had to wait a long time to be served. A broken record played a bit of guaracha that skipped at the same moment. The young man came to reset it to the beginning when by chance he noticed us.

As the man across from me sat there, his cheek flinched. He wiped his forehead again with his handkerchief and for a brief moment I saw his eyes: very bright and blue.

"Listen. I am going to show you something that might interest you."

He looked over each shoulder and dug around in his jacket pocket. He took out a little handkerchief that he set delicately on the table. At the other tables toward the back of the bar, a few sweaty sailors and factory workers huddled together in discussion. I always chose the seat next to the door in order to be able to leave if a guy got too pushy. I looked at the cloth and didn't move. In one delicate sweep, he unfolded the four

* les Saintes: the Islands of the Saints are in the archipelago of Guadeloupe. —Trans.

corners of the cloth onto the table. Stacked in the center of the hankie, right there like little chickadees, were a dozen diamonds. They were rough diamonds, the first I had ever seen in my life, but right away I understood how beautiful and how valuable they were.

Antoine: Going Back and Forth

WHEN I CAME BACK from Caracas, I didn't say anything to Dédé. I was wondering what had pushed me to agree to the deal with the feverish-looking man. My handkerchief with the four diamonds inside had burned against my chest during the whole return trip. I clenched them whenever a customs officer came near me. The voyage went by without a hitch, and once I came home, I kept them in my pocket until I found a way to unload them.

The man from the bar whose name I didn't even know had proposed giving them to me in exchange for a sum that was high but not exorbitant. He told me about a jewelry store in Pointe-à-Pitre where I could sell them for a good price, and another in Grenada, one in Puerto Rico, and if I was brave enough, I could go all the way to Cuba, where I would make even more. He seemed to know interested resellers in all corners of the Caribbean. He had noticed I was a salesperson and took a chance on me, he explained, because I'd seemed capable and determined.

Caracas gave me wings. I saw rich Venezuelans driving expensive cars on the wide streets. I had stopped at an art gallery out of curiosity where I saw paintings by Wifredo

Lam and sculptures by a man named Jesús Soto; so many shapes, creative feats that I never would have believed I'd see with my own eyes. I, who until then didn't know what an art gallery or a museum was. It was an entirely new world that I was discovering, and it drove me not to become rich or to leave everything behind, but simply to have adventures that would set my youth ablaze, stoked with passion. That man who appeared in the dark bar where I was sitting all alone—he who had shown me something magnificent and pure inside an old handkerchief—he was a sign from the Virgin Mary.

The store began to do really well. The customers stopped to linger in front of my straw hats, my tablecloths, the bolts of cotton fabric, and various items I brought back from my expeditions. It was my den of wonders. One day you'd find aprons in all sizes, on another, shirts of off-white poplin made for the colder nights in Bretagne that wealthy customers would buy on vacations away from the mainland. Bobbins of thread, bundles of zippers, sewing machines, and also tea sets, medicine jars, and leather bags were spread out between the lampshades made of conch shells.

Morne-Galant was far away, with its quiet countryside and its long, languorous evenings. I was just like Pointe-à-Pitre: brimming with energy and quiet optimism for a new era, but still with hints of poverty and bitterness.

The whole city was evolving before my eyes. You could still see some *cases* and a few nicer wooden houses in the centrally located neighborhoods, but over the years, the city had been overrun with cranes as concrete took hold as king. It showed up first in all its splendor on the buildings erected to the glory of the French government—a physical manifestation of the State that ruled over us. Heavy bags of concrete that were hoisted up by the work crews came directly from France, and little by little, concrete replaced the logwood and sapodilla that had always been used to build beautiful mansions. Wood kept interiors cool and insects away. The concrete took in heat and turned the buildings into ovens used to cook sugarcane. Centipedes loved infesting them. The walls darkened and cracked beneath the assaulting winds, salt, and earthquakes. Large fissures appeared. In short, the concrete wasn't made for our fiery island, but that wasn't obvious right away. Elected officials were all too proud: concrete was what was being used in Paris and it impressed the *ababas*, the gullible. To deal with the insects sleeping in our homes, they sold us powerful insecticides from Germany to spray every morning and night. The insides of homes started to reek of exterminating product. Eventually, poor people who wanted to imitate the rich also began to dream of cement. Anyone who could save up twelve francs would set out to build something in cement on his property. The *cases* were transformed into worksites: they would start with one layer of concrete for the floor and then add four posts, working their way gradually, penny by penny, for years. *Modernity, at last!* they said.

Twenty years later, it was an all-you-can-eat buffet, a real field day for the Lafarge concrete company: de Gaulle commissioned a Lafarge plant on the port so that concrete could be made on the island. In the 1970s, pillars with iron bars began to appear on all the houses, scraping at the sky like promises: the second story would be for the children's rooms. And when the second stories were never finished, the families held off on painting. The concrete clouded into gray beneath the sun. Even way out in the country, everything was getting covered in concrete, concrete, concrete, all of it—it was like an irresistible itch, wanting to do things the way they were being done in France.

But let me go back twenty years to when the shift toward modernity began. In the city, the constant risk of hurricanes, earthquakes, and the pummeling of waves against the foundations of the big, newly painted administrative buildings didn't matter. Concrete meant civilization. It was announced that an airport would be built. As we waited for the airport, the port carried on, sleepless.

On Sundays, I went to church. While I was there, Dédé traveled the countryside with a huge sack on his shoulder filled with items I had bought back. All day long, he went door-to-door to sell dish towels, handkerchiefs, and anything else his shoulders could bear the weight of for twelve hours in the heat. He came back at night exhausted and I would tally up the day's earnings.

I THOUGHT CONSTANTLY ABOUT THE DIAMONDS. I didn't want to go to one of the jewelry shops in Pointe-à-Pitre; it was too risky. So I calmly waited for my next trip.

On the morning that I set off for Anguilla, I took my handkerchief wrapped around its four stones with me. I sat on the outer deck as usual, near the edge of the ship. If the sea spray left me wet, I would laugh and clutch my hat. It actually worked quite well as the customs officers, upon seeing my wet blouse, would grow flustered and avoid looking at me too closely, so their inspections were much briefer—a few questions about the luggage at my feet and that was that.

Upon my arrival, I bought a few things for my store using my beginner English and Créole, which was an open sesame with all the business owners. There were not many people in that hamlet of expansive beaches, but the few hotels that existed were luxury ones. I walked along the main road all the way to the town looking for a jewelry store. There were only a few colorful wooden houses and a few cars being eaten by rust. I gave up and boarded a boat headed for Saint Martin.

I arrived at the height of the day. The air was saturated with sea spray and the sun glinted off red rocks in the harbor, which looked like molten lava. Right away, I went by taxi to the Dutch part of the island. Next to the row of restaurants, I found a jewelry store.

A tiny bell jingled when I pushed open the door, and a young blonde woman looked up from behind the counter. She didn't hide her surprise at seeing me there.

"How can I help you?" she asked politely but coldly. I told her I wanted to speak to the owner, that I had something to show him. A large man in glasses, as blond as she was but older, came out.

He looked me over from head to toe and asked in English what I wanted. I approached the counter. I would have preferred to show them to him in the back, in his office, but oh well. I slowly took out the handkerchief and unfolded it. He took his time examining them, his head down, not touching them, as though they were a venomous snake. Then I realized he was asking me where they came from. I told him I was Venezuelan and that my husband found them digging in a river, and that we were afraid of having them stolen from us there. I'm not sure if he believed me.

"How much?" he asked in English.

I left with a thick packet of American bills—the first I had ever seen. Before I walked out of his store, he called me back. I turned around, my heart slamming in my chest. He told me if I found more diamonds in my river, he had an American client who might be interested. I nodded, pretending I hadn't fully understood him.

Afterward, I realized that if the owner had called the police, I didn't even have a valid explanation prepared. I was thrilled, nearly euphoric. I wondered if I would see the man with the diamonds again on my next trip to Caracas.

Petit-Frère

THE AFTERNOON THAT TATAR MARRIED LUCINDE, he gazed at her possessively as all the family gathered around for the wedding banquet. He kept saying "my wife" and it was as though each time he said it, he grew twenty centimeters taller. My sister was nineteen. I remember her slightly tense smile—as though she couldn't completely erase a secret thought from her expression. She wore a simple off-white, close-fitting dress with a square neckline. She had sewn it herself, and it was understated and perfectly fitted. The dress was evidence of her talents but it was not extravagant. She must have copied it from an American fashion magazine she'd taken from Éléanore; she copied it so well that she looked like a famous singer from the Bahamas.

Tatar had no father, no education, and none of the good manners that are appreciated by the mothers of brides. Anyway, Hilaire was the only one he needed to convince, and Tatar received his blessing when he took Hilaire a bottle of rum and a set of dominoes one Sunday. Tatar also had the advantage of being very light-skinned, so that when the Ezechiel aunts saw him, they declared to Lucinde, "If your children are born with his coloring, they'll definitely be spared."

Lucinde was keen on having a nice wedding party in

Morne-Galant, but I knew that she was ashamed of our house with its run-down yard dotted with piles of manure from Papa's cattle. She wanted something nicer, especially when she learned that among the invited Lebecqs, Éléanore and her mother, Adose, Eulalie's sister, would be attending.

Hilaire secured permission to hold the event in the little garden next to city hall. The mayor, Monsieur Jampaneau, could deny my father nothing. So we had the party there, all of us sitting around a long white table on well-maintained sweetgrass among the sapodilla and apricot trees. As we sat in the shade of two solemn gum trees, I was consumed with a melancholy that I couldn't explain to myself at the time. After the meal, we were supposed to continue celebrating on the beach of Port-Mahon, a few kilometers from Morne-Galant.

Adose; Man Nonore; her husband, René; and their daughter, Annie, represented the Lebecq side of the family. They had all come from Pointe-à-Pitre. There were about thirty Ezechiels gathered around the table. Antoine was there, resplendent in a saffron dress that showcased her thin waist and her muscled legs. Uncharacteristically, she wore sandals, which was asking a lot of her. Dédé sat next to her, laughing affably and making toasts in honor of the bride and groom and then in honor of Gros-Vaisseau.

There was only one downside to that day. Aristippe, a neighbor who had been walking by, was invited by Hilaire to join us. Aristippe was a proud man who loved attention. When people tried to flag him down in the single street in Morne-Galant, he never turned around, but instead would stop in the middle of the street and raise an indignant index finger to decree: "Let whosoever wants to greet me stand before me!" He made us children laugh, because in addition to his theatrical ways and his elegant clothing, he knew how to tell a story. He was one of the only forms of entertainment in town.

When it was time to eat, he struck his fist down next to his plate, stood up, and railed:

"How dare you serve me rice and red peas! Do you take me for a *va-nu-pieds*, some ragamuffin that you can serve any old swill? Bring me something decent to eat!"

Lucinde, furious, pretended not to hear him. The adults joked with Aristippe, who refused to sit back down. He continued to yell at the servers scornfully, arrogantly:

"Who is trying to silence me? Who is endeavoring to disrespect me today?"

"Come now, Aristippe! This is Lucinde's wedding. You're not going to carry on like this, are you? Monsieur Aristippe, you're going to make Gros-Vaisseau very angry . . ."

After a minute, Papa intervened. Without getting up from his seat, he gave a long *tchip*, inhaling sharply and slowly so that his disdain was clear to all who were present. His eyes were closed, his forehead propped on one giant fist and the other waving a handkerchief in Aristippe's direction. "Listen, friend, eat what is in front of you! The food is very good. I made sure of it," he said, even though he didn't actually have any idea what had been stewing in the kitchen.

Aristippe sat down slowly, glad to have left his mark on the wedding, and also because he was in fact quite content to eat the excellent goat Colombo and rice. Jampaneau lifted his glass and made a quick speech, and the bride and groom were pleased.

The only thing that people asked of me, as usual, was to sit up straight and not shift around in my chair as I sat in my little dark, hot suit. I didn't move, but when Adose came to sit down next to me, something in the air shifted. I stared at her, my mother's sister. I had never seen her before, or at least I couldn't remember having seen her. She was a small and slender woman and her brown hair was pulled back in a bun. She had pale skin and the same gray eyes that her daughter had. I was burning to ask her questions about Eulalie, but I didn't dare open my mouth. Her gaze settled on me and she spoke:

"So, my boy, what's wrong with you, have you been struck dumb?"

"No, *madame*."

"Then why are you looking at me like that?"

". . ."

"Go on, answer me! Don't you recognize me?"

"You're . . . my mother's sister."

She sighed as though I had said something insolent, and then shot me a look that seemed to dissolve all the light around the table.

"Yes, I am your aunt Adose," she said harshly. "I am here to honor my sister, whom you did not know. And to honor Lucinde also, who is a nice girl. Are you working hard in school?"

"Yes, *madame*."

"Let's see about that . . . Can you recite a poem for me?"

I didn't know if she was joking or not, whether she wanted to prove to her daughter sitting next to her that the Ezechiels were hopeless illiterate peasants or if she was expressing a passing interest in me. I thought really hard about something I could recite for her. I began, a lump in my throat:

"C'est l'hiver, c'est le soir, près d'un feu dont la flamme éclaire le passé dans le fond de ton âme."

That was all I could remember. I stopped. She stared at me, waiting for the rest. When I didn't go on, she turned to her daughter:

"He looks a little like Eulalie. I'll have to show you a photo that I kept of her."

Hearing that felt like a jolt of electricity. There was a photo of my mother that existed, and we didn't even know about it. Or maybe Hilaire knew about the photo but decided it was better not to mention it. Whatever the case, I began, in that instant, to want with every fiber of my being to see the photo of her.

Adose had already moved on to another topic with Éléanore and had turned her back to me.

"Madame," I asked her, "could I see it?"

She turned back to me as though she were looking at an unwelcome insect.

"See what?"

"The photo."

"The photo of Eulalie? It's out of the question. It is a family photo, very fragile. You might damage it. And it's the only thing I have left of her. You all wasted everything you had of hers."

"But I would be very careful with it," I said.

"If you are a good boy, I'll invite you over one day. We will see how you've turned out and if you really deserve her."

"But . . . how long from now?"

She gestured evasively and turned again toward her daughter. I was furious. That photo belonged to us, I thought, despite not having any real argument for why we, Eulalie's children, had a right to it. Especially me, as I had no memory of her whatsoever. My sisters, at least, remembered her. But when I'd ask them to tell me about her, Antoine could never explain in much detail, and Lucinde made our mother out to be a celestial being of unreal proportions.

My heart was beating fast. I saw my sisters and my father

shifting in his seat at the other end of the table as though through a fog: a blur of white, yellow, and brown. I spent the rest of the party thinking about ways I could see the photo without having to wait so long. I didn't want to own it, just see my mother's face. I was a lonely child. From that day onward, it became my obsession.

Lucinde

NO, I DON'T REMEMBER any story about the photo. You say that
your father was around nine at the time? That was a little before
he left to go live with Antoine in Pointe-à-Pitre. I knew that he
was lonely in Morne-Galant, but I would have never imagined
he'd leave Papa to go after the photo. Are you sure? Either way,
back then I had other fish to fry. I never thought my wedding
would actually happen. Tatar was a boor who barely knew how
to read or count, but I really wanted to marry him because
with a skin color as light as his, people would respect me.

During our engagement, when we would walk around
town, I felt proud to be on his arm. He would pin me up
against a wall every time he got the chance, even on the porch
of his mother's house where he was living. His wandering
hands reminded me of one of our cousins on the Ezechiel
side. Antoine and I would go to sleep over at her house when
we were little. She was a "*gouine*," as Antoine would say laughing, a dyke, because she always wanted to touch us between
our thighs and we had to pin her wrists down in the bed to
keep her away. But Tatar's caresses came with sweet talk, so I
let him get away with it for a little bit before kissing him
furtively and then flitting away.

One day, he called the bakery and said that I had to come

right away to get a package at his mother's house. When I arrived, neither his mother nor the package was there.

"Come here, *ma beauté*," he said, closing the door. He was determined and I knew that I would have a hard time defending myself. Still, I protested vaguely. "But, *chérie*, we are engaged," he murmured, leading me back to his room.

I didn't want to seem unaccommodating. I don't know how he managed to lift up my dress even as he was unbuckling his pants, because I am telling you, I sure didn't help him. He pushed himself inside me and thrusted mechanically while I winced. Then he stood up and said, "Listen, I'm sorry if I hurt you. Wash yourself with vinegar water and everything will be fine."

That damned vinegar was the only recommendation I had heard since the age of thirteen for everything that could go on between your legs. I smoothed my dress before I came out of the bedroom and would you believe that a few weeks later, I realized that I was pregnant. From the very first time. What luck. When I told Tatar, he preened like a peacock. He declared he wanted a dozen children. That's when I decided I needed to marry him as quickly as possible but I would not spend my entire life with that man.

After the wedding, we moved to *l'en-ville*. Not right in the middle of town, but all the way at the end of rue Victor Hugo in a neighborhood that was just starting to be built up, all concrete with running water and toilets. I was proud because I had a shower in a little tiled corner. Since there was no ventilation in the room and we hung the laundry up to dry, it constantly smelled of mildew, but still, it was an improvement from where we lived before.

After we married, my first purchase was a sewing machine. I dove into sewing to forget the rest: Tatar, the baby on the way that I hadn't wanted to come so early. And since I was finally free to do what I wanted, I asked Antoine to go into business with me. She had the shop and I was itching to do great things. Pretty quickly, I hung dresses in the windows and the orders flowed in.

Often after his day of work at the distillery, Tatar would come by to see me at the store and find me kneeling in the middle of a pile of fabric and needles. He would shake his head and leave, saying, "I want a hot meal tonight, so don't hang around too long!" I would go home to make him a meal and sometimes I would leave right afterward. Tatar was split between liking the money that I was bringing in and lamenting the fact that he didn't have a wife who waited patiently at home for him, ready to churn out a long line of children.

Working with Antoine went well enough, but it didn't last. You should have seen the mess that she had all around her. It was really something! I don't know how she ever found anything in those piles of clothes still in their plastic bags that she stacked everywhere. Standing in the middle of her clutter, she would eat smelly fried codfish and then wipe her fingers anywhere she pleased. On top of that, I had to listen to her babbling on and on with the town gossips and pistachio vendors through the door that sat open to the street.

As soon as I could, I cut my business ties with Antoine. After a few months, I had built up a little network of customers. I told myself that I could just as easily have them come by the house and that my presence at home would also appease Tatar.

AFTER OUR OLDEST DAUGHTER WAS BORN in the apartment on rue Victor Hugo, I allowed myself to hire a maid and fully immersed myself in my career as a seamstress. My sewing machine was my bible, my daily work, the crystal ball where I saw my creative pursuits glimmering, my refuge whenever Tatar and I would fight. People would bring in a design and I would improve upon it so that it fell just right over my customers' hips.

Little by little my dresses and suits appeared at every party in *l'en-ville*. Women wore them to weddings, baptisms, tiny receptions in hotels newly opened on the seafront, or for the inauguration of the airport. First it was aunts and cousins, then friends, then friends of friends, the notary's wife, the dentist's wife, and then the high society of White Martinique who were enjoying their trips to France's colonial islands. From that point on, the *békés* and the bourgeois, who never stopped traveling, would order clothes for every occasion. And some Blacks started to want to imitate them, even those who had to choose between a suit and going to the doctor.

Remember, at that time, *la Sécurité Sociale*—retirement, and health insurance—were words we hadn't heard in Guadeloupe. Most of us only knew a world in which people didn't have actual fixed jobs and just worked in a piecemeal fashion, and the distillery workers were paid weekly. According to my best customers, who would repeat what their husbands were saying, *la Sécu* was a diabolical innovation from the mainland that would push the *Nègres* to become even more lazy if it came to the island. I look back on Nonore now with a mix of deference and triumph; I too had young girls working for me, and like her, I was no longer washing my own laundry. How about that!

Because my work took place over the course of long days of alterations and fittings, I became the confidante of many generations of women. I took good care of my most important clients. I knew how to listen to them, pins pressed between my lips, kneeling at their hemlines. I would complain about my husband and play the poor-old-me role effortlessly, making their lives seem better in comparison. It stroked their egos and reassured them. I asked questions, commented, and acted surprised when need be. For the richest of them, I knew how to fulfill their every desire, all while establishing a kind of humble familiarity, which they embraced because I made them beautiful.

I would tell the wife of the mayor of Pointe-à-Pitre, "Lift your arm!" "Get up on your tiptoes!" "Walk around so I see how that falls," "No, now lift your head!" I would interrupt the intimate stories of a plantation heiress to say out loud: "That neckline is too wide, I need to take it in," or, "A buttonhole would be better than a zipper here, it would be much more elegant—and mauve buttons to go with this pattern," or, "We'll add an invisible belt to the waistline to keep the pleats in place, but, *ma fille*, you'd better lose four kilos!"

The women talked, holding nothing back, about the troublemaking *Nègres* who had to be kept in check, about how the unions were a bad thing, about the pleasures and exhaustions of their travels to the mainland. It didn't bother me as long as they picked me to make their clothes. That's how you move up in life. Your father would get on his high horse whenever I would say something like that, but the truth is, a little bit of dishonesty doesn't hurt anyone. Your first million, you steal. I never made millions, but you get the idea: take a look at the Whites and how they made it on our island. Guadeloupe has always been a land of piracy. What I mean is those who succeed at our expense are smarter than everyone else. Oh, of course, you're going to say that they've always had power on their side, that they bend the rules to suit themselves. Alright, sure, but we have to be smart because if you don't know how to be *compè lapin*, you'll only ever end up poor.

After a while, many customers would come just to have tea in my little living room. I was always running behind on some order or another, so I'd ask them to help me prepare the hems and buttonholes while we talked. They liked spending time with me. I was pretty. Not as beautiful as Antoine, but I was much more put together! I was tireless and always had a story to tell. To get by, I charged the full amount to even my smallest clients, even the ones who didn't have a lot of money. I was less strict with the Whites, both the wealthy and the less wealthy, because in exchange they brought me their friends. *Compè lapin*, I am telling you. Those of my friends who bristled at my capitalist approach ended up forgiving me because being at my house was so entertaining. Antoine and I must have picked up the gift of gab from listening to Hilaire, the smoothest talker of all the useless smooth talkers in Morne-Galant.

Antoine: Prosperity

WHEN I RETURNED TO CARACAS, I was a bit nervous. I sat down in the same café at the same time that I had been there before. It was almost empty. The owner seemed to be away again, but you could still hear the guaracha playing. It is a lovely music, *la guaracha*—I have always loved it. I waited casually, not letting on that I was expecting someone. I don't know what I was hoping for—maybe simply to tell the man that I had managed to resell the diamonds.

The boat for Pointe-à-Pitre was leaving an hour later. I realized once again that I still didn't know the man's name, or even what the rest of his face looked like. After a half an hour, I was ready to leave—disappointed yet simultaneously relieved—when he appeared like a sudden shadow and sat down in front of me just as he had the first time.

He was a little skinnier and his face shone with a fine film of sweat. He was still wearing the hat that eclipsed his face, but I looked for his blue eyes and finding them I realized he was handsome. He didn't say anything. His suit was wrinkled and his hair was too long and made a blond halo around his ears.

"So, *mademoiselle*, how is life treating you?" he finally said.

"I sold the diamonds."

He looked up and glanced around reflexively, but I hadn't spoken loudly. He nodded. I went on:

"What is your name?"

"Armand."

"Armand what?"

"None of your business."

"Fine. Keep your name to yourself then, if it's going to be like that. My boat is leaving soon."

He put his hand in his pocket slowly and took out the same handkerchief. He sat up straight to unfold it delicately on the table. My throat tightened. We didn't say anything for a few seconds and then I asked him:

"Why are there only two of them?"

He let out a short laugh. "You think you're the only one interested in diamonds?"

The two leftover stones were small but they shone beautifully, like two teardrops of a child. The transaction didn't take long. I paid and stuffed them in my pocket. I wanted to ask him more questions but I didn't have time. He stayed at the table as I took my bag and headed off quickly toward the port.

I was careful: I didn't want to go to the same place twice to sell them. Two weeks later, I went to Nassau, in the Bahamas.

I saw yachts for the first time there, and divers playing with rays in the clear water. I slipped into an arcade that held the entrances to fancy hotels and luxury boutiques. There were White women in short printed pattern dresses, lightweight like colorful flowers. They wore sunglasses and carried giant straw bags on their shoulders. Tall, tan men wore canvas shoes with white soles. They all seemed so rich to me that I almost stopped a woman in the street to ask her directly if she wanted to buy the diamonds. A jeweler near a little square right on the water bought them from me. I took in three times what I had paid for them in Caracas.

FROM THEN ON, I had what I needed to live comfortably in Pointe-à-Pitre, and Dédé was talking about getting married, but I did not want to. As the months passed, I realized that I had never truly loved Dédé; I only liked him. He had helped me considerably. He kept the business running when I was away, but when he talked about marriage, I would roll my eyes.

We had lived in rue Schoelcher for two years. One day, he showed up with a wedding gown that he had bought in rue Frébault with Madame Pilote's advice. He was pleased with his purchase. I was caught off guard. "Oh, so it's decided then?"

"Well, it's about time, isn't it? What are you waiting for? We could get married in August before the rainy season."

"We'll see. God willing," I said, shrugging.

A while later, Man Dédé came to see me when she knew her son would be away. She sat in the middle of the store frowning. I was hanging fabric samples on wooden rings. I offered her a glass of water begrudgingly because she had been very critical of me lately. She complained to her neighbors, saying that I had turned her son into my minion. Behind my back, she called me "*la présidente*." Since Dédé didn't like it, she made fun of my big feet on the sly. The wedding gown was there, laid out across two chairs.

She started by complaining about the wedding, how we

hadn't started making the guest list, how we didn't know who was catering the meal, and how if it didn't go well shame would be brought upon her, and that she had been waiting since *an tan nanni nannan*, and a whole other list of other grievances that she went on listing for several minutes.

To rile her up, I answered nonchalantly: "I don't have time, Maman. We'll see about next month."

"Next month? When exactly are you going to get married? I thought it was going to be in the next two months!"

"No, it will be later. I have work to do here."

"What do you mean, later? How long has my André been waiting now? Four years? Five?"

"He can wait six more months."

"Fine, fine. Act all high and mighty. All this waiting! But you sure were happy you found us to take you in back in the beginning, weren't you?"

"If you want more money, just say so."

"It's not about money, it's about a date on the calendar! And doesn't your father want this all sorted out?"

"He said that he'd pay for the wedding, isn't that enough for you? Why are you in such a hurry?"

"Because you have to stop sharing a bed if you're not married. Aren't you the one always saying that you have to have your ducks in a row? You're always going off to mass—what does the priest have to say about it?"

"This is more about what the people *you* care about are saying, Maman, but I don't care what they say."

"And so what is it that you want?"

"I want to finish what I need to finish here, now."

"And beyond that? I'm starting to believe you aren't too sure about wanting to marry my Dédé after all. But you sure make good use of him—during the day as well as after night falls!"

It was that last comment that really upset me. I was the one who would lie down, waiting for it to be over every time Dédé would climb on top of me. I turned toward her, this woman who couldn't see how much the present situation that I offered to her son was better than their past. Instantly, I felt a deep fatigue and rancor toward their family. I had realized, little by little, how they were: cousins, uncles, a whole slew of people just scraping by, peasants with daily wages, except for one—and this takes the cake—who was a customs officer. My mind made up, I snatched the wedding gown, tucked it under my arm, and went out into the street under the hot sun.

Man Dédé followed me. I hurried to a dumpster filled with dirt where they were remodeling the old courthouse. I threw the gown inside. I turned back toward my store feeling very light, as though a weight had lifted off my chest, and I didn't look at Man Dédé, who was pacing all around me.

"Just look at what you've gone and done! Don't you know it's bad luck to do that!"

"Well, *ma chère*," I shouted, "how about you go and marry your precious Dédé off to Yvonne de Gaulle!" I furiously slammed the door to the store in her face.

She stood there frozen behind the glass door for a long time. I pretended I couldn't see her, but I didn't like the look on her face. After that, she didn't come back for a month. Things began to get difficult between Dédé and me. He was angry with me and didn't want to work anymore. He insisted on doing nothing, but obviously, that's not how things get done. He made me angry with his endless criticisms. One night, after a fight where I really let him have it, he took off without looking back. He screamed all the way to the end of the road. Then our relationship was over. I closed the door, ultimately pleased.

All that time, I was thinking about Armand and the diamonds in his handkerchief. I wondered whether I would see him on my next trip.

Petit-Frère

FROM THE MOMENT I learned that the photo of Eulalie existed, I began to devise a plan that would allow me to hold the photo in my hands, even if only for a few minutes. Éléanore was the person best positioned to talk to her mother, Adose, who had the photo. So I had to get closer to Éléanore in order to be invited to her mother's house on rue Achille Boisneuf, a lovely upstairs apartment with a wrought-iron balcony over the Crédit Maritime. It was convenient timing since I had been delayed returning to school in *septième*, fifth grade, because of Antoine and Lucinde, who, on a whim, trapped me in bed for an entire school year.

The previous year, they had gotten it into their heads to vaccinate me against some disease or another. To avoid taking me to the doctor, they decided that a neighbor lady would come to give me the shot. When the time came, she pinned me down and stuck the needle directly into my thigh. I screamed. The woman muttered that I was a weakling and left with her payment. Since I was still in pain, my sisters made me swallow warm milk that they had dunked a small lizard into, still alive. The next day, I couldn't walk. Antoine ended up calling Jampaneau, the mayor, who was also the doctor of the town. He diagnosed me with the beginnings of thrombosis and ordered me to stay on indefinite bed rest.

I would sit on the edge of the patio for whole eternities, my leg extended on a chair. Every night and every morning, Hilaire would apply hot compresses to my leg. My boredom and loneliness intensified since I was deprived of school. I walked again several months later, first limping slightly, then walking a bit more normally. But as I grew taller, the one leg stayed slightly shorter than the other one. As I approached adolescence, little by little, I lost interest in the luxuriousness of nature in Morne-Galant, the competitions between children to see who could climb the lofty coconut trees the fastest, and the rounds of catching crawfish. I missed my mother tremendously, violently. I spoke rarely, since neither Madame Zamuy or Papa would have understood what was wrong. Even I struggled to articulate it to myself. As long as I behaved, Hilaire was happy.

I told myself that leaving for Pointe-à-Pitre was the only way to loosen the grip of what was suffocating me inside. I asked my father to send me there for the next school year and Antoine agreed to let me stay with her. Hilaire accepted on the condition that I would come back to see him every Sunday.

While I lived with Antoine, who was fully occupied running her business, I enjoyed a bit of freedom. No one, or almost no one, knew me in the streets of La Pointe. Oftentimes I would hang around near the port. I stared wide-eyed at the crowd of White merchant ships that sat like mountains under the sun. Next to the ships was a row of a few luxury liners that brought the first waves of tourists. I imagined the ship's rooms furnished with polished wood where vacationers lazed about in three languages. They would descend onto the port, inhaling the spices from the market, allowing themselves to be coaxed along by the practiced, teasing banter of the vendors.

In the evenings, the tourists would climb back onto the liners and head off to another island. All the ports must have run together in their memories. Guadeloupe was one of the shortest stopovers, a grain of sand next to the sumptuousness of Cuba or the calm beauty of Jamaica and Haiti, whose grandeur and poverty we learned of in the stories we overheard.

It was in Pointe-à-Pitre that I met my first real friend. Yvan was three years older than I was. He was the leader of a pack of wily and clever boys, and I was drawn to his authority. When he noticed me hanging around, he took me under his wing. He was in junior high school and would go on to *lycée*, high school, the following year; for him it was certain, a future as natural as the wind in the branches. *Lycéens* were rare at the time, and his promising future made me admire him even more. Yvan wanted to become a teacher. Sure of himself and mischievous, he cured me of my shyness and swept me into epic adventures that left me breathless and thrilled. Making plans to meet up wasn't necessary; we knew where to find each other. Sitting on curbs in our neighborhood, I would lean over his shoulder as he read the adventures of Buck John and Kit Carson.

I was allowed to spend considerable amounts of time with Yvan because his older sister had just earned her medical degree, which encircled her whole family in a halo of respectability. His parents and their eight children were far from rich, but they were close-knit. They lived in one of the poorer *faubourgs* in the town's heights. His father was known in the neighborhood as Mischief because he was a captivating speaker. Papa Mischief offered advice to everyone who asked.

He was a faithful champion of the weak—undaunted, he did not hesitate to speak up when a conflict erupted in the factories—and he was continually dismayed by the lack of political awareness among the most destitute.

Papa Mischief was a deep-sea fisherman. He hunted swordfish offshore all the way to Antigua, and would leave very early in the morning on his *gomyé*, his flat-bottomed fishing boat, and often would not return until two days later after night had fallen. It was a difficult and dangerous job, wrangling that enormous creature that would feed his family. One day, he came back from sea holding a bloody cloth to his neck. While he had been out on the water by himself, the rostral bone of the swordfish had punctured his throat. We thought he'd never be able to speak again, but he was too passionate about politics and giving beautiful, rousing speeches to stop talking.

When his work afforded him the time, he read, and he passed on his taste for reading to his son. Yvan told me that in junior high school, he used to participate in *après-midis littéraires*, reading groups with friends, which I found fascinating. At Yvan's house, you could speak freely about what you were reading and what you were deeply interested in. For that reason alone, I couldn't wait to start the sixth grade.

SIXTH GRADE MEANT THAT I WOULD RETURN to blotting paper covered in advertisements, chalk, and fountain pens thirsting for ink. I was happy. Yvan would wait for me after school so we could kick a soccer ball around, feinting left and right all the way to Antoine's house. One day as we were sitting on the sidewalk, I told him the story of the photograph. He immediately recognized the potential for adventure.

"*Frérot*, I swear to you that we're going to get that photograph back!" he cried as he leapt to his feet. The next day, he insisted that I show him where Adose lived. From the sidewalk across the street, he guessed the height of the balcony with a knowing eye.

"It wouldn't be hard to climb up the gutter."

"Are you kidding me?" I asked, my heart pounding. I shook my head vigorously. "No way." I was too fearful to implicate myself in such a scheme, and I could already imagine the retribution if Antoine, Lucinde, or Hilaire caught me trying to pull off a feat like that. I quickly schooled Yvan about the streak of suspicion that ran in the Lebecq family against our side, the Ezechiels. He listened distractedly and then, with his gaze steady on my aunt's house, I heard him recite, savoring his own words as I listened, astonished:

"*Le logis est plein d'ombre et l'on sent quelque chose qui rayonne à travers ce crépuscule obscur.*"* Then he turned toward me, frowning: "It's not right that she's holding on to that photograph of your mother. That woman has fallen prey to the mean-spirited avarice and the prejudice of the bourgeoisie. Meet me tomorrow after school. I'll have a plan."

The next day, I hurried up the narrow, labyrinthine streets on the hill where Yvan lived. Halfway up, the roads turned into muddy alleys. His house sat at the end of a dead-end road paved shoddily with tar. Hens nested beneath their front doorstep. I knocked. Yvan's mother answered with her usual wide smile. She liked me. She offered me some soursop juice

---

* Poem by Victor Hugo. Translation here by B. P. Alexander:
  'Tis night—within the close stout cabin door,
  The room is wrapped in shade save where there fall
  Some twilight rays that creep along the floor,
  [And show the fisher's nets upon the wall.]
  —Trans.

and had me wait in the shade of the living room where Yvan's youngest brother was playing. I looked out the window downhill at the enormous construction site of the Raizet airport whose runways stretched out, packed with cranes and excavators.

Yvan came in smiling and out of breath. He threw his backpack into a corner and motioned for me to follow him behind the house under the big mango tree.

"Carnaval is in two months. Your aunt will probably be out all day. All you have to do is figure out where she'll be, and at what time. With that, I'll be able to calculate what time I need to get to her house."

"Yvan, I don't really think that—"

"Listen, I am just going to get what is rightfully yours." He smiled.

Right then, Papa Mischief called us inside. He liked to engage his children in conversation and gladly included me. He would earnestly ask our opinions, and insist on knowing our views on a variety of subjects, which for me epitomized an exotic household. These long debates often turned into exhortations. Mischief was a staunch communist. He spoke eloquently about union struggles and one's duty toward the rebellion. He told us of bloody confrontations between bosses and laborers, and even though it was hard to believe, he told us that these struggles were also taking place in France between White people. He told us about Jaurès. Yvan and I would listen to him, enraptured. Papa Mischief had come back that very day with a new story that he wanted to share with us.

"*Frérot!*" Mischief called to me. "Isn't Madame Chanzy your schoolteacher?"

"Yes. What has she done?" I asked curiously.

"She hasn't done anything. But have you ever wondered why she seems sad whenever you see her?"

The woman who taught our class was slender and petite and always looked serious, betraying no emotion. She was half-African and half-Portuguese and it seemed as though she heard some kind of bad news every night. She often, in the middle of the day, would go rigid, cataleptic, between the rows of school desks. After a few minutes, she would make what looked like a superhuman effort to take one step forward and then the next, shake her head, and then return to the lesson.

Papa Mischief was using his storytelling voice. As always, he expanded his tale to connect it to the misfortunes of Guadeloupe. Listening to him, I seemed to understand a little better the world in which my father was fighting to survive.

Madame Chanzy had married Edmond Chanzy, who was also a schoolteacher and a well-known speaker among the sugarcane workers. A few years earlier, when the planters were delivering their sugarcane to the Darboussier factory, clashes broke out with the owners. Harvest days were always very tense. When I was little, I had witnessed several of these scenes without understanding what was happening. The sugarcane would arrive in trucks or on oxcarts, which meant that the planters had left their fields at four o'clock in the morning with their cargo. They were waiting in front of the factory for their harvest to be weighed so they could get paid. The men stared at one another and said nothing. That day, the foreman, a mulatto, announced abruptly that the scale was not working and that they would have to wait for it to be repaired. The small farmers from Grande-Terre had paid for the delivery of the sugarcane to be transported all the way to the port. All of their worldly wealth was sitting there in those heavy bundles that the women had worked for days to tie together.

The farmers stood there, clenching their fists, powerless. After two days, the cattle were thirsty, the sugarcane was giving off its foul-smelling odor of sugar and sap. After three days, the harvest was starting to dry out. After a week, it weighed much less, and that's when Darboussier announced that the scale was working again. The planters had lost a third of the price they had hoped to get. This merry-go-round happened often, but this time, the farmers from Grande-Terre decided to protest and were backed by activists, factory workers, dockers, and a few teachers. They all gathered in front of the huge gates of Darboussier and Edmond Chanzy stepped up to speak on behalf of all of them. Since he spoke elegantly and buoyed the energy of the protestors, the army intervened. A soldier shot him with a single bullet right in the chest.

I looked at Yvan, engrossed in his father's story. And I understood that for him, recovering the photograph of my mother was an opportunity to perform an act of bravery for a worthy cause.

I returned home shaken, but I said nothing to Antoine about the photo or my teacher. At best, she would have shrugged. At worst, she would have slapped me—she thought it was poor manners to ask anything of the Lebecqs, even for a photo of our own mother.

Antoine: Love and the Wind

I RETURNED TO CARACAS, but not to buy fabric. I just wanted to see Armand again. For months, I had thought of him often, as a kind of mystery to solve. I was driven to know his story beyond the diamonds. I was also ready to buy a few more to satiate the taste for risk I'd developed since meeting him.

At first, I didn't find him. After waiting for a long time at the café, I wandered the port to see if I might run into him, but he was nowhere to be found. I couldn't stray too far by myself because it was a dangerous area, and I could feel all of the men nearby undressing me with their eyes. I was angry when I left.

When I came home, I had words with Lucinde, who from time to time displayed one of her dresses in my store window. She irritated me, bringing her haughty demeanor into my store. She didn't think my clientele were chic enough and she wasn't shy about letting me know it. Well what did she expect? Anyone could come into my store, even if all they could afford was a half a candle. But Lucinde and her *créations*, as she called them, her *original designs*, required their own space as well as rich customers. If she could have, she would have sold her dresses exclusively to the *békés*. A real Banania, that one.* That's how I see it. Anyway, that day she told me that all my mess was giving her a headache and that I needed to sweep it up, and I told her that if she didn't like my mess, she could see herself out. I was the boss in my store. Not long after that I caught another boat to Caracas.

This time when I went into the café, I found Armand sitting near the door. It was as though he knew I was looking for him, even though I hadn't said anything to anyone. I sat down across from him and this time I studied his face.

"Take off your hat," I said before even saying hello. He looked at me, surprised, and took it off slowly. I could see all of him, and his eyes were on me. We looked at one another without saying anything for a minute, then he ordered his *ti punch*. His eyes looked feverish. His bony cheekbones jutted from beneath his tanned skin. He wiped his forehead. He shifted in his seat uncomfortably and murmured:

"So, *mignonne*, what brings us here today?"

I shrugged. "I'm guessing you have something to sell me. If not, we could just have a chat like old friends."

He laughed his noiseless laugh, a single upward heave of his chest.

"No diamonds today. Can't draw too much attention our way. Besides, we shouldn't stay around here too long."

"Is someone looking for you? The police?"

"Maybe. If so, you'd be my cover. I could tell them that I'm here to walk along the port with you. What do you think of that?"

---

* Banania is a historically controversial brand because the images used in its advertising campaigns are colonialist and racist. Frantz Fanon mentions how the depictions of Black people as the object of marketing and colonialism amount to a minstrel-style performance for White consumers. —Trans.

I shrugged again and after he finished his glass of *ti punch*, he suggested we take a walk.

We strolled the length of the dock in silence, him hunched over, looking up at people suspiciously. I was ready to test the limits of my bad luck, to risk perhaps more than I should. I suggested he show me where he was living. He hesitated and then looked at me. "Why not?" He took me through the little streets where concrete houses stood in a row. I remember a red church, and then a green one with lovely rounded facades and white molding.

His "place" was a lush park with trees, benches, and fountains. I had never seen anything like it up close, maybe from far away and only through the gates of a large house. No, there was nothing like it, and I only saw that kind of park again in France, a bit like the Buttes-Chaumont, but much bigger. He sought out a wooded area, planted himself in front of me lighthearted, nearly laughing, and kissed me. It was the first time I had ever been kissed like that, voraciously and delicately at the same time. Dédé knew nothing of how to kiss like this and neither did I.

Then he explored the whole of my body with his hands. It didn't bother him that I was much, much taller than he was. He dove into my chest as though he were drinking from a spring, so I laid my hand on his head, like the Virgin Mary does with her baby. He grabbed my buttocks, sucked my nipples until he was breathless, and then turned me over on the grass.

A half an hour later, we stood up. He smoothed out my dress and handed me my shoes. He seemed surprised that someone so young had offered herself to him, but behind his wonder was a sadness where I would have expected to see joy.

He walked me back to the port, his hands in his pockets. Before I left, I told him that I was still interested in the jewels since I didn't know how else to say that I wanted to see him again soon. It was only then that he smiled slightly as he looked up at the sky.

I RETURNED SEVERAL TIMES and with each meeting, he took me to the park. I enjoyed it but I wanted to know more about him. I sensed that I wouldn't have him for very long, so I wanted to know everything. Piece by piece, I cobbled together his story. I quickly ascertained that he was not from les Saintes as he had told me. I knew the islands very well, you could see them perfectly from the southern coast of Basse-Terre. The fishermen who lived there had the same eyes that he did, but Armand lacked their assuredness, a kind of certainty they shared of being in the right place. It was obvious he'd seen more of the world than just the insular and traditional island community of les Saintes; he didn't look at me the way the people from there usually look at *Nègres*.

"You're from France, aren't you?" I asked him pointedly as we walked the streets of the port one day.

"Bordeaux. You've never been, have you?"

I shook my head.

"A lovely city from what I can remember. Big, with straight roads and ancient buildings. An old city, more sophisticated than Caracas. There is a port, much bigger and more beautiful than this one, with a broad river flowing into the sea. I come from along that river, behind the city."

He looked down at his feet with a bittersweet smile. He spoke more about Bordeaux, which was, according to him, a fabulous place. And then he slid his hand around my waist, which was the first time that he'd ever shown any tenderness outside of the little woods in the park.

"All that has been over for a long time, so no more questions about it," he said.

The next time, he sold me two diamonds. On the boat for Pointe-à-Pitre, the customs officer wasn't the usual one whom I had gotten to know, the one who smiled affably each time I climbed aboard. This officer was short with gray hair and more meticulous, you could tell by the way he moved from one passenger to the next. He asked everyone to open their bags wide and carefully listed everything that was to be declared, down to the tiniest bottle of perfume.

This time I hadn't hidden the diamonds. I had grown overconfident. And clutching my handkerchief with the tiny gleaming stones inside, I felt like I was with Armand again. The officer was going to ask me to unwrap all of my parcels and I would have to set down my tied-up hankie, and he might also ask me to open it. He was only two seats away. The sea was calm. I had a small moment of panic and anger; *how stupid to get caught like this*. So, just before he came over with his cap, his mustache, and his old, wrinkled face, I threw them overboard. The wind carried the handkerchief a little ways as though delivering some delight unto the sea, and then it landed in the water, and danced gracefully in the wake of the boat before dropping like a jellyfish into the blue water.

Later, sitting in the little bar where we always met, I told Armand how I had lost them.

"That is the stupidest thing you've ever done." It was one of the longest sentences I'd heard him utter.

"You don't know the stupidest thing that I've done. Stupid things, I've done a lot of them, tons of them, and it's certainly not the last one. I'm the queen of stupid things. I have done more stupid things than you will ever know. And for the record, you don't know anything about me, so don't tell me what the stupidest thing I have ever done is, because that would mean that you know me, that would mean my life is some clear pool of water inside your little glass. Is that what you think? Lord no, you don't know anything, you don't even know why I take the time to answer you or even explain all this to you. One thing's for sure: you are also on the long list of stupid things that I've done, but you're nowhere near the top."

I don't know why I directed that lengthy tirade at him. I was annoyed at the way that, sooner or later, a man will use the word *stupid* when referring to a woman. After that, I threw back his glass of rum. He seemed amused but not surprised.

"Very well, *petite*," he said. Then he stood up and teetered a bit. And then it came to me in a flash of clarity that this man was not going to live much longer. He was older, first of all, and much too skinny. I could feel his delicate bones beneath his skin when he was on top of me. The hollow of his chest seemed deeper each time I saw it.

And just that once, he took me to the place where he actually lived, at the end of a road and up many stories in a dark, charmless building.

There was just one room with a bed, a wooden box on the floor, and a glass next to it. A strange, thick odor wafted through the room that reminded me of the plants that we would burn around the veranda to keep the mosquitoes away. I learned afterward that it was the smell of opium. His bed was old and dirty and covered with a stained, yellowed sheet. We laid down on top of it and he fell asleep drawing one finger lightly across my breasts. Out the window, I saw two alba-trosses gliding, the same ones that accompany the boats into the harbor at La Pointe.

IT WAS ONLY ONCE Armand died that I learned most of his story. It's often like that, I know. One time, I asked him how a man with diamonds lining his pockets could live in such a pit. As always, he evaded the question, saying that it wasn't a young girl's business. But that didn't stop him from selling plenty of his diamonds to me!

One day I had waited too long for him on the port and I knew that something had happened. I ran to his building. The door was open. An older woman with bare arms wearing an apron was mopping the floor. I asked after him and she ex-plained in a Spanish mixed with Créole that Monsieur Ar-mand had died the night before. She was the one who had found his body. Caracas authorities had taken him God knows where, but she did know that no one knew of any family. The woman's tobacco-colored face was expressionless. She pushed her mop into the corners of the bare room.

"But he is French!" I shouted. "You have to tell the pre-fecture!"

The woman shrugged and continued cleaning. I stood there and began to detect a trace of empathy behind her rough exterior. "From what I know," she said quietly, "the bodies of convicts are never claimed, especially an old man like him."

She allowed me to come inside for a moment. I sat down on the bed, trying to remember every detail of his body, his eyes, his gestures, the sound of his voice. I tried to rebuild his personality in my mind, but I knew too little to do it properly. Then I commended his soul to God and I left.

I returned to the café where we'd met. I sat down alone at a table and ordered a beer. The loud guaracha music was still sounding from the back of the room. When the owner brought me my drink, I told him straightaway, "Armand is dead."

He shook his head and didn't look very surprised. Then he paused, and I think he was taking pity on me. He told me what little he knew about Armand.

It turns out that my Armand had arrived from a French penal colony in Cayenne, in French Guiana. He had been freed after the war. For a few years, he had not done much, hung around like a vagrant near the Maroni River, before ending up, God knows how, in Caracas. I figured that the diamonds came from Cayenne, that he must have taken them with him from French Guiana or someplace else.

I was sad to learn all this only after he was gone, as you can imagine. I was angry at myself. I found out later, thanks to friends in the Armée du Salut, what it had been like in the prison colonies of Cayenne—how the people were treated worse than animals, how they died like flies. It reminded me of slavery. Armand survived only because he had arrived as a very young man, maybe eighteen or nineteen years old, and because at that time he was probably very strong.

There was nothing left of that vitality by the time I met him, and yet, he hadn't even been so old, only in his forties. Only the slightest trace of it remained; you could see it in his eyes. He was stuck in Caracas with no way to return to France or even Cayenne, all his money going to opium.

That was how I learned about drugs. They weren't common at that time in Guadeloupe, in the 1950s. It's very sad to see how young Antilleans today are succumbing to this plague. I may be old, you know, but I still know what's going on.

I admit that yes, I was scared that the police would some-how implicate me in their investigation into Armand, which, according to the café bar owner, was uncovering a lot of infor-mation. So I boarded the boat and I left completely changed— or perhaps it was the world itself that had changed, now that Armand was no longer walking around in it.

I never went back to Caracas.

Petit-Frère

LIVING AT ANTOINE'S HOUSE was quiet and pretty monotonous. After I finished school, we would sit together in the evenings when she had pulled down the rolling iron shutter of her store, united in our solitude, like two drops of oil in a bottle gourd filled with water. I would sit in the corner of the room preparing the eighty stitches that she would instruct me to mount onto her knitting needles. I'd watch her out of the corner of my eye. Antoine was a calm and resolute monster who busied herself with task after task, amid heaps of things that were never put away properly.

In this clutter, continuously built and rebuilt, I saw the mysterious tumult that inhabited my sister's mind. I knew how not to trigger the volatility that could overcome her. When she drowned me with her words, I feigned attention even as my thoughts ran elsewhere. For her, I felt both fear and admiration, the way a person does in the presence of a great natural phenomenon—a torrent or a gaping hole in the earth. In exchange, she granted me a kind of distracted attention that could float to the surface in bursts of tenderness: a stroke of my head, a lovely unblemished fruit given to me for lunch, a new shirt. In the evenings, she would welcome me home with a warm greeting, with that piercing voice pitching upward that she used for friendly chitchat.

I was still preoccupied with the photo and I awaited Carnaval in February with nervous energy, because Yvan, very excited, had been giving me meticulous daily reports on his observations of rue Boisneuf. He knew the hours each person worked by heart and could predict the comings and goings from Adose's house or nearby businesses. In order to try to speed things along on my end, I went to Éléanore's house and knocked on her door, claiming I wanted to visit my young cousins. I couldn't just arrive empty-handed, but what could I possibly offer a family that, from my perspective, already had everything? I racked my brains and ended up bringing the thing that was most precious to me: an issue of the comic book *Buck John* that wasn't too crinkled, as well as two brand-new packets of blotting paper. I headed toward the rue du Cimetière without knowing what I was going to say. The point was to make a good impression.

A girl about my age opened the door and frowned at me.

"Hello, I am Petit-Frère Ezechiel. Is your mother home?"

From down the hallway, a woman's voice called out, "Annie? Who is it?"

"A boy named Petit-Frère!" she scoffed. Little Brother.

I blushed and didn't answer. A young woman appeared behind her, probably the maid. I followed her to the kitchen, where she left me with Annie, who peered at me with curiosity. I heard another child chattering inside the house and a baby crying upstairs. When no adult showed up, I awkwardly held out the blotting paper to Annie.

"Here, these are for you."

She took them without saying thank you and looked at

them carefully. I remember that on one of them there was an advertisement that I really liked—a drawing of a magnificent yellow convertible with a driver wearing matching gloves and sunglasses. I heard Éléanore bark an order. She came into the kitchen with a baby in her arms, and recognized me immediately.

"Oh, hello there! What are you doing out this way?"

I held out the issue of *Buck John*. "This is for Marino."

She tossed it on the table and sat the baby on her lap.

"Is someone sick?"

"No, I just came to visit. I . . . I wanted to see Annie and Marino. And the baby."

Her face softened a bit. "That's nice of you."

The infamous Marino was about seven years old. He burst into the room like a rocket. After looking me over, unimpressed, he grabbed my *Buck John* and disappeared. Annie had already started cutting up the advertisements on the blotting paper. After the customary small talk and questions about the health of Hilaire and my sisters, Nonore sized me up as her daughter had done, and called Marino into the room.

He reappeared in the doorway, scowling.

"Do you remember Petit-Frère?" Éléanore asked. "He's come to see you. How lucky, now you have someone to play with."

She turned to look at me again with her greenish-gray eyes, making me uncomfortable.

"Marino is a bit agitated these days. His father is never here and he misses him. It would be nice for him to play with a boy older than he is. You could come over from time to time after school and keep him company."

"Sure, of course."

"Very well then. Go on out into the yard."

I FOLLOWED MARINO RELUCTANTLY. The first thing we did in the yard, which was more like a narrow square of grass with an outhouse at the far end, was take stock of each other. He shifted from one foot to the other.

"Do you want to read *Buck John*?" I asked.

He shook his head, still eyeing me suspiciously. Annie came over to us. She had slid up behind me without me hearing her. "Don't talk to him!" She blurted at her little brother, "His father killed his mother! *Mamie* told me so!"

I was stunned. It took me a moment to realize that their grandmother was Adose, my aunt. I didn't know what she meant by her accusation against my father, but I knew it wasn't helping my mission. With a lump in my throat I told them as calmly as I could:

"My mother died of an illness when I was little."

Marino looked from me to his sister. He didn't know how to interpret any of this.

"I'm telling you it's true," Annie continued. "And Papa told me that their family is scum. One day, Antoine spat on him."

"Who's Antoine?" Marino asked.

"She was the nanny that took care of me when I was little." She thought for a second. "She's your sister," she declared, staring at me.

Marino drew closer to me, smiling, and when he was an inch away from my face, he spat on me. I felt the glob run down my cheek. Annie laughed. Pleased with her reaction,

Marino was winding up to spit again but I firmly and calmly pushed him backward.

"If you do that again, I'll break your nose."

"See?!" Annie cried triumphantly. I wiped my face off quickly with my palm. I was trembling with indignation.

"If we are such scum, then surely your mother wouldn't want you to play with me, now would she? Come on, let's go play soccer in the street."

"I can't go outside of the yard," he said with a twinge of regret in his voice. He kicked at a small rock. It was only at that moment that I realized that he was wearing well-fitting short trousers and a shirt that was much newer than mine.

"Why not?"

"Maman doesn't let us play in the street," Annie answered.

"So what else could we play?"

Marino shrugged. "I could bring my marbles out here."

We started playing marbles on the grass, which was not ideal because the marbles couldn't roll straight. Annie watched us from afar but I made a point of ignoring her. After a half hour, I stood up.

"I have to go home."

"So when are you coming back?" Marino asked.

"I don't know. Sometime."

I WENT BACK several Sundays in a row. I was bored stiff by Marino's toys, which were for children his own age, and they were even more boring since I knew I could have been running in the streets with Yvan. Marino's sister continued to glare at me as though I were a mangy dog, but I managed to win him over enough so that he completely forgot her story about my parents. In the meantime, I asked Antoine why Adose would say that about us. She shrugged, muttering that people didn't know what they were talking about.

"Papa did not take care of Maman, that's a fact. But for the rest, it was God who decided to call her to Him and nobody else."

FEBRUARY ARRIVED, the season of Carnaval. Despite my objections, I couldn't get the idea of the burglary out of Yvan's head. He had decided to put the plan into action on the first day of Carnaval to take advantage of the distraction of the big parade at the Place de la Victoire and the widespread joy that coursed through the town. All of the brass players, *tambouyés*, and other drummers in La Pointe would gather on that day after weeks of perfecting their costumes and practicing the complicated rhythms and songs they would play all day and all night. Antoine and Lucinde were not planning to attend. For Antoine it was a good day for business, and Lucinde had too much work, and her second pregnancy was wearing her out.

"You should just come with us," Éléanore suggested. It was hard to figure my cousin out. She oscillated between caring for our family and holding a grudge against us. In the end, I understood that her earlier scorn stemmed more from the cultural codes in Grands Fonds than from her own personality, which was relatively warm.

Adose was also supposed to come with us, which cleared the way for Yvan to make his attempt to steal the photo.

I walked through the streets trying to concentrate on the dances and the jubilation around me. The beats on the *kas* and the stridulations of the shaking *chachas* resonated in my chest. The celebration would last for one week, with Carnaval balls unfolding one after the other. Each neighborhood was more musically imaginative than the next. The region's best musicians were all there. The closer we got to the center, the denser the crowd became. We followed each other single file into the packed streets—René, Éléanore holding Annie and Marino by the hand, the nanny dressed in white lace with the baby in her arms, and me.

The Place de la Victoire, lined with trees swaying in the sea breeze, had been invaded by a joyful and captivated crowd. We arrived at the meeting spot and found Adose, who was sitting on a folding stool. The cooler between her feet was full of fruit juice and spongy cakes that she had brought for us. We were planning to stay there all day.

Next to us, the *tambouyés* changed their rhythm wordlessly, without even exchanging a single look, their drums communicating directly with one another. The more the music swelled, the more my worries dissipated. The beat of the drums pulled me into a trance. Fascinated and still, I became inhabited by the tangled rhythms that echoed and layered themselves on top of one another, unraveling and then synchronizing anew, guiding the crowd little by little toward communion, toward fusion. Everyone was clapping to and exulting in the triumphant sounds of the *gwoka*—this was Guadeloupe. The parade advanced slowly. The dancers would pause their dancing, open their arms decorated in gold, sing, and then spin, flowing together like a stream. As they danced, they offered their backs and gleaming necks to the onlookers, and then advanced to the sound of the trumpets and conch shells trailing behind them.

When the sun had gone down, I followed Adose, ever imperial, as she walked home with her daughter, her son-in-law, and her grandchildren behind her. We had not yet had our fill of music and dancing, but the heat had made us thirsty. I managed to peel away from them before rue Achille Boisneuf and I ran all the way to Yvan's house.

IN HIS NEIGHBORHOOD up the hill, a different Carnaval was going on. More raw and down-to-earth. The drums rang out, calling to the crowd, from everywhere at once. The entire hillside quivered with the sound. The earth vibrated. All the residents of the quarter were outside, answering in unison the calls of the *ka* drum leader. The circles of *tambouyés* would open and in the middle a dancer pulled from the crowd, male or female, would twist like a flame, leaping, transforming an everyday gesture into poetry, and then would fall back into anonymity. Unrecognizable faces coated with cane sugar and soot sprung out in the dark. Children danced with the grace of adults, their faces exultant.

I sat beneath the mango tree and listened, prepared to stay there all night long in the firelight of the torches brandished by those moving in the shadows. Yvan's father was there, clapping, yelling, and encouraging the drums that seemed to beat out a call across the centuries. Down the hill, Carnaval was effusive, a display of pure joy. Up here, it was a wild warrior.

After an hour, I saw Yvan coming. I stood up and waved to him. He came over and sat down without a word. The flames flickered across his face. He looked tired and disappointed.

"Did you find anything?" I asked. I already knew the answer.

He shook his head.

"I didn't. All the shutters were closed and I only had my little knife to force them open. I waited until dark to go around the back of the house to find a way in without anyone seeing me, but nothing worked. At one point, I cut across the roof and I almost slid all the way down to the street. But I managed to pull myself up onto the balcony. I would have needed a large rock or something. And then I heard Adose come home so I jumped to the balcony next door, and from balcony to balcony until I reached the end of the street!"

A childlike triumph, a joy had returned to Yvan as he recounted his adventure. I had never really believed that he would find the photo, and after all, how could he have even identified the right one? But I shared that moment of triumph with him—we burst out laughing together, reveling in the pleasure of transgression that was shuddering through the entire town. Thinking back, sharing that childhood secret with him is one of my fondest memories of La Pointe.

The Niece

AT FIFTEEN, I WENT TO GUADELOUPE without my parents. I was glad to be going alone; this was the beginning of my freedom. I hadn't been back for a long time and I was eager to see my grandfather again.

Over the span of a few years, many things had changed. A superstore complete with a food court had dug its heels into the heart of Pointe-à-Pitre, sending small, local growers into ruin, fueling the local desire to mimic mainland consumer culture, and doubling food prices compared to those in mainland France. Of course, people protested here and there with unions advocating resistance, but it was in vain. The race toward overconsumption was on, and the island was becoming utterly dependent on the outside world.

The beach I'd frequented as a child, which had been the childhood beach of my father, Petit-Frère, and Antoine, had been destroyed. A manufacturer had polluted it without repercussions and a Dutch hotel consortium had dug up the bay and then abandoned the project, resulting in unexpected and deadly holes that filled with water and pooled incoming waves in the sand, and leaving behind cement sheds for the crabs to colonize. What had been one of the most beautiful bays on the coast, fed simultaneously by the sea and by a freshwater spring, now resembled a dangerous brown backwater.

During the first days of my stay with Hilaire, I went from house to house to pay the necessary visits to cousins, uncles, and aunts. If I had not, my grandfather would have heard about it: "*I ka akoué i tellement.*" She's so arrogant. I felt my actions would have reflected negatively on Petit-Frère. I liked talking with everyone. It was often the case that afterward a child I didn't know would bring me a well-ripened breadfruit or a bunch of bananas, a gift from an aunt hanging back in the shade of her own small *case.*

And yet, I heard people saying that I was not a real Guadeloupean. The third time that one of my distant cousins said it, I was hurt. I was actually surprised that I was hurt; I didn't think I would be. I didn't think I would care about what a fat woman sprawled out in her small folding chair would say from her concrete patio. I protested, reminding her of my pedigree, of the name of my grandfather who everyone knew, invoking also my father and my aunts. It didn't matter. This woman, whose own children had left to live on the mainland, insisted I was not Antillean.

Frustrated, I shot back, "Well, anyway, just four short centuries ago, no one was here. Not you, not me, not our forefathers, not the *békés* with their money, not the old plantation mills or the rusty railway lines built by our ancestors who are now buried under the mangrove. Not even this sugarcane all around us was here—it was imported, just like almost everything else."

She shrugged. It did not change the fact that I was a mainlander on vacation.

She was right.

I was not born in Guadeloupe, I traveled there only once every two years at best. Even though I loved the island deeply, and loved Créole society, my life was elsewhere. That was not to say that this land had given me nothing. On the contrary, I felt it in my body, in my words, in my way of understanding the diversity of the world. In Morne-Galant, my ancestors had had to fight for their survival. This was the case for the majority of the island's inhabitants, with the exception of the *békés* who had battled to hold on to their power, even going so far as to violate the law and ignore the principles of justice.

When I was speaking with Antoine fifteen years later, I understood that I needed this same freedom; I needed to acknowledge the past without endlessly looking backward. This was, after all, the hand that French Caribbeans, the *Antillais*, were dealt: they were lost travelers voyaging across all continents, from New York to Saint Louis to Senegal, from Caracas to Shenzhen. I learned to love my history and what constituted it—a succession of violence, of destinies forcibly intertwined, of submissions, and of revolts.

1960–2006

The Niece

I WAS BORN under a gray European sky, so, for me, the island is a world of sensations that I kept secret, that were out of reach most of the time. The moments I spend there are interludes that suffuse all my senses—where everything, all of it fleeting, is brought into sharp focus. In Guadeloupe, I touch, I taste, I smell. The soles of my feet bake. The day slips through my fingers. I am stunned by the stars.

When I was a teenager, I had my first kiss there, a kind of trial run before anything serious. One month in Morne-Galant and I grew stronger, my skin shone a deeper copper, my muscles worked. Then I came back and forgot nearly all of it until the next time. Small amnesias.

When I entered adulthood, the island faded even more. Guadeloupe came to mind only intermittently, when people would mention my skin color, in innocuous remarks about the freckles dotting my brown face. So it was the little things that tethered me to Guadeloupe: a complicit smile offered to the young mail carrier with long braids, an evening at an Afro-Cuban restaurant where a zouk song swept me back to my vacations there.

After I married, I realized how few concrete details I had about that side of my family. Even down to our last name,

Ezechiel, which has its own history independent from those who bear it. Our name—invented or agreed upon in 1848 during a brief discussion at the crowded office of a civil servant. In front of the desk, a line of emancipated slaves would have stood eager to make their newly acquired freedom official with a name inscribed at a registry office. Behind the desk, the agent's pen strokes would have sped across the thick register. Perhaps my ancestor, steeped in biblical stories he'd learned during wakes, would have insisted on taking this name. Or perhaps the registrar, out of ideas for last names after assigning them all morning, had come back from lunch with the parish priest and the name of the Mesopotamian prophet came to mind.

My fiancé became interested in genealogy. He knew his own family's history in great detail—he had deeds, photographs, old jewelry. Sheet music composed by a grandfather at the beginning of the century. Bound journals from his great-grandfather. His parents had bought the first video cameras available to the public. Their VHS tapes were well-organized in a giant cabinet and he could behold at will the glowing youth of his uncles and aunts, father and mother.

To conserve is an instinct of the wellborn, those who are careful to transmit the radiant trail of their family's line from generation to generation. I didn't possess that instinct. No document sat sheltered within the thick stone walls of my family home. No record of ancestors. We were too busy surviving. But I had a ledger of experiences, of gestures, of words that nourished me in subtle ways from beneath the soil.

I had my own memories. All my vacations spent on the island. Hilaire was calm, settled into the quietude of the days in Morne-Galant, his gestures always the same. The years passed by and his habits never changed. Hitching the cattle up in the morning, working on the land in the afternoon. Time passed and gently left behind signs of the progress the world had made throughout his *case*: a large television, a fan with golden blades. These objects sat at the edges of his existence. All I had to do was step into the reddish shadows of his home to converse with ghosts from 1923. An old rag hanging in the open window seemed to be animated by Eulalie's ghost brushing past it. The dusty boater hat forgotten on a plank above the bed sat waiting for a good party. During the midday nap, Hilaire's eyelids twitched to the rustling of the three coconut trees in front of the open door. Two were tall and one was slightly smaller, one planted after each of his children had been born, the placentas buried amid their young roots. In the silence of this stifling hour, I would seize the chance to touch my grandfather's face, furtively caressing the stretches of his moist skin, feeling the birthmark standing in relief along the ridge of his skull, tracing his strong jaw, home to few teeth. An ample smile would unfold beneath his large nose. He would invariably open his eyes, straighten out his wiry body, and snip, "Alright, Eulalie, alright!" He was pleased that I bore his wife's name.

In the afternoons Maman would dunk me in a large zinc washbasin filled with rainwater to rinse off the salt and sand from the beach. The neighbor children would draw closer. They were barefoot, scruffy, their skinny knees powdered in tufa rock dust. They were mostly cousins and second cousins whose names I didn't know. They would line up obediently next to the washbasin and smile for my mother's camera.

In the evenings, against the backdrop of frog song, I would listen to my father and my grandfather speak for hours on end. They were making up for lost time, rushing to head off the long separation between those moments and the next long vacation—conversations in Créole that during the rest of the year would collapse down to a few minutes on the telephone each Sunday. I understood only one word out of every ten they said. What music! Hilaire's voice flowed over words rough and resonant. A voice of hard rain on stone, of a tumbledown door, of the motor of an old junker. Petit-Frère would answer him lightheartedly. There was a tender complicity between them. They discussed their land, Lucinde, Antoine, life in mainland France. Hilaire would ask him about something he had heard on the radio, that a man had gone to the moon. "*Ka ou pé comprend?*" Do you understand all that? Petit-Frère would present Hilaire with arguments and find analogies that were likely to convince him. Their debate about space exploration sounded out of place in Créole, a bit funny, a bit stubborn. Then they would move on to the solar system, to the galaxies. Hilaire would listen, laughing as though the universe were simply a funny joke made up by the Americans, although he believed everything that his son was explaining to him.

When I compare my memories to what Antoine, Lucinde, and Petit-Frère tell me, I can see that Hilaire embodied a rural Guadeloupe that was vanishing. None of his children belonged to the same world he did. They were from the modern era, far removed from sugarcane, diving into *l'en-ville*, that state of consciousness inhabited by Créoles living outside the Créole world.

Antoine: The Big Rumbling

I SAW THE HOUSES literally going by outside my window, rolling past right in front of me. Man Dédé's little house, old Bilar's house, the one that belonged to Yvan's family—Yvan, that smiling little boy, full of promise, with whom Petit-Frère spent most of his time. Papa Mischief seemed worried and was talking with the truck driver who was slowly pulling the little house where Papa Mischief's eight children had been born. The modest *cases* filed along the cleared streets that circled the center of Pointe-à-Pitre and then faded away into the dust, on the other side of the mangrove toward the sugarcane fields. Five, ten *cases* at a time, perched on top of carts pulled by two large oxen each, with the distressed inhabitants inside, watching the countryside go by.

I recognized Man Dédé on one of the carts and I ran toward her. She was clutching her windowsill and staring at the hillside that had held the neighborhoods where she had lived for fifteen years, the hillside that she was slowly rolling away from.

"*Oh!* Man Dédé! *Ka ou fé ou bien?* Are you okay?"

She turned toward me, her eyes full of tears. She was too upset to remember that she was still angry with me. In a voice that she tried to keep steady, she called out, "Yes, yes, everything is fine!"

"Where are you headed off to like that?" I asked, worried for her.

She thought for a moment, as though she had forgotten where she was going.

"I'm going to my brother's house. He has some land near the Abymes."

"That's a good thing," I said, hoping to reassure her. "It's not very far, and you can easily get to the market by bus."

I had to practically run to keep up with the rolling cart. She shot me another worried look from high inside her house, which pitched and swayed above my head, and she smiled sadly. I stopped running alongside her because it was becoming dangerous, this parade of carts with houses stacked on top like matchboxes, fragile but steady. I took out my handkerchief and waved it at her. She waved back from her window until I could no longer see her troubled face. An entire neighborhood was moving.

All of this was the result of the giant construction project that the authorities had started just after General de Gaulle's first visit in 1960. It began with the strange *cité* Henri IV, where giant concrete squares that would hold a hundred families at once had sprung from the ground. It was as though they were stacking people on top of one another, but in a way that left them no space to walk around, no room for a garden of even just three yams, and no hidden nooks to gather and talk. No more outdoor kitchens in the open air. No more dirt under your feet. And for what? Half of the families seemed to be happy to leave, but the other half were worried.

I went to see how it was happening in the area near where Man Dédé used to live, because I had heard that they were making everyone move, willingly or not. The *cases* were easy to transport. The city authorities took them as they were, without making any effort to learn what kind of life was being led inside of them, and they asked people where they wanted to be dropped off. Those who had a bit of land in the country found themselves relocated in no time at all. Those who didn't have any place to go, well, their houses were destroyed and the residents washed up in Lauricisque, the other new concrete *cité*.

When I arrived in the spot where I had lived with Dédé and his mother, I found a giant hole in the ground. Bulldozers were already scraping at what was left of the boards and the detritus of the families who had lived there before. It was difficult to climb the rubble to the top of the slope where before there had been a path beaten down by thousands of feet pressed into the dirt.

In the place where Man Dédé's house had been, all that remained were the giant stones upon which the house had perched for years. My head was spinning. It was as though the house had been lifted up into the sky, or that it had abruptly disappeared. Bilar's house was also gone. The stretch of the muddy river that I had bathed in many times remained, out in the open air and stripped naked, no longer crisscrossed by makeshift bridges and surrounded with little gardens. There were no children shouting or flying kites.

My heart beat faster. I looked down toward the center of town and off to the left. You could still see the parade of *cases* like tiny sugar cubes being carried farther and farther inland by invisible ants. From where I was standing, I could imagine the rumble of motors and the jostling of the carts on the tufa roads. Down below me, I could see the Place de la Victoire bristling with cranes, stretched out in front of the sea.

The city revealed its layered skins to me: the old, the very old, the newest. There were clear strata: the old houses around the port built for Norman fishermen or Dutch traders, perhaps even built by some strapping ancestor of Hilaire's. There were the *cases* of the city center, ravaged a hundred times over by the Anglo-French wars through the centuries, then the *faubourgs* that for sixty years had welcomed all the unemployed from the countryside. And in the midst of all that, the new concrete roads extended like giant fresh scars and the first HLMs, the French public housing projects that clashed with all the rest, crushed the vegetation that everywhere else had invaded each available centimeter between the houses. I stood there frozen, taking it all in.

SUDDENLY, I HEARD THE BREATHING of someone behind me. I turned around and saw a man walking slowly along the slope, ignoring the commotion down below and focusing instead on a point on the blue line of the hills of Basse-Terre. He seemed to have risen out of the ground, like a spirit coming out of his tomb.

He had long, curly hair and a nose that was hooked like an eagle's beak. His eyes, sunken deep into their sockets, were a piercing black. He walked as though I were not there and I looked at him closely because his clothes were not the typical clothes you'd see people wearing during the day, not even the clothes we'd see on the backs of the very rich. They were Carnaval clothes, and yet he didn't seem to have been in costume or off to dance *la gigue*.

He was wearing a thin white shirt and I recognized the quality of it immediately since I had been in the business of buying fabric for years. The collar was embroidered with mother-of-pearl buttons and the sleeves as well. Over the shirt he wore a vest with a red-and-pink pattern in thick velvet. His short brown pants were tight at the knees and beneath them he was wearing thin gray wool stockings. Next, his ankle boots were made of a gold-and-brown damask, unlike any I had ever seen before, tight and finely crafted, and the heels enhanced his extraordinary height. He was clutching a metal-headed cane and dug here and there in the ground with it. He was pale despite the heat and the sun, as though he had covered his face in a light dusting of flour.

It was just the two of us on the ravaged hillside. He didn't seem to want to leave; he wandered around and looked up occasionally, seized by a deep thought. But each time I saw his face, I didn't like the smirk on it. After a moment, I called out:

"*Monsieur*, are you looking for something? There's nothing left here."

It was as though I had spoken into the wind.

"*Monsieur?* Can I help you with something?"

He turned his head slightly in my direction and shot me a hostile look and murmured something in a gravelly voice.

"I beg your pardon? I don't understand."

This time he looked straight at me with his raptor eyes. He scared me at first, and then he made me angry. I bore the weight of his glare with all of my strength, and then I shot him back the darkest, most defiant look I could muster. We stood there staring at one another for several long minutes. And then he shot toward me like a cannonball; I never would have guessed he could walk that quickly on the freshly unearthed soil of the hillside with his heeled boots. He bounded closer, his cane shaking in his fist. I understood instantly that it would be a fight to the death. He could throw me into the sky, off the edge of the hill, and I'd end up crushed on the

unfinished road. Or else I would be the one to send him rolling into the giant acacia thorns and cactuses on the hillside. I
was ready.

"Mary, Mother of God, protect me!" I cried, making the
sign of the cross.

He was three steps away from me, and then he turned
and took long, authoritative strides toward the meadow. He
splashed across the river and disappeared into the leaves on
the other side. I wasn't that scared. Right away I knew that
that powdered white man had been a spirit sent by the Virgin
Mary to warn me of danger ahead, and I thanked her. I knew
I would have to be on my guard and I committed to staying
vigilant.

Petit-Frère

I FINISHED THE FIFTH GRADE and spent the dry months talking with Yvan about what we would do when school started again. Now that I was going into junior high, we were full of plans and laughed excitedly just thinking about them.

But my joy was short-lived. In December, the principal decreed that given my age, I would go directly to trade school because I had fallen a year behind when I was sick in Morne-Galant. It was useless to try to discuss it with Hilaire or with my sisters. They would have each shrugged and simply proceeded with their day.

I finished the school year in a review course meant to prepare me for the sixth grade, where I stewed in my anger and my humiliation about falling behind. I couldn't see where school was going to lead me and I felt trapped. Then a friend told me about an apprenticeship to become an electrician that he was going to begin when the school year started. It was even paid.

I went to his employer, a jovial heavyset man who came from La Marne and had lived in Guadeloupe with his wife for twenty years. He hired me as his apprentice, too.

In the years that followed, I installed electricity in the most modern homes in the city center. I repaired transistors for residents who furnished their homes en masse from my boss's store, Radiola. I continued to visit Éléanore and her children. Marino had become like a little brother to me. He listened, rapt, to my adventures in the streets of Pointe-à-Pitre. When he was ten, I was allowed to take him out in the street to play marbles. One day I asked Éléanore again about the photo, feigning a casual, easy tone. She shrugged.

"Well, if I remember, I'll ask Mother about it."

I was full of hope, even though Adose continued to eye me a bit suspiciously.

It was around that time that I fell in love with music. One Saturday after work, I was walking near the huge construction site in the Henri IV *cité* where the first low-rise buildings of the town's public housing were starting to go up. Nearby, there was a record store where I would go and press my nose to the window. I remember every detail of that moment as though I had seen it on-screen, shot in a close-up. The rain at night had left mirrorlike pools in the ditches. The wind was gently nudging a herd of clouds onward. A half-blind beggar was sitting on the bumpy sidewalk delivering a series of monologues to his dog. The door to the record store was open, covered by a multicolor beaded curtain. I had never before heard sounds like those coming from inside.

At home, Antoine listened to whatever came on the radio; the *biguines* of Ernest Léardée's clarinet music, songs for paso doble, rumbas, and Édith Piaf. She loved to dance. Sometimes while I did my homework, she would stand in the middle of her clutter and I'd watch her twirling around like the blades of a windmill. She would do little steps, gracefully rounding her long arms and bending her thin waist, fully concentrated, a faint smile on her lips.

What I heard that day was something entirely different. It

whizzed around with the speed of an automobile with cut brakes barreling down a steep slope. I could make out the spirited song of a saxophone. A trumpet soared and scratched against the dirty windows of the store. Elegant and understated chords tumbled from the piano. It felt like I was in a perfect bubble where there existed an answer to every question.

The record player spun in the window with a record sleeve displayed alongside it, like courtroom evidence. Who were these Americans? This Miles Davis, that John Coltrane? I stood there frozen, staring at the crazy eye of the center of the record. On the face of the man with his hand curled around the trumpet you could see the rage he held inside. I didn't dare buy a record that day, but I was a changed person when I stepped out into the street. That trumpet. And that rage. A beauty with no name; joy and light piercing through the fog. I wanted a trumpet also, and maybe a record player.

I could see clearly that everything in the city was evolving. New appliances, still rare where we were, arrived by boat: televisions, radios, electric lamps. The sidewalks had been gutted to lay down cables and pipes. With the arrival of the brand-new airport, all of the young people of the island dreamed that it would be possible to see what the rest of the world was made of—I was not the first one and I wouldn't be the last one. I was thirsty to meet people, to read books, to have encounters. On the island I was suffocating.

Antoine: *Nèg Kont' Nèg*[*]

I HAD BEEN IN A DEEP SLEEP for maybe two hours when it happened. I'd stayed up late to count the money from the store and do a little cooking. Petit-Frère was sleeping on his fold-up bed at the back of the store. All of a sudden, I woke up to the racket of something metal being violently heaved against the door. A horrible smell rose up, thick and strong. I recognized the stench of *Grésil*,[†] mixed with something I couldn't define. Peat moss? Giblets? Something rotting? I couldn't tell you what it was, but it got you right in the throat and wouldn't let go, not even if you breathed through your mouth.

The stench invaded the first floor and spread to the second. Petit-Frère woke with a start. I ran to grab a kerosene lamp and turned it on high to go down my little staircase. Downstairs, I saw a dark liquid creeping underneath the door and spreading its tentacles all the way into the middle of the room, almost to Petit-Frère's bed.

[*] *Kont'* refers to the French *contre*, against, but the Créole term *Nègre* is more pejorative in French, therefore the Créole term *Nèg* is used in this instance. —Trans.

[†] A distortion of the disinfectant brand Crésyl.

"Come here quick!" I ordered. He stood up, still drowsy, and joined me near the stairs. We stood like that silently for a few seconds, and then I understood.

"It's a curse. Get dressed fast!"

I had never gone near witchcraft, but I knew it when I saw it. Witchcraft is like a strong woman from the country brought into the city, like me. Witchcraft lives alongside Sunday services, confirmations, and the Day of the Holy Innocents. Even the most Catholic of *Nègres*, Indians, Syrians, and Chinese still seek out witchcraft if it will help them out. Even the *békés* in their big houses hiding behind their white shutters will try it if they need to.

I knew certain people resented me. They thought that my business was a little too successful. Man Dédé maybe, because of the canceled wedding, even though many years had passed. Most of all, I suspected a *chabine** my age who thought that I wanted to steal her boyfriend, simply because he was teaching me about accounting—a guy with slicked-back hair who I wasn't even interested in!

Anyone could have been the culprit. The streets were rampant with tales of vengeance exacted between neighbors, former lovers, rivals, each hexing and jinxing the other. There was generally low employment in La Pointe, except for short-lived gigs; anyone's small victory became fuel for large-scale jealousy. That is how it was back when Maman had her *lolo*. We say *Nèg kont' Nèg*, which means that an unhappy *Nègre* can never tolerate another *Nègre* getting along better than him. He can accept the success of Whites, but could never swallow the success of a brother in misfortune. And women—

---

* *chabine*: a *métisse* girl of Black and White parentage, with visible signs of mixed ethnicity. —Trans.

who are the most badly treated in all of Creation on this little island where immorality reigns—bicker the most, like chained fighting cocks that strike out at one another as soon as their owners, hovering above them, let them loose.

I ordered Petit-Frère to hurry up, tied a scarf around my head, and put on my old rubber boots. We grabbed the biggest *kannaris* that we had in the kitchen. We stepped around the nauseating puddle in the store with our pots in hand and didn't stick around trying to identify the soft gunk spreading out in the middle of the room.

Outside, the road was perfectly silent. The moon was veiled with large ribbons of clouds. We started to walk quickly, the pots in hand. We walked the length of the port, crossed through the abandoned neighborhoods, keeping close to the sea whose thrumming waves covered the sound of our footsteps.

Beyond the limits of the town, it was all nature, wild and tainted, with deep ponds in the mangrove swamps, fallen trees and all kinds of trash hanging from the roots that dug into the brackish water. We arrived at the tiny beach strewn with sharp, broken lambi conch shells that had been eaten away by the salt water. I had decided to head there because there was a little cemetery that bordered the beach where people went to set down candles on All Saints' Day. It was a spot that was respected by the dead and the living alike.

The palms of the coconut trees slapped against each other like whips. Have you ever seen how at the edge of the water the roots of these trees grow close to the ground's surface, as though they are about to crawl right into the sea? That night, we bumped into their shaggy roots that had been partially ripped out of the sand, our pots clanging.

We stopped near the rocks that bordered the beach and set the pots on the sand, then filled them with seawater and headed back the way we came. The moon was barely shining when we returned to the house, our arms trembling with fatigue. But I didn't stop there. We threw the water into the room and onto the front steps and I swept vigorously with a broom with my teeth clenched tight. Petit-Frère sat on the steps watching me and then fell asleep. In the early morning, the smell of *Grésil* was gone, but there remained a dark mark on the doorstep that reached all the way to the middle of the store like an eternal stain.

THE NEXT DAY and the days after, I carefully stepped around the stain as I came in and out of my house. Every time I looked down I shuddered. To protect myself, I stopped my accounting lessons with the neighbor with his slicked-back hair. I thought back to the evil spirit that I encountered where Man Dédé's *case* used to be. The curse could destroy my business, or bring on an illness, or worse. I couldn't live in limbo like that.

So one afternoon, as soon as Petit-Frère came home, I took him through the poorer neighborhoods of Pointe-à-Pitre to a place called "Réhabilitation," so named because in one week nearly all of the *cases* surrounding the main road had been torn down. Nevertheless, the poorest were still there, dayworkers, homeless children, and women of ill repute, those left there after a hurricane or by bad luck. We crossed a labyrinth of bandit-run alleys until we arrived in front of a hut that was different from the others—it had a raw cement facade decorated with bottle shards.

This was where the *gadèzafè** lived. I'd told a friend of mine our misfortune one Sunday at church, and she advised me to find the *gadèzafè* to reverse the curse. I knocked on his door and after a few minutes came the sound of sliding locks, then the door opened. A heavy man with bloodshot eyes and sideburns appeared, wearing a long tunic with geometric patterns.

A red square cap sat cocked on his head, just like the Senegalese and Tunisians wore in Hilaire's memories of the military. The orange and brown hues of his tunic blended into a dancing fire every time he moved. He wore bracelets made of shells and black goat hair. Across his large chest lay gold chain necklaces. Until then, I had seen them worn only on the necks of women.

I was hoping that he could help me quickly and effectively, so straightaway, I declared that I had come for a consultation. The man nodded silently and invited us into the tiny hallway. He strode into a small room that was mostly dark with just a few candles flickering on the ground.

He gestured for us to sit on the cushions on the irregular tile floor, and then sat in front of us and looked at me intensely. I explained it all: the curse, who I suspected was responsible for it, but did not explain about the spirit that had warned me a few weeks earlier. That was between me and my guardian angels. When I finished my story, he remained silent for a few moments and then pulled out a small box that had been sitting behind him. He took out three big, gleaming, flat seeds

---

* *gadèzafè*: Also known as a *quimboiseur*; a well-respected interpreter of the gods who does not foretell the future, but deciphers what cannot be understood and consults with residents about their problems. From the kenbwa syncretic tradition in Guadeloupe equivalent to santería in Cuba or candomblé in Brazil. In the Antilles, reductively referred to as a sorcerer and caster of spells. —Trans.

that were white and dark red. The shimmer of the candlelight reflected off his long fingernails.

"What you're experiencing is very serious," he said sorrowfully. As if I didn't already know that! Then, with the seeds in his hand, he closed his eyes and started swaying back and forth chanting a list of saints' names mixed with other names that I didn't know—Erzulie and Mami Wata. The seeds scuttled in his palms and took on the glow of precious stones. His voice jumped an octave, and he hummed in a woman's range.

As he chanted, I prayed silently: to the Holy Virgin, who would help me with this trial—how could she possibly allow such an affront to her daughter? No, it was not the Virgin who was to blame, nothing bad could happen on her watch. I was the sinner here, and I needed to *m'attacher les reins*,* take up the challenge, and retaliate against this malevolence. I was a sinner among sinners, but all the saints laid their gentle hands on my shoulder, caressing me, and wove for me a shroud that I would don again one day. The *gadèzafè* prayed in his own way, and I felt the good tingling at the tips of my fingers.

My sense of injustice about my situation was washed away as the light rained down on me. All those tears created a protective, loving bubble in this man's little house, and even he disappeared into the wave of love that was going to protect me like a kind of armor.

The man finished his prayer. His eyelids remained closed on his baby face, and he continued to knead the flat seeds in his palm. He waved a stick across the biggest of the surround-

---

* *m'attacher les reins*: Literally, to buckle up. An expression from Guadeloupe and Martinique meaning to prepare to do something difficult, most likely originating from putting on a large belt to carry heavy loads or to cut and lift sugarcane. —Trans.

ing candles and it gave off a sweet smell. It reminded me of the perfume from Paris that I had sold to a British tourist the previous week. He passed his hands gently over his face and at last looked at me. He had recovered his deep voice.

"Listen carefully. A journey is required to put an end to the curse that was put on you. I am going to foil your enemy, do you understand? I am going to *touyer* his curse! I'll kill it! I'll crush it!" He pretended to squish a bug on the ground and then waved his hand threateningly, his reddened eyes open wide, his finger pointed right at me. "No one will come for you after I have finished! Your enemy will be crying out for her mother! The evil will come back upon her and she won't be able to do anything about it! Nothing at all!" he said, nearly shouting. Then he calmly gave me these instructions:

"I am going to travel on your behalf to Marie-Galante Island. When I am there, I will buy a kid goat. I will bring it here and I will prepare it. I will do it properly. You will come and you will eat a piece. You will give me nine hundred francs for the trip, for the purchase, and for preparing the goat. When you have swallowed down what I've prepared, your enemy will be the laughingstock of the neighborhood!"

The tone of his voice revived me. I agreed to his plan. He told me to come back in a month to eat the goat. I paid him and we went home. I was not completely at ease, but I was hopeful, and the next morning I opened my store feeling full of energy, ready to face any enemy headed my way.

Petit-Frère

I REMEMBER very clearly the abrupt noise and the horrible smell in the room, Antoine in a yellowed satin shirt getting me up quickly so we could go and fetch seawater. And I remember the *quimboiseur* that we went to see a few days later.

We went down a little road deep within Pointe-à-Pitre. In the dark room where the man seated us, I was worried about all the candles that could at any moment have set fire to the dried palm leaves that lined the walls. There were taxidermy animals and all kinds of little statuettes. The candlelight was impressive, but it all seemed ridiculous to me. Antoine told him her story, and the *quimboiseur* launched into incantations that went on and on, his eyes closed, his full lips parting, then closing. I watched him, astonished, and then after a while I couldn't hold back any longer and I burst out laughing. He stopped short and shot me a look with his bloodshot eyes.

"The boy must leave."

Antoine tipped her chin at me and I stood up partly in shame and partly out of relief. I sat outside the door, my ear cocked to what was happening inside, but I couldn't hear anything. When Antoine came out, she seemed satisfied.

"Well?" I asked. "What did he do? What did he tell you?"

She told me the remedy that the *quimboiseur* had proposed. I didn't say anything, but the price he had named made my stomach turn.

"Do you think it will work?"

"It can't hurt," she answered as she stepped over the muddy waters of a brook. Such stories of curses and countercurses that I never believed in, by the way, poisoned my childhood. You could never tell anyone, for example, that you were unhappy in love. With my sisters, if I was unhappy because of a girl, it meant that someone had put a curse on me. So it was better to keep my agony to myself.

I was not willing to accept the way of life shared by everyone in our town. I could not buy into their optimism that had them opening their shutters in the morning and lighting their gas lamps in the evening as though nothing was wrong. My experience was riddled with pangs of fear and distress. Nothing was right. I knew it as I walked alongside my sister. I hated everything, that night that we had to go haul back water from the ocean. When I imagined Antoine sliding a bundle of bills into the hands of the *quimboiseur*, a deep disquiet settled over me. The town was growing in opposition to the landscape. The humidity was in opposition with the hanging sheet metal and the awful cracks in the concrete. I think I was on the verge of a depression.

I continued to visit Hilaire on Sundays, including the Sunday after we went to see the *gadèzafè*. As always, first I told Papa stories from my life as an electrician's apprentice. He sat on his bench and gently congratulated me for being reasonable and hardworking. And then I told him, glancing distractedly toward the end of the road, everything going on in La Pointe, including how we went to meet the sorcerer. Hilaire listened attentively without interrupting.

"So tell me," he asked casually when I had finished speaking, "where does this man live?" I tried remembering as well as I could.

Much later, he told me that the Monday after my visit, he left his house early in the morning. He arrived at the house of the *quimboiseur* around two in the afternoon. The man opened the door in the splendor of his multicolor tunic. Hilaire sat down in the little living room and the man sat across from him.

"You are going to hand over the nine hundred francs that my daughter paid you," he stated calmly. The man sat for a few moments without saying anything, and then the memory of the tall woman with a teenage boy at her side came back to him.

"You are going to give it back, and if you've already gone to Marie-Galante Island, you are also going to give me the goat that you allegedly went to get."

"But this is a very serious situation," the man started, shifting on his cushion.

"Listen to me very carefully. If you don't give back the money right now, I will come back for it tonight and I won't be as nice about it. And if you try to run, I will find you, even if you run off to the caves of the Soufrière."*

He started to protest, but Hilaire's granite expression and serious tone shut him down. He stood up, rocking backward as if someone had spat in his face. Hilaire stood up quickly, clenched his fists, and straightened his neck, his lips pursed.

"It would have taken too much time anyway," the *quimboiseur* said. "What a pity, a father intervening like this!" he muttered as he brushed off an imaginary fleck from his chest.

---

* Soufrière: a volcano in Basse-Terre in Guadeloupe. —Trans.

He *tchip*ed again and shook his head, lamenting the situation, but nevertheless he pulled out a bundle of bills from under his tunic.

"The poor girl comes and begs me for help, and this is what I get." The money changed hands. Hilaire left without saying goodbye.

With the bills in hand, he decided to have a good time at the cockfighting ring on rue Lacrosse.

The following Sunday, he explained his remedy for the *quimboiseurs*, *gadèzafès*, and all other sorcerers: "I took the nine hundred francs back from that crook and here I am standing right in front of you, just fine." I was overjoyed. It was useless to ask for the money to pay Antoine back—that was the price of the lesson.

For once, I admired my father—I held no bitterness and no list of grievances like I typically had against him. Strangely, Antoine concluded that the curse had definitively been broken. She bad-mouthed Hilaire, saying he had gone rogue, and the nine hundred francs were out of her mind, as well as her habit of stepping around the stain as she left for the day.

Lucinde

I WAS A MODERN WOMAN. I kept up with all the latest styles of clothes and furnishings in Pointe-à-Pitre. I influenced what was up and coming. And do you know why? Because I was the one that made the clothes for every woman chosen Miss Guadeloupe for an entire decade, from the first year of the competition until I grew tired of it. Oh, you should have seen it!

To look at Antoine back then, despite her successful business, you would have sworn she was still living back in Morne-Galant. At thirty years old, she dressed as though she were fifty. What a waste! All of that beauty and she took no pride in it! If only I'd had her figure!

I made clothes for dozens of contestants in keeping with the standards set forth in photos in American magazines imported from Miami; fashion photography inspired by what was happening in Paris. My designs became more and more sophisticated—I sewed each one with the best hue for each girl: fuchsia for the one whose arms were the shade of dark soil, light green for the one with copper undertones on the skin of her neck.

The pageant organizers could no longer do without my services. The whole island's petite bourgeoisie, all the way up to the *békés*, was desperately in search of elegance and they all came to see me. Once I was even invited to a baptism in Grande-Terre, not too far from Morne-Galant. I was the only Black woman there. Now tell me, who would have believed that Hilaire's little guttersnipe would end up at that kind of shindig, *hmm*? The nights before a gala I would work on my knees until I was exhausted. The next day, from backstage, I would watch with pride as my designs graced the shoulders of the pageant contestants and the backs of the richest women on the island. Sometimes, the announcer would say my name for such and such a cocktail dress going by onstage.

The committee was overseen by Georges Coulange—you know, the heir to the rum company. The Coulange family owned more than just the main distilleries of the island. They also built the hotel that hosted all the fashion shows as well as the entire marina for the tourists in Le Gosier, and all the major restaurants of Grande-Terre, where the rose-colored beaches spread out toward the sea like silky sheets. They also opened the first supermarket in Guadeloupe. At first, they hired only Whites. And then a few hardworking Black women were able to get jobs as cashiers. It was certainly better than working sugarcane.

Père Coulange was not an easygoing man, but the business world was unforgiving and he had to keep his employees in line. I watched him rage during strikes and protests, and I felt bad for him since he had to navigate his employees through it all, stay alert on the front lines, all while competing against the Americans. Anne, his wife, a delicate blonde woman whom I often dressed, confided in me about their struggles and boasted about her husband's firm leadership.

If the workers went on strike at Darboussier or in the distilleries, Père Coulange would tell his friends: "When the

Nègres get hungry, they'll go back to work." He thought that this type of remark would stay between him and his wife, but Anne would tell them to me. I wondered if she did it to test me or because she had minor misgivings about it, sitting there on the edge of her couch, holding a teacup between her thin fingers.

The other company leaders in the steel, banana, and concrete industries stuck by Coulange and liked that he would represent them. The conflicts would go on sometimes for months, and sometimes people died during the strikes. I forbade Tatar from participating. Most of the time, they would return to work in the end. When it was over, Anne would come to see me for another order as though things were fine. Yes, I would say that Anne Coulange was my friend.

The day that de Gaulle came to visit, she asked me to go with her. See how far I'd come? I wasn't able to sit with the officials though, because for once Anne wanted to spare herself the stuffy encounters with the other important families. It was fun for her to walk among the crowd on important occasions like that. I was a little disappointed, but it was fine. I was her chaperone; she was reassured having me at her side. We walked through the streets arm in arm all the way to Place de la Victoire. I wore a handsome cream suit that I had made especially for the occasion. We sat down unnoticed, both of us far from the stage underneath the red-orange flowers of the peacock trees that lined the square, sipping our *sorbets à coco*.

Not far from us, I saw Antoine climb onto the top of a small pole, lifting herself up to catch sight of de Gaulle and the military parade. She looked like some kind of statue. If Anne hadn't been there, I would have laughed seeing her up there on her lookout spot with her scraggly *fildidine* dress and those huge, worn-out shoes she always had on. Tall and towering over the crowd in the cheerful afternoon light, she looked both self-satisfied and frightening. I didn't want to introduce her to Anne or even to admit that Antoine was my sister. Can you imagine what Antoine might have done upon meeting her? Taken Anne's slender wrist into her own hand to measure whether or not she was a good Christian woman? I would have been so ashamed.

Antoine: Second Winds

YOU SHOULDN'T BELIEVE EVERYTHING that my sister tells you about her fancy customers. Even though she said that she used to work on commission for the island's richest citizens, it was actually her less wealthy, faithful clients who kept her in business. The others, the truly rich ones who would go off to travel at the drop of a hat, went to the biggest couturiers whose names were always dropping out of Lucinde's mouth— les Courrèges, Dior, and God knows who else. Some of the women were all too happy to have her admire what they had bought and then flit away after giving her two quick kisses on the cheek, the kind you would give to a distant cousin.

The day de Gaulle arrived, I was at Place de la Victoire and I saw her arriving with her precious Anne Coulange at her side. Lucinde's poor old tongue never got a break yapping about that Coulange woman, and right away I could tell it was her. Lucinde saw me too, but she turned the other way. I am telling you right now, if that *béké* Coulange was with her, it was not because she was Lucinde's friend, it was because she had another rendezvous planned that she didn't want her husband suspecting.

From my perch I saw it all. As soon as they slid under the shade of the peacock tree, a redheaded man who looked like a sailor on vacation with his beret and his blue-and-white sweater approached them. It was clear that Anne Coulange and the man knew one another. She told him something and then went off with him. Lucinde sat there in her lovely fresh-butter-colored suit. I can just imagine how Coulange must have politely directed her to stay put: "Could you wait here for me for just a moment please?" Lucinde's face fell, her expression dull like opaque cotton, before she pulled herself together and nodded at Coulange's back as she was walking away. She sat there stiffly, on guard like a wading bird in front of a crab hole. I was sure that she was thinking back to all her preparations from the night before, to her fight with Tatar when she had refused to let him come to see de Gaulle with her. Right then, she looked in my direction and I was the one who turned away so as not to humiliate her further.

WHEN I WOULD GO to see them, Tatar would complain that Lucinde was making more money than he was. In his mind, that wasn't how things were supposed to go. After his work-day, he paced around the kitchen, unhappy that it was the help in the kitchen cooking their children meals and not his wife. "Who cares?" Lucinde shot at him from behind her sewing machine. "I'm the one who pays to keep the stove on, aren't I? And I'm also the one who dresses the children and the one who pays for your Sunday suits!"

That Tatar, he did like for his wife to dress him. He would find a suit in a store and she would buy it for him right away, or if she had the time, would make one just like it. All the same, he couldn't stand the dynamic between them even though he would show off his gray anthracite suit with a matching hat on Saturday nights. He talked more and more of leaving Darboussier and going to work in France, where, according to him, he would find a better job and be paid twice as much.

Lucinde shrugged. She pretended to scold Tatar for what he was: a simple man, somewhat boorish. She pretended that she wanted him to come with her to the Renaissance, the movie theater that had just opened in Pointe-à-Pitre. The owner's wife, a customer of hers, had invited them to see movies there for free. But truth be told, all Tatar wanted was his wife, his dominoes, and the neighborhood dances on Saturday nights. And ultimately, that was fine with Lucinde. Because despite her airs, Lucinde is still a girl from the country, a hard worker but not as refined as she thinks she is. And you can go and tell her that, if you want.

One day when I was with them, Tatar, who was looking once again for something to fight about, started criticizing the parade of regular clients who would come by to see her at all hours, and he started to complain about the bobbins of thread spread across the floor of their apartment. From behind her sewing machine, Lucinde pulled out a ten-franc bill from her bra and held it out to him without looking up from her work: "So why don't you just ask me to pay a fine for every bobbin you find. That would make a nice little side-hustle for you."

Tatar rushed over to slap her. Lucinde pulled away quickly and knocked over a vase on the table. "Come over here and just try to hit me!" He froze and turned toward me, an opaque look on his face, picked up the money, and slammed the door behind him. I shook my head and called them both idiots. After an hour, just imagine who charged back into the house declaring that this time their lives were going to change, that he was going to really be somebody and she would respect him in France, if only he got his chance.

Avoiding that *bitin an kouyonad'*, that nonsense, that's why I never wanted to get married. In any event, Lucinde ended up giving in, maybe also because there was nothing more left for her to gain on the island. According to her, it was so that her daughters could get a better education.

Guadeloupe lacked schools and teachers and we barely recognized a student when we saw one. Well then again, yes we did—I would see the handful of Black high schoolers leaving the Pointe-à-Pitre high school, walking stiffly, almost haughtily in their suits, preoccupied with projecting their superiority to the crowd of Whites and mulatto high school students.

Those educated Blacks would come to our neighborhood meetings sometimes in the evenings where they would parade around their fancy ways of talking and their big ideas for the people from Montesquieu and Diderot, and *Trotkisses* and *Communisses*. I would listen to them talk as I licked my Floup popsicle, loving the fancy French that spilled out of their mouths so easily. One day they wanted us to take up arms in the image of our African brothers in the march toward independence. Another time, they wanted us to become *anarchisses*. Still another time, it was a disciple of Guevara who spoke, who then was quickly countered by a *Maoisse*. There was even one who gave his speeches in Spanish, punctuated all throughout with "*hasta la muerte.*" In the middle of the astounded crowd, that young man with a gift for languages was quite encouraged by me smiling and nodding, but really I was just remembering my good times in Caracas. Ultimately, those students didn't really know what life was like for poor people. They dreamed of going to France too, but they didn't have a lot of contact with normal young people on the island who were all unemployed or under apprenticeship. Apprenticing felt normal to us. It was better than sugarcane. Like with your father, where all anyone wanted was for him to find a job quickly. All this to say that according to Lucinde, on the mainland, it would be different for her daughters.

I WATCHED EVERYONE LEAVE. It had begun with a few of my customers who came to the store to tell me goodbye, their suitcases in hand. Lucinde was getting ready. She entrusted Tatar with a hefty sum and sent him on a recon mission to find a cozy little apartment in France. Ha! As though that would change the way they felt about each other. The plan was that he would begin working for La Poste and then she would follow him.

We heard that on the mainland, the economy was going strong and they had full employment. Here, factories were closing one after the other. Bananas and Antillean rum were no longer profitable. There was some new business activity on the island since people can't just sit around watching the boats go by. But those buildings popping up in Pointe-à-Pitre, the tourism, and the electricity were all driven by investments in businesses owned by mainland Whites, and the profits bypassed us entirely.

None of the company owners were Black, despite that good old bone called French citizenship that they have been throwing at us to gnaw on for centuries, and maybe it was for the best, since there was nothing worse than a Créole dog raising his hackles to try to pass for a wolf.

My employee at the store was a girl named Martha who

cost me only a little bit each week. She was a thin young thing, barely eighteen, and was raising a baby on her own. Martha told me that she was also preparing to go and would leave her baby with her mother. She wouldn't stop talking about BUMIDOM.

"*Bibidom, ka sa yé?*" I finally asked. What was that? While I was washing my window, she explained that it was a French program that encouraged young people overseas to come work in France, where there was a need for manual laborers. She was hoping to get training and a good job.

Martha left full of hope and many others did the same; young people whose parents I saw at church, and older people too, who couldn't find work on the island. It was endless. Those with land sold their plots for cheap to have a little nest egg for their arrival on the mainland. The airport was up and running at full speed.

But from the news that I gleaned here and there, things were not looking good in France. Martha's grandmother told me, all choked up, that Martha had to take a job as a maid in the sixteenth arrondissement. For her and the other young women who arrived on the plane with her, the only thing they received in the form of job training from BUMIDOM was a metro ticket and a few instructions about how to properly scrub floors.

In the factories over there, it wasn't much better than at Darboussier. Our men shared the same fate as the Algerians and Africans on the automobile assembly lines; they were mistreated and humiliated. In order not to fail the same way the first group had, most of the newly arrived went into administrative roles; at hospitals, the postal service and tele-communications, the RATP public transport operator in Paris, and big companies like that because they helped the workers get housing. When I ran into their parents at church, they said, resigned, "Well, why not?"

But in the housing projects in Sarcelles or Saint-Denis, I know that all these *ti-moun* were feeling isolated and lost. I know they weren't being paid enough to come home to Guadeloupe. A few started the long process for family reunification in order to bring their children over, others gave up on it. People kept leaving, but at the meetings in my neighborhood or on Saturday nights around makeshift cookouts in the *faubourgs*, I could hear the worry in their voices.

The trade unionists proclaimed that BUMIDOM was only good for spiriting away the young people and so reducing the threat of revolts on the island. In Martinique, there were huge protests, large strikes that provoked bloody fights, and the owners had to concede small improvements to the workers' circumstances.

Do you know Réunion? I have never been to that tiny island, but I know it's French like Guadeloupe, and back then, I would hear horrible stories about the thousands of children who were taken from their families there to repopulate a part of the mainland they called La Creuse.

This wore heavily on my shoulders and added a layer of tension everywhere, even though I had neither a husband nor a child to worry about. When I think back to it, all of Guadeloupe was in the grip of anxiety at that time; the poor as well as the richest. The company owners monitored the people, organizing sports clubs to prevent the youth from joining political groups. The prefect kept a record of activists who had made speeches in public squares and sent off reports. High school students at the *lycée* ended up in prison, and a bomb thrown in the middle of the night blew apart the wrought-iron bars outside of the courthouse.

I'm not saying that it was any better when I lived in Morne-Galant, or even back in my twenties. But the mid-1960s, it was quite intense. I was worried and saddened to see everyone leaving. And also, with unemployment and factories closing one after the other, business at my store had slowed down. Sometimes I would pace between my blouses and rice paper fans and would chide myself: "Stop it! You're whirling around like a top spun by a bunch of kids!" I was tired, *pffff.* It had been a long time since I had felt the pleasant tingling in the tips of my fingers, as if my *fluide* had all dried up. I was truly disheartened.

I needed some fresh air and a good talk with Mary, Saint Victor Schoelcher, and my dear Saint Michael. Fortunately, I knew where to find them; at church, they told me about a new congregation of sisters who had just opened in Basse-Terre, four hours by bus from Pointe-à-Pitre.

Petit-Frère

"*TCHAP*, how are you?"

"Hello, son. I'm good. You?"

"Yes, I'm well."

"How are your sisters?"

"They are well also, Papa. Lucinde seems happy with her husband."

"Of course she is happy! We chose her the best husband there is! And Antoine?"

"She's doing better. Still in her store. The other day, I opened a bank account for her without her knowing. All of those wads of bills she leaves laying around—I had to do something. I told her as much but she shrugged each time. So I opened her a savings account and I have been putting money in it from time to time. I don't think she even notices."

"Very good, son."

"Papa, on that topic . . . You know, I've been talking about a trumpet. I saw one in Pointe-à-Pitre. A nice one that I really like. But with my apprenticeship stipend, I don't have enough to buy it yet. Would you lend me the money? I would pay you back each month."

"What's that?"

"I work hard, you said it yourself, didn't you?"

"I sure did."

Hilaire chuckled a bit like a hen clucking at her chicks. I persisted.

"Do you remember a few months ago, you promised that if I worked hard, you would buy it for me? Do you remember? I don't want to lose a lot of time, so if you are okay with it, it's not a gift, just a loan. I could buy it for myself tomorrow."

"Son, I'm going to do you one better. I am going to buy you a tractor! A nice new tractor that will run for a long time. Now *that's* something your father can buy for you, and all up front, nothing on credit! I'll just sell off a bit of land. That's worth more than a trumpet."

"But, Papa . . ."

"Listen, son, one day, you'll come out with me to cut sugar-cane, right? You will come out and the two of us, we'll be like a team of ten! You'll see, I'll give you a nice plot of land."

"But you promised me the trumpet!"

"Forget the trumpet, son. Think on it and come back to see me when you're ready. I will be here for you."

That's how it was, Sundays with Papa, on the little patio in front of the house in Morne-Galant. My adolescent self, enduring a mix of tenderness with him and also disappointment about never being understood. From the moment I moved in with Antoine until I left for the mainland, I went to see him every Sunday. Hilaire never understood that I wanted a different life from the one he had. If you decided that's what you wanted, he wouldn't be opposed to it, but he wouldn't help you out, either. That was his perpetual role of being there for us but not available for anything beyond on our basic needs, and he felt it was the right way since he was there for the important things: your wedding, the land where you'll want to build your house, an ox to help you get started in life . . . He was getting older, but he was still just as strong as he used to be.

At over sixty, he was as muscled as he was at twenty-five. His legs, smooth and round, were the color of melted chocolate and extended far beyond his washed-out shorts. There was not an ounce of fat on his torso. His hat protected his shaved head, solid like wood. It was always best to sit next to him and watch the hill's shadow advance toward the house while discussing this and that. That was what he preferred. A father like that could be very frustrating but helped you build character at the same time, since you knew that you couldn't expect much from him, good or bad. Antoine and Lucinde had a hard time understanding that that was how he worked. Perhaps they harbored such bitterness toward him because they had lived with him longer than I had.

In Morne-Galant, Hilaire had long been a figure of local life, surrounded by his brothers and sister and all those sweet-talkers who always needed something. Take Mayor Jampaneau, for example. I saw him do it. He was an ambitious socialist who dreamed of being the next Gaston Monnerville. He had created the branch of the party in Morne-Galant and the party had put him in charge of reversing the influence of the communists, their rivals, and converting the hardworking farmers—who were both illiterate and capable, who worked in a silence that nonetheless stoked a rage toward those in power—and lastly, tasked him with convincing them to rebel in one violent and ridiculous bang.

These descendants of slaves came out in droves to vote and send this champion who would carry their hopes and their love of the party off to distant France. In his most magnificent dreams, Jampaneau would climb through the rows of seats of the Senate. His chest swollen in pride, he would let out an authoritative cry in the middle of the assembly and all of Guadeloupe would celebrate their native son. He had given himself twenty years to rise through the ranks of the island. Next up, Paris!

When I was little and still living with my father, I often witnessed Jampaneau's visits to the house, especially during his very first municipal campaign. He would come on Sundays, a pot of crab *matété* under his arm smelling of garlic and lime that his wife had gotten up early to make.

"Well hello there, Mr. Gros-Vaisseau!" he would say as he arrived on Hilaire's doorstep.

"*Oh!*" Papa would yell from inside by way of a hello, his voice booming and cheerful.

The future mayor would stride over, heavy-footed and relaxed, like a war hero coming home, his shoulders buckling slightly over his long torso, his bandy legs, his hat hanging at his fingertips. Let me do an impression of him so you can imagine what he looked like. There, you see how I'm standing? That was Jampaneau exactly. He would sit down in slow motion on the wooden chair on the patio and straighten out his neck, pensively looking out at the end of the dusty road. He tossed his hat down onto his knee.

"So!" Hilaire would say, popping out of the tiny kitchen and buttoning up his shirt that he had taken from a nail on the wall.

"Ah, my old friend. Here I am. I'm hanging in there!"

"I heard that! Keep on going . . ."

Hilaire sat down on his favorite stool, stretched his legs out in front of him, still wearing boots from when he hitched his oxen early that morning. Jampaneau sighed and began.

"Gros-Vaisseau, I'm tired."

"Is that right."

"You know the region better than I do; you'll be able to tell me. Why are people in Grands Fonds so stubborn? Do you know the Icare family? The ones who live in Blanchette."

"The ones in the old house or the ones in the village?"

"The village. You know, the ones with a son who's a captain."

"I know them."

"Why do they shut their door when they see me as though I was a ghost, hmm? You know me, you know what I'm trying to do in Blanchette. If they truly want a road, they need to show themselves more often, so the rest of us will know they live there!"

"Yeah, one of them got hurt last month. The youngest son of the Icare family's neighbors. He was on a moped when the road collapsed right in front of him, and *woup!* It was after the rains. He ended up in the ravine."

"You see that, Gros-Vaisseau? And I went the other day to the departmental council to talk face-to-face with Servil about it so that we can finally get money for the roads, that's what's going to happen when I'm mayor."

"Yes!"

"Their son could ride a bike all the way to Gourbet!"

"I used to ride there on horseback."

"All the way to Gourbet? Oh, Monsieur Gros-Vaisseau! You've really been everywhere!"

Jampaneau laughed loudly.

"It's really my mare, Vini, who's been everywhere. She could have taken me all the way to the moon."

"Your mare Vini. I remember hearing about her when I was a kid. You see, that's what I've been telling the men in the party. At the departmental council, they're over there writing memoranda with their fountain pens. But me, I'm out here with the people. I know Morne-Galant down to its tiniest potholes."

"That's right."

"The people here in Morne-Galant, I love them, Gros-Vaisseau, I'd do anything for them. They criticize the Whites, but sometimes they should follow their example."

"That's right."

"Now I'm not saying that the *Nègre* has to necessarily find someone with lighter skin and follow their lead. Not at all. I see all too well how they behave at the top. Do what I say, not as I do, am I right? But still, sometimes . . . Let's just say that it's in the *Nègre*'s best interest to take a critical look at ourselves. I'm a *Nègre* too, I know what life has in store for us. If I could, I would do what you're doing, Gros-Vaisseau. I would get on a horse and I'd go everywhere to talk to everyone, even to the Matignons that we only see on a full moon. But I have too much work to do to beat Mr. Lanseing in the next elections. And he's got money. He has his businesses."

"I understand."

"You're a real socialist, Gros-Vaisseau. So I'm telling you, if I'm going to win, we need a massive turnout on election day. We need to be a united army! Organized!"

Jampaneau knocked his fist on his thigh with each point he made. Hilaire lowered his head, his hands between his knees, and grunted his approval. Then the two men listened to the silence of eleven o'clock in the morning, punctuated with the lowing of a thirsty ox. At eleven thirty, Jampaneau seemed to wake up with a start.

"Oh Hilaire! Look at what my wife made for you!"

He extended the tightly closed pot wrapped in newspaper. The *matété* was still warm and Papa simply putting it on the gas stove perfumed the air with lard and spices and the dominating musky odor of the juicy shellfish. Hilaire, flattered and galvanized, made it his mission to see Jampaneau's career succeed, and promised to recruit the entire neighborhood to come out on election day.

WHEN I LEFT Guadeloupe, Jampaneau was in his third term. People who needed a favor at city hall would go to Papa first, who would then play the middleman. He would put on his hat, holding his largest handkerchief in his calloused hand, and head off with the petitioner to help them plead their case.

Each time that he came through the neighborhood, Jampaneau always stopped his car in front of Hilaire's house for five minutes, which filled Hilaire with pride. The mayor had received a bit of land as a gift from my father upon which he was planning to build a cafeteria for the community school.

Years later, Hilaire gave Jampaneau's successor a hectare of land on the other side of Morne-Galant, in the heart of Ezechiel territory. He ran an access road into the new neighborhood. Antoine was furious and called Papa a bandit and a squanderer. At the time of this arrangement, Hilaire was eighty-nine years old. He must have received his pot of crab *matété* and shared it with the town councilor along with a *décollage au rhum*, the first rum of the day. When Antoine came back to Guadeloupe a few months later to take care of Hilaire, she had a dump truck full of gravel unloaded onto the unwanted road. I agreed with her. I wrote letters certified by mail from Créteil to the mayor to make him pay my father what he owed for the land. The letters went unanswered. Alas, he who is absent is always in the wrong!

If someone negotiated nicely with Jampaneau—and later

on the mayors who succeeded him—they could get a contract for the installation of utility poles, no inspections needed, for the arrival of electricity that had already been promised. There was a businessman from Port-Mahon who was persuasive enough to drain the big crawfish pond where we would go to play as children in the clear water and fish for our supper; he turned it into a gas station.

As a teenager, I observed crooked deals like this but never thought too much about them. However, Antoine was incensed and called Hilaire a good-for-nothing grifter. "What will be left for us?" she would say. Papa listened to her criticism and hunched his shoulders. He waited for the storm to pass. But your aunt could pour out her grievances for hours on end, to such an extent that even the most patient listener, let's say me, for example, or Dédé while he was still around, would end up pitying Hilaire.

Now with decades of hindsight, I understand that what my father needed most of all was for us to be there at his side. But none of us, none of his children, were there.

I was the second to abandon him, after Lucinde. Several factors drove me to leave. There was my disappointment and alienation I felt about the photo of my mother, which remained a mystery. Then there was my interrupted schooling and not knowing what I was going to make of my adult life. Lastly there was the feeling, day after day, of having to lower my head in resignation. It never ended—you had to "come to an agreement" with one authority figure after another, from the postal clerk behind his counter with just a bit of power, to the mayor, all by going through smaller players first, all the way up to the powerful *békés* who themselves also negotiated, with the State and the big American factory owners. I felt ensnared like a fly in a spider's web. You know, I had a friend at the time who tried to start a yogurt factory there. So what do you think happened? All the stores on the island started offering deals on yogurt that was imported from the mainland. People were quick to take advantage of the sales. Owners sold their yogurt at a loss, just like that, for months. This went on until my friend, with his local, small-scale setup, threw in the towel and closed his business. That's how it was and it hasn't changed since. You know the Bob Marley song? The one that goes, *Every time I plant a seed, sheriff said kill it before it grow.* Every time I hear it, I think about my friend's yogurt business.

The first trap from which I had to extricate myself was my family. At that time and still today, I struggled with my sisters. I struggled with their irrefutable talent for making consistently terrible choices. With their love for me, which was like some kind of marionette theater of tyranny and manipulation. With their advice, which I felt was careless and delusional, even as a child. They lived in a permanent fantasy in which I never grew up, where I was the mirror that reflected how respectable and responsible they were, where corporal punishment was rare but delivered even more forcefully and in public. I suffocated under their loving touch as well as their slaps. I think that ever since I was a child, I knew that I would leave Guadeloupe. That motivation was the only thing that kept me from screaming at them what I thought about the way they were raising me—an approach fueled by a deep fear of God and concern for what others might say.

I WAS TWENTY YEARS OLD in 1964, and I was working, at last, as an electrician with steady work. General de Gaulle's second visit was kindling excitement throughout the entire island. It was the most talked about topic on the radio and in the newspapers, the main story reported on ahead of the Algerian war that was beginning to end, and the Vietnam War that was only just beginning. Well ahead of the revolution in Cuba or the struggle for civil rights in the United States, these revolutions were happening at the same time, right next to us, but we heard practically nothing about them. It was Yvan's father, Papa Mischief, who explained to us what was happening in Havana and in Alabama. He felt very hopeful about Fidel Castro. He talked to us about the struggles of the people. He removed a book from his bag, one by the Martinican author Frantz Fanon, whom I knew nothing about. He handled it carefully as though it were a treasure and read it in secret, since books by Fanon were seized by the French police.

The night before de Gaulle arrived, I worked with another electrician until two in the morning preparing the sound system for his speech the next day.

When de Gaulle walked onstage with his cries of love for overseas France, everything went according to plan. We spent the next night dismantling the equipment. Satisfied and relieved, the boss held out twenty-five francs to each of us in congratulations.

I forced a thank-you; I always had trouble smiling at him. At the end of the week, when we came to the office to retrieve our pay, his wife coolly handed us our checks. She had deducted twenty-five francs from our compensation. It threw me into an icy rage.

"This is twenty-five francs short," I told her. She looked at me with feigned surprise.

"I think my husband has already paid you that amount, isn't that right?"

"I didn't ask him for an advance. He paid us that amount after the ceremony."

"So you got your twenty-five francs, then."

"But that was paid to us as a bonus. We did not ask for it in advance."

"Listen, I'm paying you the amount that was agreed upon. If you want more, you'll have to ask later."

I was going to argue further, but my coworker shot me a look begging me to let it go. I left furious, and three days later I signed the necessary papers to enlist in the army.

Those last few years, many of my friends had enlisted in the army before their obligatory years of service to avoid ending up in Algeria. There, France's "peacekeeping" consisted of sending conscripts rather than career military men. So officially, the army had lost only a few men in that war that at the time did not have a name. Guadeloupean families learned about the Algerian conflict only when the coffins were unloaded with military honors in the port at Pointe-à-Pitre. Young Antilleans had perished under a different sun, thousands of kilometers from the island, for a colonial France where indigenous people were treated like slaves. The conflict was over, even though some of my friends were still being sent there a few months before I left, and even after the Évian Accords. When it was my turn, I enlisted early; it was either that or slide slowly toward an emotional breakdown. The contours of the island were the walls of my prison. I feared that my shorter leg would cost me the recruitment exam, but in the end I was declared fit to serve. Much later, when I gained access to as many books as I wanted, when my colleagues and professors helped me to put words to what I felt, when I myself learned how to find a path through the tortuous words of my patients that I treated—then I understood that at twenty years old, the army had saved me.

I returned to see Hilaire the Sunday before I left.

"*Tchap.*"

"Yes?"

"I'm leaving next week."

"After your service, you'll be a man and we will sit down and drink a glass of rum together."

"Yes, *pa'.*"

"Be careful, take good care of your health. Don't fight like Gros-Vaisseau."

"No, *pa'.*"

"Where are you going?"

"To Germany. A town called Rastatt."

". . . The army! I'm proud of you. Don't you forget it. For how long, did you say?"

"Eighteen months."

"It will pass quickly. When you come back, we'll work together."

"No, *pa'.* You know very well that we won't."

"So what will you do, then?"

"I don't know."

"Don't forget to take a clean shirt."

"Yes, *pa'.*"

When I said goodbye, I saw that he was crying quietly. We didn't know then that we wouldn't see one another for fifteen years, but we both knew that it could be a long time. No one on the island boarded a plane only to come back just eighteen months later.

When I told Antoine I was leaving, she looked at me, one fist set boldly on her hip, and quickly rattled off advice on the theme of how I needed to be a good boy no matter the situation. I didn't listen to her, but I examined her pretty face with that half-crazy expression. I saw a tenderness there, and pride at seeing me don a uniform, and a soupçon of sadness.

It was only then that I told her about the bank account that I opened for her. She had never once stood in front of a bank teller. She seemed skeptical, so I tried to explain how it worked.

"You see, it's like your house, but safer. You can go there whenever you want."

"Mm-hmm. You're a good boy. I'll think about it."

"Well, it's already opened, the only thing you have to do is keep depositing money there and check with the teller to see how much you have saved each month."

"Yes, alright."

"And pay your taxes with that money."

"Mmm," she said offhandedly.

BASSE-TERRE IS THE OPPOSITE of Grande-Terre and these two sister islands are as different as Lucinde and me. And yet there is only a tiny arm of the sea between them, and a large bridge that has collapsed on several occasions since the times when Hilaire would travel around on horseback, but they would always rebuild it because the people wanted the two sisters to be holding hands.

Grande-Terre, where the Ezechiels are from, is flat-chested, made for big distilleries and beautiful mills that today are falling into ruin. Basse-Terre is mountainous and mist-covered, and has always been the land of those who escaped slavery or who were never enslaved. It was a refuge to the Maroons escaping slavery in the seventeenth to nineteenth centuries, to the dissidents who rejected the Vichy regime and hid along the sides of the volcano, reclaiming ancient footpaths left by the Carib people before them— undetectable paths that nature quickly swallowed up, that they would keep hidden. The people there are perhaps more proud than in Grande-Terre because they carry a legacy of freedom.

I boarded my bus before daybreak, as is my habit. First, you leave La Pointe and its progression of little tired *faubourgs* being eroded by demolition. Then you return to a land that is relatively flat and then abruptly takes shape. Hills, peaks, and mountain chains. We named this part *route de la traversée*, the crossing road, and along the length of it, fern-laden slopes and nettle trees emit a sulfurous mist that makes you think of ancient times. Huge banana plantations descend on the first slopes all the way to the sea. The wealthy landowners took the hot and humid lower slopes but left the heights to the waterfalls.

While the bus was climbing the hairpin curves, loudly sputtering its *biguine* music, I thought back to Dédé's old dream of wanting to work his own plot of banana trees. That fool, what did he think would happen? You could see clearly that everything here was controlled by those with powerful hands—they had money to pay dozens of men, bent and broken in half working in the furrows, money to pay for the machines to bag up the banana bunches to protect them from rats, and for the vats of insecticide that seeped deep into the earth and leaked into the tiniest streams, making its way to the vegetables and to the fish from the sea and the river, all the way into the milk of the women breastfeeding their children.*

Above the banana plantations were the real mountains, a paradise of wild herbs and warm springs. That's where I was headed. But first, the bus had to stop in the town of Basse Terre, which was too sleepy to compete with Pointe-à-Pitre. I

---

* Note from the author: Banana plantation owners used so many pesticides that all of Basse-Terre is contaminated by chlordecone and residents cannot eat the fruits and vegetables that they grow. Residents of Guadeloupe and Martinique have the highest levels of cancer in the world because of this. It is a crime of the plantation owners but also the State, since these pesticides have been forbidden in mainland France but authorized for a long time in the Antilles.

saw the gray line of the austere, crumbling fort that extended the length of the town, along with its two pathetic towers used in the war between the French and the English.

I waited for another bus at the foot of the newly constructed concrete Préfecture. It was maybe nine o'clock in the morning. I liked how the sea took on a darker, greener tint than what I was used to in La Pointe. Still another hour zigzagging on the road and then I arrived where the sisters of Notre-Dame were living like pioneers: the very spot where a thousand years ago the Caribs smoked their meat.

Three nuns welcomed me beneath the gum trees of a large, brand-new house with big open windows. To start, I prayed fervently and paid to have a mass said for Armand. I was thirty-five years old and I had come to catch my breath at the foot of this volcano, so I thought over particular moments of my life.

I loved having the sisters nearby, their heavy white habits contrasting with their dark foreheads and hands, much darker than mine. I felt lighter than I ever had before. I slept in their freshly painted dormitory. I was beside them at dawn, in a church built from lava stones, and I was with them at night for the evening prayers.

THE DAYS PASSED. Two weeks maybe. I wasn't counting. But I didn't receive any signs from the Holy Mother of God or from the angels that surrounded her. It was only Armand who ended up visiting me.

One afternoon I was picking fruit with a hunchbacked sister who was out of breath and panting because of her bad knees. I stood up with a nice avocado in my hand to place into the wicker basket between us, and who do I see standing there, smiling, magnificent in front of me? It was Armand, who had recovered his copper skin tone, his jutting pink cheekbones, his playful blue eyes, and his golden curls. He looked at me teasingly, but not unkindly.

*"Oh oh! Sé ou ki la aló? Ou fé kè an mwen soté oh!"** I told him with a smile. He didn't move and stood there before me with his shirt halfway open revealing his chest, still skinny, and his pants rolled up over his ankles. I wanted to introduce him to Sister Josépha, who was gaping at me, but I wondered if he would like that or not. So I gently set the avocado into the basket and asked Josépha to give us a moment.

We sat there for a long time next to a quick-rushing stream lined with arborescent ferns. I held his hands in mine and he told me what I had not wanted to know before: how he arrived at such a young age in the Cayenne penal colony, how he saw prisoners around him collapse and die of scurvy. The guards who mistreated them and the White settlers who looked down on them as they crushed stones while carving a road through the forest. How, when he got out, he wandered along the Maroni River, letting himself drift along, how he had hallucinated with fever and then scraped by for a time in the village of Oyapock, where the Indians had saved him.

Our conversation lasted for at least an hour. And then I hugged him tightly and he told me he would come back the next day. For four days in a row, I found him curled in the large trunk of a buttress-root tree or squatting in the river. After he had told me his life story, he talked only about fruit and wild animals. He looked around as he sat on a rock in the middle of a low spot in the river and pointed to a flower and told me its name. He complained about how quiet it was.

* "Is that you? You scared me!"

"You don't know what a forest is," he said. "There is nothing here, no more animals. All you have here are bananas and coffee." I didn't understand what he meant. There had never been anything else on this side of Guadeloupe. Or maybe a very long time ago there had been more, when the ancient petroglyphs buried beneath the moss meant something to the people who lived here.

On the fourth day I asked him why he had come to see me. I had read a clear warning in his eyes, and I was waiting for him to tell me more. He looked at me with his strange smile and told me, "You won't be better off there." I didn't want to understand. I had no plans to leave.

I washed my feet in the cold water; I took my shoes and went to the convent feeling anxious. On the terrace, the sisters shot me questioning, leery looks. For a few days, they avoided me as I walked past and I felt their reticence when I sat down on the same benches with them to pray.

Here's what actually happened: they chased me out. First, Josépha, the sister I had gone out collecting fruit with, started to whisper behind my back that I was *La Diablesse*.* I caught her a few times eyeing my shoes as though inside them I had cloven feet. The Mother Superior reprimanded her, saying that that kind of superstition was not Christian. However, from then on, even with all her authority, she who had been so welcoming to me, looked at me with shock and disapproval.

And then one morning very early, when we had barely opened our eyes in the dormitory, another sister, a tiny woman with thin little legs beneath her long white cotton dress, cried out as she looked at my bed. Sitting on her mattress, she pointed at something on the ground. I had been lying down

* *La Diablesse*: a beautiful, evil woman in Antillean folklore who has one cloven foot. —Trans.

and sat up with a start. Leaning over carefully to see what she was pointing to, I squinted to see more clearly in the dim light of dawn. Wet footprints circled around my bed as though multiple people had danced there.

I hadn't heard anything in particular that night, not one of the sisters had noticed anything, and there were no footprints anywhere else on the floor. So I shrugged and tried to make light of the trick that one of them had played on me. But the sisters were not having it. It was as though they were waiting for some kind of permission to unleash their imaginations. A few began praying, their faces strained in anguish; others clasped their hands and looked at me.

No one dared come near me, but there were still people buzzing about it in the dormitory. The Mother Superior, who had her own little cell at the corner of the building, came to investigate. The footprints around my bed were fresh as though the feet of the person who left them had been covered in dew. But all the sisters were there and their sandals were dry. So the Mother Superior gravely declared that I must leave, because I was causing trouble in their community. I knew that there was nothing left for me there anyway. Armand hadn't shown up for eight days.

SITTING ON A PEACOCK TREE STUMP at the bottom of the main road of Basse-Terre, I waited for the bus home. There, worry overtook me, as it had prior to my trip there. You know how I can sense things. The air was heavy with a tension that weighed upon the road and the people, and I felt it in my entire being. It was a very hot day and the sea at my back was silent.

In front of me, from the other side of the road, there was

a shoe store called Sans Pareil. Laying out on the ground in front of the window was a disabled old *Nègre* who called out to people passing by saying he would resole their shoes for a few coins. I was overwhelmed by the heat, and my gaze wandered toward him as I used one of those pink fans I sold in La Pointe to cool my face, but it was torn from tumbling around in my bag, so it didn't really help me.

I heard shouting and looked back at the disabled man. A hefty White man sweating in a long-sleeved shirt was standing in front of him, his legs spread wide, shouting at him to go away. I deduced that the White man was the owner of the store. The old man sitting on the ground refused. He bent his atrophied leg as best he could, swearing in Créole and settling his skinny rear end a little more comfortably on the asphalt. The store owner yelled and then sent the man's supplies flying with one swift kick. The nails and the box of wax rolled into the gutter.

Next to me, a woman watching the scene hissed something indecipherable. Passersby drew closer. Without standing up, the crippled old man slowly picked up his nails and his little metal box.

"An di a-w an pa a bougé!" he declared loudly. This time, the kick caught him in the lower back. He fell backward, cursing the White man and all of his ancestors. As he realized a crowd was forming around him, that John Wayne rushed into the store and locked the door behind him. The woman next to me shook her head and *tchip*ed her scorn.

It happened just like it does onstage at the theater. At least I imagine it's like that. A window of the Sans Pareil store opened over the storefront. As though on a spring, a sweaty head, red like a chili pepper, popped out and spat, "Get out of here, you baboons!" He pointed a gun down at the street.

People had helped the old man up, and leaning on a young woman, he walked away lecturing about his right to use the sidewalk as he pleased.

Instinctively, I searched for a safe spot. The group of onlookers was crowding slowly around the store. When the first stone was thrown at the window, a shot split through the air. It was as though the owner had been waiting for it. I slid behind an old cannon that hadn't moved an inch since the era of Spanish pirates. I was protected behind its big stone base, but felt icy snakes running down my back.

John Wayne shouted again, "I'm going to go crazy on these *Nègres!*" With three stones, just like that, *blogodo!* the window shattered. At the second shot, the boys from the street spread out toward the homes a few roads over and higher up. Again, I saw the old man and the young woman quickly moving away underneath the peacock trees. She had slid an arm around his skinny frame and was roughly pushing him forward. I prayed that he wouldn't encounter any further trouble. Five minutes of silence. Then fifteen or so people of all ages came out of the alleys behind the unevenly lined houses. I could see them from my hiding spot. Twenty, thirty. A little group started rocking a white Simca, probably the store owner's car. It ended up roofside to the pavement, flipped over like a fat turtle. The store owner waved a gun wildly in the window. This seemed to have inflamed the people below. They were just children who didn't yet believe in death. A frenzied group struck at the car with boards. Through my shock, I heard rallying cries mixed with the revving engines of police cars.

The Compagnie Républicaine de Sécurité arrived at the moment when the Simca caught on fire. I was still huddling behind my cannon. I wanted to stay tucked and roll all the way down to the calm sea below. The police fell on the crowd like wickedness upon the Earth. Billy clubs rained down and bodies dropped to the sidewalk. I saw the owner of the Sans Pareil, terrified, dragged out from his store and stuffed hastily into a police truck. My bus appeared in the distance, calmly climbed the coastline, and then stopped in the middle of the battlefield.

The bus doors opened mechanically. I hurried in without thinking. Inside, the radio was blasting a feverish melody. From the window, I saw another police officer shove an angry woman into a wall with his shoulder. She was yelling something in the direction of the patrol wagon where John Wayne was hiding away. Four teenagers were lying on the ground in handcuffs. Inside the bus, everyone had stood up in protest and was eyeing the windows. The police signaled to the driver to start the engine and leave.

The CRS swung their clubs to clear the road. I clutched the strap hanging from the ceiling of the bus. Some of the agitated passengers yelled out that the driver had better stop if he didn't want to be a traitor to his people, but the driver continued on his way, objecting that he had no choice. Two men, however, were able to force open the latch on the door. "No, no! Don't go out there!" I yelled at them, but they jumped out and I saw them run toward the Sans Pareil. The bus pulled away in a cloud of blue smoke, leaving the scramble of people behind us and our stricken faces looking out from inside the bus.

Ôôô . . . I couldn't believe that the situation had exploded like that, all in the silence of the afternoon. The trouble had ripened there without us having realized it—silently, discreetly, but ever-present. And I had just been blind, which had prevented me from seeing it in time to prepare for it all.

The bus, swaying, crossed a bridge and drove around the

statue of the general from the French army who had re-instated slavery under Napoleon,* and then bounced toward the heights where I could see only a few *cases* without doors or windows. The popular *biguine* music continued to fill the bus, permeating the space like an awful lie.

* The French Republic had abolished slavery in its colonies in 1794. In efforts to establish a French Empire and meet labor shortages on sugar plantations, Napoleon Bonaparte reestablished slavery in France and the French colonies in 1802, the legal structures of which were not entirely dismantled until 1848. —Trans.

Antoine: May '67

WHEN I RETURNED to Basse-Terre, my life returned to normal for a while. But I kept an eye out. After the *quimboiseur*, the apparition of Armand, and the incident at the Sans Pareil, I slept poorly. Despite the undercurrent of sadness that slowed me down, I tried to pull it together. I would open my store and chat with the people who came in. I was on the lookout.

Things started to get worse in La Pointe. It seemed like the youth had *zozio* chili pepper in their veins, ready to challenge their place in society. On the one hand, our traditional industries were in decline. On the other hand, there was a newfound appetite for items from France: washing machines, automobiles, popular records. There was not a lot of work. The women worked as cooks or seamstresses. But the men—what would they become without the factories? Concrete was springing up everywhere, but the workers were paid next to nothing and they were pitted against each other: Haitians against Guadeloupeans, Blacks against Indians, Indians against Chinese, and on and on, in a dance with the devil.

For a few years, there had been separatists who would give rousing speeches on their nights off at social clubs. Even though in the *France-Antilles* newspaper that all the mamans used to wrap their fish with nothing was being written about it all. Guadeloupe had its clandestine ways of passing along information. Those who wanted to know what was going on in the world could listen to underground radio stations. What the young people heard filled their heads with questions.

One day, I went back to see Madame Pilote, who was getting quite old, sitting at the back of her store. I saw a large gathering at the Place de la Victoire. I walked closer. Construction workers were on strike. They explained that a meeting of the company owners was happening at that very moment in the chamber of commerce to determine whether the strikers would get a small raise. The square was locked down by the Compagnie Républicaine de Sécurité riot police and French naval officers.

Coulange, that boss of all bosses, came out on the little front steps and sized up the crowd. At the foot of the steps, someone threw a giant conch shell at him. I didn't see what happened, but apparently the shell went right into the eye of a CRS officer who had taken off his helmet in the heat.

Very quickly, everything was a blur. People started running all around me and the movement lifted me up like a wave. And then, shots rang out, sharply, repeatedly. It happened like in Basse-Terre, but this time, not like on a theater stage but like the movie version, and I was right in the thick of it.

Two men fell down next to me. I rushed toward the port. Charging toward us from behind was a powerful dark mass of policemen that spread panic within seconds.

"They're doing what they did in Algeria!" I heard someone shout. I found myself in the rue Alexandre Isaac; the exact opposite of where I wanted to be. A jeep full of police officers drove onto the sidewalk, barely missing me. All I wanted was to get far away from the swelling rumble, return to my house, draw the curtains, and lose myself in prayer with the healing novenas.

I was assailed by the smell of smoke and gasoline. I jumped over objects that must have been used as projectiles. Vats, broken coconuts, and empty shoes as though their owners had suddenly disappeared into thin air. I ran all the way to the cemetery to wait for things to calm down, but many others had the same idea. When I got there, a whole group of women and children was talking nervously at the entrance. The gates were closed. I couldn't just stand outside like a stupid *ababa*; I summoned all my courage and headed back to the center of town to try to get to my house. Around the war memorial, young people were running around, yelling to each other. They shouted that the police had killed two separatists. One window, then another, had exploded in broad daylight. Men rushed in and ran out with anything that they could swing or use to cut.

I dropped to the ground, flat like a butterfly frozen in white-hot fear against a wall. Two strong men with shaved heads who looked like legionnaires closed in on me and called out in gruff French:

"What the hell are you doing here?"

With their awful sea-dog breath, I realized that they had started on rum that morning and hadn't stopped. When I didn't respond, they grabbed me by the arm. My feet scraped the sidewalk. They brusquely released me because a delegation decked out in the blue, white, and red of the French flag had appeared in front of us.

It was the mayor of Pointe-à-Pitre, a tall *Nègre* full of

confidence, being escorted by policemen, walking down the road trying to calm people down. Seeing him like that, walking calmly in the sea of the officers' flat-topped képi hats, was surely not going to solve anything or appease any of the anger.

Seizing the opportunity, I backed farther away, but a rock destined for the tone-deaf procession hit me in the head and my vision swirled as though I, too, had drunk too much rum. Blood ran down my ear. I zigzagged in the street, spiraling in disaster.

My store was my Promised Land. I swore that I wouldn't come out until Christmas and it was only just May! I took a road that ran perpendicular to the harbor, I don't remember which one. I remember a car across the street from me with a White woman at the wheel, terrified by the crowd that had formed around her. Blows to the roof of the car, the car rocking violently, it must have felt like heavy rain pouring down on the sheet-metal roofs of the *cases*; a ferocious roar that I loved under normal circumstances, but this was wartime. Even as I loped along with my mangled ear, I still ran to help the woman because she was crying. "Stop!" I shouted, and a few of the young people around the car turned toward me. I shouted again, "The police are shooting! They are shooting! Get out of here! Take cover!" One guy rushed toward me, looking threatening. I stayed planted where I was in the street. He continued toward me and spat, "You, lady! Are you Black or are you White?"

At first I didn't understand what he wanted. "What am I supposed to say to that?" I answered defiantly. He repeated his question and pointed a menacing finger at me. My life depended on how I responded. But all that talk of *négritude* that

Césaire and Senghor had waxed poetic about and that had captivated our young people had always left me indifferent.

More than anything, I considered myself a woman, and also a Guadeloupean, that is to say, someone of mixed-blood, like all of us here on the island, this tiny piece of confetti in the vast ocean, where everyone has come from somewhere else and has kept only a bit of blood from the native Carib people. For me, this kept any notions of grandeur or purity at bay. I was proud of my life's trajectory and all the twists and turns that I alone had chosen. The man grabbed me by the neck and I spat at him in Créole:

"What, do you not have eyes to see?"

He hesitated and then let me go. The others had abandoned the car and the woman had run away. A siren rang out and they *pris un toufoukan*, took off running in the alleys. No one else was in front of me. I was attacked twice in one minute—once by the White legionnaires and then again by the Black protesters. I was disoriented, terrorized, numbed. I started to walk, found my bearings despite the disarray, the blood, gravel, and tear gas that stung my eyes.

I had almost arrived home when a young woman emerged from the other side of the sidewalk. She was running and holding the hand of a twelve-year-old boy. A police car appeared around the corner behind her. They fired a single shot that spread a round red stain on the boy's shirt. He fell under his own weight from the shock, chin-first, as the car disappeared.

The woman leaned over the boy's trembling body, then grabbed at her undone hair, rocking back and forth. People slowly drew closer and called blindly for help. Ten minutes later, the medics arrived with their sirens wailing. Two men loaded up the boy and helped the young woman covered in blood into the cab. I imagine that they headed off to the hospital, but I knew the boy was already dead.

I ENDED UP AT MY DOORSTEP by feeling my way there. A martial voice decreed the curfew by order of the prefecture from a loudspeaker. Everyone was ordered home before five o'clock in the evening and was told to stay put. I sat down on the ground, my hands over my ears. I continued to hear the bursts of machine-gun fire and shouting. Lord knows how long I stayed there like that, frozen in my doorway.

When I opened my eyes again, it was pitch black. I slithered to the small window on the first floor and pulled myself up just enough to see into the street. A human form appeared on the other side on the sidewalk, barely discernible. I thought back to the boy who had caught the bullet in his back. It couldn't have been him since they had carried him off, but I couldn't imagine who else it could be. I looked again. There was certainly someone who had been left there, lying against the curtains of the grocery store across the street.

Without knowing what I was going to do, I slid back toward the door. I murmured to myself: "Virgin Mary, Holy Mother of the living, protect me," and I advanced on all fours, even down the stairs. I half opened the door, still chanting. The road was silent. I waited a few minutes and then dove toward the shape laying on the ground.

It was a young man. His head was bloody but his chest was still warm. I lifted him up by the shoulders and pulled him to my door. I froze when I heard the motor of a car. I could be taken to the police station for less than this. I pulled the man into the entrance and locked the door from the inside. I had hoped that it was the boy, that he wasn't dead, and that I was going to save him. But this boy was older, over twenty.

I placed a wet cloth on his face. There was a giant crack from his hairline down to his nose. Blood pearled as soon as I moved him. It looked like a split in the side of a bottle gourd. I was afraid of seeing his brain underneath, but the bone was not broken in; just clearly split in a straight crack that ran from his hairline to his nose. It had no doubt been a billy club. He would have to get to a doctor very quickly.

When I was little, I once saw a steer kick a man who bent down to grab its chain. The man was thrown a meter away and stood up as though nothing had happened, took a few steps, and then fell down dead. I was afraid the same would happen to the boy. I didn't know what to do. Exhausted, I hauled him onto my armchair. He still was not moving, but he was breathing. That was when I recognized him. It was Petit-Frère's friend Yvan.

Lucinde

TINY COLLARS in fluffy fabric, all exactly the same, that's what I made when I first arrived in Paris. Cutout gloves with a die cut from shagreen that I stitched under the cold, watchful eye of the boss, an immense woman in flats. This was on rue Amsterdam, at a place called Sainte-Croix, an atelier that supplied stores of the Galeries de l'Opéra and, from time to time, the Chanel fashion house. I had passed it by chance, and seeing the way the women were bent over inside, I instantly guessed they were cutting fabric.

Without giving myself time to think about it, I went inside. A lanky woman asked me to bring photos of my designs. I came back with a few newspaper articles from the time of the beauty pageants. She sized up the images blankly and barely opened her mouth when she offered me a job as a tailor. Still, I was very pleased to have found the spot. That's how it was back then; you could easily get into the field, but then you had to forget everything you knew and begin again.

I brought work home. Fifty buttonholes on dresses to deliver the next day or two hundred labels to embroider on the back of flannel blouses. Tatar didn't really think I was working, because he left every morning at seven o'clock for the Orly postal-sorting office. He came back at 5:25 exactly to slump down on the couch in front of his television. We were renting an apartment near rue de Rennes.

I found more than a few acquaintances from La Pointe, wives of *békés* also. Tatar was able to buy a car. Antoine tells you that he bought it with his money. I don't know, maybe he did, I can't really say. But he dipped into my savings, that's for sure. I didn't care; I was happy to be on the mainland, far from the jealous people and glaring eyes. I was finally going to be able to rub shoulders with people of my caliber. You have to admit that La Pointe was a huge heap of ignorant and jealous people where a *Nègre* couldn't walk by with a bag over his shoulder without being suspected of secretly having a fortune. There, people frowned at my daughters simply because I would slip on delicate ankle socks to go with their polished shoes. It's true, I liked to dress them like princesses—what's wrong with some elegance? Here, I was finally going to be able to live at my level.

Couture at Sainte-Croix was, nevertheless, a kind of coordinated exploitation. The pay and the work were not stable; nothing for two weeks and then all at once you'd get an order to fulfill the next day, paid per piece. I didn't see myself going on like that for long. So when a friend offered to get me a job at the Palais de Justice, where she was a secretary, I jumped at the opportunity. There, I had a regular salary, and, in turn, I also became a civil servant. Of course, I always regretted not being able to dedicate myself fully to my couture, but the Palais de Justice was quite an improvement and ensured stability for the children. During my evenings and on my days off, I was able to keep sewing for my regular clients; I even sent a few dresses back to Guadeloupe.

I wasn't allowed to use Tatar's car, but I quickly became

more independent. I got my driver's license. I took my daughters to London, without their father of course. I'd always dreamed of learning English. From time to time, I still read a few lines here and there from my old Oxford dictionary, figuring they might come in handy. A few years later, we bought the apartment in Champigny. There you have it; we had made our start on the mainland.

The more I blossomed, even little by little, the more I noticed that Tatar was not thriving. He had wanted to get to the mainland as much as me, but I could see that this new life was not fulfilling for him. At home in the evenings, he would stare at the television and not say a word. The girls would bring him his *ti punch* and he wouldn't speak until dinner. He was suspicious, sullen—the Tatar I knew was disappearing bit by bit.

At work, he spoke only with other Antilleans, and in Créole, of course. As though they needed to comfort one another. He would say nothing to me; everything seemed normal, except that he was talking more and more to the nanny we had brought over with us. Anyway, as long as I could carry on with my own business . . . Back then, I looked at other men too. Men who had been wooing me for a while and whom I saw again once we came to the mainland; the dentist from rue Frébault, a very light-skinned mulatto who was shyer than a little girl; the hotel owner from Marie-Galant who would invite us over when we still lived there. I was starting to have fun; it was as though I had left a whole slew of rules on the plane when I stepped off of it.

Still, in the end, Tatar became so short-tempered that I forced him to talk to me. He was very homesick. He missed the Saturday nights around the table playing dominoes and the dances where he could dress up and show off. Deep down, he was still a fatherless son who lacked self-confidence. In Guadeloupe, he knew the social codes and had his place—a modest one, but a sure one. Even just his yellowish skin tone made it seem as though he was disappearing completely here. He had always been so loudmouthed, but turned soft-spoken because of his accent. He wanted to hide his provincial ways, had the impression that people were making fun of him because they laughed at things he did not understand. He spoke increasingly about leaving. For me, leaving was out of the question.

Time went by and Tatar became more and more angry. I didn't want to know anything about it. Even back before we were married, his backward manners had struck me like a slap in the face. As time went on, I found the strength to scold him for his lack of education. He blamed the mainland for making me insolent, but it was really just that I was over thirty by that point. In bed, he had to fight to get what he wanted, especially since I refused to have more children. That, too, was easier on the mainland. More than once I ended a pregnancy I did not want.

Later, Tatar admitted to me that barely one year after our arrival, he had asked for a job transfer. But it wasn't that easy. On the mainland you could easily find work. In Guadeloupe, civil servant jobs were rare; rarer still if you had climbed the ladder. Let's say that you started on the mainland at the lowest rung of the ladder and little by little, as you advanced, you became the office manager or something like that. In Guadeloupe, that kind of position was reserved for Whites. All the managers in public service were people from the mainland. For an Antillean, it was basically impossible. So, Tatar—that idiot—fearing he'd see his transfer request rejected, continually turned down any promotion that came his way. He stayed at Orly in the same position in the sorting room, from the first day until fifteen years later, when he at last got his transfer. In the meantime, we had divorced.

Petit-Frère

I STAYED IN GERMANY for three years, assigned to the Forty-Second Army Signal Corps of Rastatt. Those were good years. Freedom and frivolity. I shed my anger like an old skin. I had thought I was angry at all White people, but I came to understand that discrimination wasn't always about skin color. Injustice existed outside of Guadeloupe, and that realization both relieved and toughened me. By letting the world in, I developed a social consciousness.

My friends in the army came from all over France. Some guys could barely read the easiest word scratched on a door. It saddened me having to see them concentrating in order to even understand a spoken order. Others, who displayed a real strength of character, told me about working-class *cités*, the mines in the North of France, about their future children, who would be, they hoped, the first college graduates of the family. Poverty mixed with hope and solidarity—a whole world I couldn't imagine given the caste society I had come from.

I didn't know about all the trouble in Guadeloupe. I didn't know what Yvan was going through. Antoine was confronting the end of innocence—all the violence and the repression of the State—and I was spending time in the noncommissioned officers' mess hall. On Saturdays, I would invite the German girls to dance to the Rolling Stones. Pretty, carefree blondes who asked me to speak French to them and who were up for a good time, fueled by the bliss of youth, of being well-fed and fearless. I learned how to laugh, to be mischievous and careless, to suspect nothing.

Guard duty in the freezing cold of the Black Forest, bad cigarettes to warm my blue fingers in the snow, even the early-morning chores—none of it bothered me. I received no news from my sisters. I wasn't angry about it. Just once I received a package from Antoine. A bit of money and a strange dark-purple-colored sweater that she had unearthed from who knows where. As I unfolded the sweater, a little wooden cross tumbled out. I stuffed it all in the back of my wardrobe.

The only thing I would've liked to have was the photo of Eulalie that I was still dreaming about. I thought about it when friends passed family photos from bed to bed in the barracks, eliciting jokes about a grandfather's baldness or the snub nose of a younger sister.

With my first paycheck, I bought myself a trumpet in a wonderful music store in the heart of Rastatt. Indeed, it was a carefree time, a time of opening to the world, and Paris was my next stop.

I had wanted to see the capital city for so long! I arrived in June of '67 and stayed with Lucinde and Tatar. I found a job as a radio repairman. I wanted to move into my own place as soon as possible, because in addition to Lucinde and Tatar's incessant arguments and the drama of their preteen daughters, they were asking an exorbitant amount for rent for the privilege of setting up my cot in their living room.

———

IN PARIS, I looked up Éléanore's son, Marino. Seven thousand kilometers away from his mother, he was thankful to have even the smallest connections to Guadeloupe. Lucinde and I were his strongest links to home as he was starting his life in Paris. He was no longer the overprotected and spoiled child I had known. He was tall and handsome, his skin the color of aged rum, and he had acquired a self-confidence bolstered by the generous financial support of his parents. He was a student at the Sorbonne, which made him interesting to me on several levels: first, he was meeting smart, passionate people, and second, he was surrounded by many pretty girls. We began to wander around Paris, almost the way we had done a few years prior in Pointe-à-Pitre. We were equally hungry to go out on the town, find parties, and explore. Imagine it: just a single movie theater in La Pointe. In Paris, there were cinemas aplenty, theaters, bookstores, concerts on every street corner. I was happy. Every day I realized more and more how life on the island—with its colonial hierarchy, its closed-mindedness, and its lack of professional prospects—was oppressive.

I'm not embellishing. Life was really more beautiful then than it is now. It all went downhill after the Trente Glorieuses. I would say that we became Black around 1980 on the mainland, from the moment when having work was no longer a given.* Before then, being securely employed and young had been enough to bond people—those who didn't have much—

* Note from the author: Antilleans truly became Black around this time of economic struggle. Before then, during the Trente Glorieuses, their skin color was irrelevant, even though there was a minor degree of racism. Mixed marriages were never illegal in France like they were in the United States. The notion of "becoming Black" is essential to understanding that skin color is an idea that appears and disappears according to circumstances.

with the same raison d'être, the same dreams. Sure, racism existed, but not enough to ruin the party. Our biggest problem was finding an apartment to rent. As far as renting went, though—yes, the prejudice was considerable. I knew families who had spent several years living in a hotel. But on the whole, in the 1960s, we blended into French society. In Paris, we were just small-towners along with the rest, free at last and carefree like everyone else. Thanks to Marino, I discovered a whole network of Black and White students—with them we discussed class struggle and philosophy, exchanged ideas about the world, and developed our dreams and ambitions. We went to La Cigale together, to the Antillean dance parties where Al Lirvat played his jazzy *biguine* and *wabap*, listened to more tropical jazz by Robert Mavounzy, and the Créole songs of Moune de Rivel, who had returned from a two-year tour in New York. I discovered Antillean writers, actors, and musicians who had lived in Paris since the beginning of the war and were a part of the French and international cultural elite. With Marino, the good times never stopped.

One day we were strolling toward Montparnasse, and I casually mentioned the photo of Eulalie and the distant promise that Adose had made. He offered his help.

"After all, Eulalie was my great-aunt. Grandmother never denies me anything; she will show it to me."

He was planning to go back to Guadeloupe for the academic break. He promised to return with the photo.

At the summer's end, he told me to meet him at the Place Saint-Michel. September was dry in Paris, the sun's heat beating down relentlessly and radiating back up from the dusty cobblestones. The mist from the fountain provided a welcome coolness. Marino's skin had turned a dark copper. Nevertheless, he looked pleased to be back in Paris. He now had a nice afro and smoked cigarillos. He offered me one and we settled into the patio of a café. We were soon surrounded by gray curls of smoke. After telling me some news about his family—he hadn't seen my father, Antoine seemed a little thin to him—he came around to the subject that I was so eager to hear about.

"Listen, I talked to my grandmother about it. I insisted. I even went to her house to dig around in her cabinet drawers. Mother told me that the photo must have been lost a long time ago. Even still, I looked. Nothing. I came to the conclusion that the photo must have never even existed."

"Maybe it's still in Grands Fonds?"

Marino shook his head sadly.

"I think my grandmother was just talking. That was her way of spitting in your face, on all of you, one more time, her way of avenging her sister's honor, as she put it. It was easier to hurt you than to hurt Hilaire. I think that she took pleasure in seeing you hope for all those years, of one day getting to see it."

"But surely you must have found other family photos?"

"A few. I took out all the old photo albums that I found in the apartment on rue Boisneuf, and I asked her to name the people in them, their names having faded on the reverse. She pointed out my uncles, my cousins, a load of cousins twice removed. But she never named your mother. I think that back then, they just didn't have the money to have their photos taken, or that they never thought to do it."

"Are you sure?"

"Very sure."

I knew he wasn't lying. I was distraught. The photo—the one that had kept me up for nights on end when I was a child, with my mother's features that I had dreamed of seeing one day, delicate like chalk—had not survived her death. I was left alone with this absence. Hilaire, Lucinde, and Antoine had their memories of her, reworked and embellished though they may have been. I had nothing: no keepsake, no echo of her voice in my ear. Not a single image of her, only a ragged tapestry of memories built on shreds of anecdotes from others who had known her.

Marino saw my face fall. Wanting to cheer me up, he invited me to a party that night. I had nothing else to do and it was better than listening to Lucinde complain about Tatar. I followed him.

That night, in a basement in Saint-Germain, I met your mother, Valérie. She was from northern France and had never seen the ocean.

Antoine: Second Departure

I SPENT THE ENTIRE NIGHT at Yvan's bedside. He lay unmoving on the armchair where I had awkwardly set him down. His pallor worried me, but I didn't dare go outside to find a doctor. He began moaning softly, so I blotted his forehead with an infusion of leaves I used to massage my sore feet. I figured it couldn't hurt.

The next day, in broad daylight, the protesters began hanging their flyers, painting their slogans, and raising their fists, but this time the army and the police were better organized. I heard bullets whistling by again like carpenter bees. I kept one foot inside, one foot outside. As soon as a suspicious car drove by, I pretended to be checking the metal curtain on my storefront. Above our heads, the beating of helicopters kept time. At the end of the day, the stories I had gleaned of neighbors from my doorstep were as inconsistent as they were troublesome; from mouth to ear, parents spread appeals for information about a son or a daughter who had disappeared.

Joyful music played on the radio, but there was no commentary about the turmoil—on to the next song. But in town, the authorities urged people to stay in their homes; even the countryside was becoming dangerous for those who insisted on risking gatherings. Rumors ran that the bodies of the separatists were floating in the harbor, holes in their stomachs. People simply passing by were being arrested and taken en masse to the police station. I pushed water between Yvan's tightly closed lips.

On the second night, since it looked calmer in the street, I left to go to a doctor at the end of the road whom I knew and who agreed to come back with me. He was an educated Martinican whom everyone respected. I explained what had happened.

He examined Yvan with precision and skill. After a long silence, I couldn't keep from asking if he would be okay.

Yvan's eyelids fluttered beneath the doctor's fingers. While the doctor inspected his wound, his swollen forehead, he said yes. I took out a poorly preserved cinnamon rum *shrubb* from Christmas from my pantry, and asked him about the situation in town. He gently answered, but did not look at me. He spoke with difficulty and thanked me, but did not touch the glass that I had set down next to him.

"The police arrested the ringleaders as well as activists who were not even in Pointe-à-Pitre yesterday. Many had been under surveillance for months, since the incident at the Sans Pareil in Basse-Terre. There are many wounded, and even more who have disappeared."

My unsettled expression must have saddened him, because he placed his hand on my arm and attempted a weak smile.

"This *ti-moun* here will thank you."

We went to my door and listened carefully. The road was deserted and he took the opportunity to leave. Instead of scurrying off like a cockroach along the wall, he set out walking slowly and straight, right smack in the middle of the road. A few months later, he went back to Martinique. I light a candle for him each time that I go to Sacré-Coeur because, even as of now, I have no idea if he is dead or still moving among poor fishermen like us.

In the middle of the second night, Yvan fully woke up. I had prepared a yam purée without butter for him, something substantial but dry, so as not to wear out his stomach. He forced himself to eat, and then insisted on listening to the news on the radio until morning, which didn't give us much to go on, like I was telling you. At dawn, I hugged him and he left, still unsteady on his feet.

Later on, I learned that Papa Mischief had looked for him the entire evening prior, despite the curfew, and that he had been caught. A month later, no one had seen him. His wife combed the hospitals on the island to see if he wasn't among the unidentified wounded. She didn't dare complain to the police because of Yvan, who was surely still in hiding. In the end, she was relieved that her children were all still alive.

If I had been a stronger woman, I would have found a way to inform Mischief that his son was safe. I was too empty-headed to think of it. Yvan never saw his father again. Maybe his battered body is rotting at the bottom of the Salée River, under the Gabarre Bridge.

AFTER THAT, life went pretty much back to normal. What I mean to say is that I would open my store as usual and that the customers more or less showed up. But the town was still recovering. People remained afraid. For my part, I feared being arrested one day simply because I had taken Yvan in for two nights. I had only just learned that he was one of the ringleaders of the young separatists on the island. None of that had interested me before then.

There was no question for me: *bon Dyé*, we were French!

Guadeloupe was France, as Hilaire and the people we elected proclaimed, just like my teacher in school drilled it into our heads, just like the story that the priest and the mayor of Morne-Galant had repeated to us our whole lives. In theory, we were all children of the Republic.

I could sense a sadness underlying the movements of every inhabitant of La Pointe. When I passed by the World War I memorial at the Place de la Victoire, the new bullet holes I saw left me distraught. At night, I slept poorly. Every night I had the same dream that would haunt me for years to come: Very high above my head, a *lambi* conch shell swung through the air continuously. Little by little, the shell turned into a comet with a pink tail. And the comet threatened to crash into us, into Man Pilote, who I saw sitting on dry land with her legs out in front of her like two dry tamarinds. I wanted to warn her, to shout to her to get out of the way, but she didn't hear me and sat there watching me, not moving. The red dot of the bindi on her forehead got bigger and bigger. But she was looking at me in pain. And then an uncountable number of hands rose out of the sea. They were holding a frothy wooden statue of the Virgin Mary, sliding it from hand to hand. I recognized it as the statue of the Virgin Mary from the procession that Lucinde and I followed when we were just little girls deep in Morne-Galant. I was trying with all my might to throw my coin into the lap of the Virgin Mary, like I had tried to do back then, but the fingers fanned out and blocked my way, and the Virgin Mary went farther and farther above the dark water. Among the open hands, I recognized Papa Mischief's hands—huge, strong hands that had lived through so much.

Oh là là, even just telling you about it makes my scalp tingle all over again with dread. I would wake up with my heart racing, my head buzzing. All I could do was rub my scalp until it bled, until it ached like it was in a vise. Feeling the pain would bring me back into the darkness of the room and out of my own thoughts. I would stay unmoving on my bed with heavy shoulders, my palms turned toward the ceiling. Every time, I would have to go over the events again and untangle them in order to hope to fall back asleep. From the outside, you would have thought I was a woman suffering for want of sex. Do you know how that goes? A woman without a man . . . But that's not what it was at all.

There were trials held for people who were caught by the police. France considered them dangerous instigators inciting *manjékochon*, chaos. Despite objections, the trials took place on the mainland, to avoid more riots, they claimed. In the more politicized trials, those who would have brilliantly pleaded their cases weren't allowed to speak. All of them, even the youngest ones, were sent to unknown prisons from which they wouldn't be released until their hair had turned gray.

On the island, it was impossible to count the number of people who'd died, but we know that it was more than the official count. In the street, we regarded each other with distress, as if the infected, darker sides of the island had been abruptly exposed.

What everyone already knew proved to be even uglier when it was illuminated by those events. Whites laid low but didn't relinquish any of their power. Blacks lowered their heads, incapable of creating a unified front.

Blacks, Whites, Indians, Chinese, Syrians—we knew we were all connected, mixed together, but we were ashamed of the *créolité* that was, however, the only reality, the island's only history. The mainland was turning into a lifeline: there, life would be easier; there, equality would be real. There, we could become civil servants and could take comfort in having a solid roof above our heads.

I went to church. I prayed for Papa Mischief and for his entire family. And then one day, I couldn't take it anymore. I knew my island inside and out. I no longer wanted to accept its landscapes of misfortune or its contradictions. I didn't want to wake up anymore with a start and live with my head like a grumbling volcano, like Soufrière, ready to blow. Armand was right. Like Lucinde, like Petit-Frère, and like so many others, I packed my bags and hurried off to the Raizet airport.

Antoine: France . . . Paris at Last

I ARRIVED at the Orly airport very early in the morning, at the end of the fall of 1968. The first fall of my life. I had only heard about this in-between season in poems at school that I had long since forgotten. A sharp little ray of sun illuminated the runways, and poplars seemed to orchestrate the tumbling of their vibrant leaves in unison against the airport roofs. I was struck by the way that nature on the mainland was kept at a distance, as though they wanted to see it only from afar, as though projected onto a huge screen. I exited the airport through the automatic sliding doors.

I let Lucinde know I was coming. I had sent her a hefty sum in advance so that she could find me a place to live in Paris.

Tatar was waiting for me, leaning against a blue Citroën DS that he was clearly very proud of. I would later learn that a part of my money had helped to pay for this car he bought on loan. He barely said hello and stuffed my bags in the trunk in a hurry. I asked him his news since moving to France a few years prior, but he only answered vaguely.

In the car, I clung to a small medal of Saint Rita that had been blessed three times, radiating her good energy for lost causes against my stomach. I prattled on about who knows what while I looked out the window. The fields in France are so big that they meld into one another into an infinite bland skyline, no contrasting colors, just a thousand shades between pale yellow and gray.

In that car, I felt tiny for the first time, like I was dissolving into the air, giving way to the tufa-stone-colored sky.

"Here, spread this across your lap," Tatar told me as he held out a large map in folds. I opened it but didn't read it. I wouldn't have understood a thing on that map. I had never needed one to know where I was going. But here, I was lost. Tatar could have taken me wherever he wanted; I would have had nothing to say about it.

"So where is it that I'm going to live?" I asked after a while.

"I found you someplace good," he said, nodding without taking his eyes off of the road, frowning. His driving was questionable but, once again, it wasn't my place to tell him how to do it; I had never touched a steering wheel.

After the airport, the car set out on a road lined with trees with golden-brown leaves. I read *A86* on a sign. It was a highway that straddled roads and houses and made me feel like we were moving forward on a flying carpet.

There was no one in sight, as though the landscape had been designed to disorient me. I gave up trying to understand the scenery—slate bell towers, short buildings that reminded me of the newer neighborhoods in La Pointe, red cranes, and little houses, some of them enclosed with their yards hidden behind hedges, others huddling together against the cold. They all seemed to be completely out of reach.

I saw concrete roads snaking between towers where balconies were stacked one on top of the other, much like the Tower of Babel described in the Bible. It occurred to me that in Guadeloupe, God had allowed us to invent Créole for us to understand each other, and it was probably what happened to Nimrod's builders, too. While we passed a giant construction site riddled with holes and surrounded with red-and-white construction tape, I imagined the supreme African leader Nimrod dressed in a toga, looking down from a sandy hillside onto the crowd of his builders. They were creating a magnificent city, all while joking in Créole. I almost shared my thoughts with Tatar, but he wouldn't have understood.

A fine rain dotted the windows of the car. We passed villages that all looked the same through the rainy curtain: Sucy-en-Brie, Pontault-Combault, Torcy. Then more departmental roads that crossed two-lane highways cutting through interminable flat fields that were crisscrossed with tractors trailing exhaust in the distance. In one hour, I saw more road signs than I'd seen in my entire life. I wondered when we would finally get to Paris.

The Citroën DS was moving along quickly and it made Tatar smile. He'd lit a cigarette. After a town that was called Lagny, we came to a village around lunchtime that was being beaten down by the storm.

"Here we are!" Tatar declared as he looked for a place to park.

"But how . . ." I said. "We're not in Paris."

"Paris? Are you out of your mind?" He forced out a little laugh. "With the money that you sent us, you could never live in Paris. You'll be much better off here."

We parked at the foot of a charmless building that was four or five stories tall, and that had been erected on a pitiful square of grass at an intersection with only a *tabac* and a driving school. I was stunned. If we hadn't made it into the capital, where was I? I couldn't find the words to even call Tatar names—an idiot, a lout—because I felt even more stupid than he was. I hauled myself out of the car in a stupor. He took out a small ring of keys from his pocket that he swung around his finger as he hurried to the entrance of the building.

THE APARTMENT was on the fifth floor with no elevator. After the brown-tiled staircase where our footsteps reverberated, Tatar put the smaller of the two keys in the lock. The door was the color of dried blood and looked like the entrance to a tomb. "The big one is for the basement," he told me like some kind of professor.

We walked into a dark vestibule that opened to a kitchen, the only room that had a bit of light, about fifteen square meters. The room had a window to the left with flaking paint and the walls had a fresh white coat. On either side of the central wall where an old cast-iron radiator clung were two little rooms: a bedroom to the right with a sink and a bidet, a tiny kitchen to the left with a window that faced a wall.

The toilets were on the landing. Everywhere there was an odor of chalky dust. The space was so sterile, it was hard to imagine that anyone had ever lived there before. According to Tatar, it had been occupied by an old couple who had moved out to the country.

I walked on the carpet that looked like a giant used doormat and I went to look out the window. Still no one in the street. Spirits didn't even live here. I took a big breath and turned to Tatar.

"So explain this to me, how you settled on this place? And how much did it cost me?"

"It's not bad, right? I paid three months in advance. You'll have to pick up the rent from there."

"You didn't pay anything at all," I told him, holding back

my anger. "I paid for it. But I told Lucinde to find me something in the city."

"You're in the city!"

"This? I wouldn't call this a city. It's not even a crossroads where we're from, not even a *carrefour à lolo*! There is nothing here but people sitting around betting on horses, and a bank! Do you think I left Morne-Galant to come to this desert?"

"Listen," he said, sitting on a bench covered in orange carpet between the wall and the radiator, "I did my best and got you a good deal as quickly as we could. Lucinde will tell you—"

"Has Lucinde seen this place?"

"No, she hasn't been here, but—"

"Lucinde hasn't seen it, then. And where do you both live?"

"In Champigny."

"Where is Champigny? Why aren't you in Paris?"

"It's right next door."

"So what about this place? Why is it far from everything? There wasn't even a little attic near where you both are? Lucinde told me you were well set up!"

He tried to hide how proud he was of their place. I understood the trick; this place he'd found for me must have been passed off for a low price without them even locating it on the map. It wasn't the apartment that disgusted me, but the soulless way of life that seemed to go with it.

Can you picture me in a place like that? I can't imagine who could possibly scrape by in this tumbleweed town. You could tell that not a single Antillean lived there. It looked nothing like the French countryside that I had seen in my schoolbooks, with the rooster on top of the bale of hay and the postman's bike, and definitely not like the *misié-dames* from the *grands boulevards* in Paris. It looked like an imitation of a city.

"Lucinde is always exaggerating," Tatar said, holding up his hands, trying to calm me down. "Champigny is fine, but we're not on the best side of town. It's full of Portuguese in the slums. And it's thanks to my job that we found it . . ."

I didn't understand anything he was saying since I had yet to find out that slums existed in France. And I wanted Paris or nothing. So I started screaming a whole slew of insults and reproaching him in Créole because I suspected that I wasn't going to get my deposit back or the three months of rent that I had paid in advance.

What was certain was that I wasn't going to stay despite the words Tatar flung my way, his "*sa ki ta'w ta'w*" that insinuated that I should have been happy with what I had. We went down the flights of stairs in a duet of curses that made a few noses spring out surprisingly from behind their coffin-like doors. Downstairs, I ordered him to take me to Lucinde. He didn't want to, but nevertheless opened the door, all the while spitting insults at me. I sat there *tchip*ing and I continued complaining while he started the car.

WE DROVE on the national road, and then the highway. I could see better out the window, and I was not at all reassured when I didn't see *Paris* on any of the road signs.

"You and Lucinde are absolutely worthless. Have you forgotten all I did for you back home? I was the one who got Lucinde her first job! And you who worked at Darboussier just last Christmas, now you fancy yourself bourgeois."

"Oh come on, who told you we were acting bourgeois?" Tatar answered weakly. "All of this fuss when we found you a nice place to live!"

"So where will I work?"

"You didn't even give it a chance. They have stores there. You could have applied to be a salesperson."

I nearly jumped out of my seat with rage. Me, a salesperson? The only job that I'd had since working with Man Pilote was being the boss. I'd love to see the first person to give me orders, ha! I retorted that he had better give me his car to pay me back for the money that he cost me. I called him a dumb rat and a bastard child, which really got a rise out of him.

We were on our millionth overpass that crossed over a bit of highway still under construction. He drove a few meters toward an exit and stopped the car right there. He got out, opened the trunk, methodically set my two suitcases and my purse on the ground. Then he turned the DS around and opened my door, ordering me to get out.

What else was I supposed to do? Well, I did the only thing there was to do, of course. I stepped out of the car like a queen.

Petit-Frère

ANTOINE CALLED ME from a pay phone. I had just left my job as an electrician to begin training to be a psychiatric nurse. I had found it almost by accident, reading through ads in the paper. The training was paid, the work was guaranteed when the program was over, and I felt, at least somewhat, like a student. Understanding the contradictions and the pain of other people—I think that was what I had been trying to do all my life. Hilaire, my sisters, and all of Antillean society had been quite the training ground. At that point, I was discovering that you could access the depths of the human mind with specific tactics and methods. I immediately became passionate about psychiatry. And it reminded me of what Papa Mischief had told me about Frantz Fanon, that as well as being an important thinker he was also one heck of a doctor. So I set out to be a nurse.

I wanted to make my own way in life. I had left Champigny to move in with Valérie in the sixth arrondissement. Lucinde had sewn her wedding gown. The ceremony took place at her parents' house in the North. We were expecting our first child.

Antoine explained her altercation with Tatar briefly on the phone. I figured out where she was and went to pick her up in the car we had just bought on credit. I pulled into a place on the outskirts of Chennevières, a wasteland being gnawed away by a city under construction. I parked and walked around the heaps of gravel, giant holes left by bulldozers, and teams of workers in helmets. I saw the tiny bistro where my sister had taken shelter, on the ground floor of a new set of buildings.

She was sitting in a dark corner of the room, facing the swinging doors. Seeing her there, I thought immediately of a live fish nailed to a wall. It was strange to see her outside of the environment where I normally saw her, far from the Catholic meeting places in Pointe-à-Pitre and the Saint-Antoine market. Nevertheless, she sat up straight and I was quickly reminded of her ability to twist reality to her liking.

She kissed my cheek warmly, chattering like a bird. We hadn't seen one another in four years. She told me the story of the apartment in the far-off suburb. I didn't need her to explain that it would have never worked out. I knew that Antoine's place was in the turbulent hearts of never-sleeping cities. She asked me to help her find something in Paris.

She went on to tell me about what had happened with Yvan. I felt myself turn to molten lead. I hadn't heard anything about those days in May of '67. I had been a part of demonstrations for the Prague Spring. I had fallen out with the communists. I had supported Plioutch at the Mutualité. Listened to Russian dissidents talk about the dark times and glorious hours of Soviet psychiatry. In '68, I had occupied the hospital where I worked, demanding more rights for the patients as well as the nurses. But I had heard nothing about May 1967 in Pointe-à-Pitre. No one was talking about it, especially not on the mainland.

Listening to Antoine's story, I imagined what Yvan and

Papa Mischief must have had to endure. For Antoine, it was above all a question of humanity; she had protected Yvan because, for her, he was just a kid. She had never been a revolutionary; she would have told off Angela Davis back then, and called bullshit on both the Gaullists and the communists. With time, she grew critical of protests, wanted law and order. But she is upright in heart and she saved my friend, that much is true.

A year earlier, after getting out of the army, I think that right away I would have looked for a ticket to Cuba and met up with Yvan, perhaps come to know the struggle at his side. But I had started down another path. A job that, at last, had been my own choice, a wife, your older brother on the way.

I never heard from Yvan again, and it weighs on my heart. Not even his family knows what became of him. A few secret letters from Havana and then nothing. But Yvan can't die, because I love him, and I don't know anything about what happened to him after his separatist network exfiltrated him to Cuba. Whenever I see an article or special report about Cuba, I look for him. Is he still alive? Will the waves return his bones and his secrets to the shores of a beach in Santiago or elsewhere, in Bolivia, in the Congo?

The first time that I went back to Guadeloupe, you were three years old. The first person that I went to visit was Yvan's mother. She wanted to give me a photo of Yvan, but I prefer keeping him with Eulalie, in the special place I'd created for them in the sanctuary of my mind. With Yvan at least, I can see him clearly. He's remained the boy who broke into my aunt's home—that heartless old woman—and he's still there, dancing to the sound of the *ka* after scaling her balcony.

Antoine: Wintering on Morne Montmartre

PARIS WAS WHAT I EXPECTED. Absolutely beautiful. Especially near Château-Landon, where I discovered a giant market that had everything. It was ten times the length of the Saint-Antoine market. With tomatoes, leeks, and fat lettuce like the kind that Mister Seguin's goat used to eat. Potatoes in giant crates. At first, I thought they were much less flavorful than our *madères*, but in the end I got used to them, and because fries are, of course, delicious. Kebabs and mint tea. And then Tati, where I have shopped now for ages.

I told Petit-Frère I wanted to live near Sacré-Coeur. It was the other place in Paris that bewitched me. We searched for weeks. I never tired of going up and down the stairs of the butte. In the end, it was your mother who found me a place through a rental agency. They had a commercial site and were renting it at an affordable price at the bottom of rue Poulet. It was perfect.

"But what will you do to get by?" Petit-Frère asked.

I was going to do what I always did! Sell merchandise. I was excited. But after a few weeks, I understood that it wouldn't be easy. First, I didn't have a lot of money. And second, I didn't know how to stock my store. Paris wasn't Guadeloupe; I couldn't board ships on Fridays and tour around the markets of the Caribbean. No junk vendors coming to stock up at my store to resell items in the country. Here, it was big grocery stores along the avenues and big chain stores once you hit the outer belt. Huge trucks driving around endlessly. I couldn't compete with my little store full of knickknacks tucked away in a corner of the city. Once I paid the first six months' rent in advance, I found myself seated in my tiny new place, not even another chair across from mine, with nothing but empty space that echoed, some running water, and a sink.

I wondered where I should start in order to get my footing. I searched my old memories—how had others figured it out, their heads held high after starting from nothing and against all the odds?

Thinking back to my start in the *faubourgs*, I remembered one of Man Dédé's stories. One Sunday, she took me to one of her friend's houses. A beautiful woman named Olympe. Not chatty, more soft-spoken if anything. She had very dark skin and was taller than other women, with strong arms. She had a lovely red madras tied around her head, which she always held high. What struck me was that she lived alone. And where, you want to know? In a magnificent place. One of those old windmills in Grande-Terre that we say are cursed because of the huge fig trees growing inside of them, strangling the stones in between their enormous roots and beheading most of them. Just looking at them gives you a feeling of redemption, seeing those windmills being suffocated by vegetation, mills that had been turned by the sweat and blood of hundreds of slaves. The Ezechiels, like other inhabitants of Grande-Terre, eyed them meanly and wouldn't go near them. There are still ghosts tied up in those ruins.

Olympe didn't care about that kind of superstition. She tore out the fig tree from her windmill, cleared out the courtyard all by herself, and fixed the roof. People said she was a Kongo; a descendant of those who had been brought to slave away on the island even after the official end of slavery, when trafficking was still taking place between Nantes and African kingdoms. They said that she spoke a language in secret that was not Créole, that she practiced strange rituals. The Kongos had always been rejected by the other *Nègres*. It was the same misfortune, though, that had brought them there, but they said that they spoke *wani wana* and that they were dirty people. Anyway, I think that she had first moved in out of necessity, before making it into an imposing tower surrounded by a magnificent garden, full of flowers and carpeted with sweetgrass. I was delighted by her after our visit, but when I asked Man Dédé how this beautiful woman made a living out in the middle of the country, she laughed and told me that Olympe was selling the factory workers her lovely plump *bonda*. Her life must not have been as pleasant as I thought. Either way, I admired her for her independence.

I WOULD SIT AT THE BACK of the Sacré-Coeur for the 6:00 p.m. and 10:00 p.m. masses. I observed. I felt confident because my fingers were tingling and voices were murmuring to me what to do. When nothing interesting happened, I would pray. The rest of the time, I would size up the people who came in: tourists, families having a good time (of no interest to me), women by themselves.

They were the ones I wanted to see. For two weeks, I categorized them in my mind: those who were too old, too well-dressed, those accompanied by others, and the rest. Those who were young, very lonely, with a sad or desperate air about them. One or two came per day. The only one I talked to was

Chantal. A sumptuous woman of twenty, soft skin and heavy hair in curls pinned back, the kind of blonde with hints of red that you don't see every day. Her eyelids were red and swollen when I sat down wordlessly next to her. She cried for about half an hour. She turned her head slightly toward me and then, to hide her face, leaned forward enough to rest her forehead against the wooden pew in front of her, as though she were falling asleep in the silence around her. I started talking to her softly. I had no problem getting her to lift up her chin to answer me; she needed me to, and wanted it.

Hers was a common story: the love of an older man that she fought with her parents for, parents who then kicked her out of the house. The man quickly left her. Impossible to go back home because of her shame and her father's violence. She came from Annecy. She never wanted to go back again.

We walked together to my store. I made her a good, warm soup and at that time I recalled what I had learned from the *quimboiseur*: low lighting, intense eye contact. All that was very natural for me. I comforted her for most of the evening. At nine o'clock, I suggested that we go to mass, but she was tired. So I told her that I would pray for her and I went back to church. She had the choice to either leave or stay, but when I came back a little before midnight, there she was, lying on my mattress, prettier than anything.

Chantal didn't want to work in a factory, or as a cleaning lady, not even in a department store. Very well. She wanted to help me at my store, but I told her how stupid that was:

"Look around you. Do you think that I'm in need of help right now? I'm lucky if I can find a reason to keep my hands busy the whole day. Business is tough."

She watched with a stubbornness about her as I hung two blouses on a rack. And then I cast out my line:

"A lovely girl like you could have all the money she wants without owing anything to anyone."

She seemed intrigued, so I went on.

"While we wait for my store to fill up, we can pool our strengths and our skills. You are lucky to have found me, and I can teach you things that will be of use to you later, when you'll want to go out on your own."

I asked her to come closer to the window and we rested our foreheads against the gray chiffon of the curtains. Half-hidden, we watched the street and the inimitable spectacle outside. We scrutinized the men walking by. We poked fun, we laughed, we compared our tastes. I spoke about the money we could pocket with her youth and beauty and my authority and the protection I'd gladly provide her. She was contemplative, but not scared or turned off by the idea.

I let her think about it for the rest of the day. She stayed glued to the window nearly the entire time, her knees curled into her arms and her feet in my slippers. When I brought her a nice salad that I had gone to buy at the market, she nibbled the leaves without taking her eyes off of the sidewalk.

The next day, we came to an agreement as though we were establishing the rules of a game: she would work when she wanted to in the street, and together we would convert the space into a little boudoir in the back of the store. I would always be there to make sure that no one hurt her. I would prepare her meals. Most importantly, I would manage the cash and write out pay stubs for her. She would give me half of what she made. We celebrated with red wine and then went to the Marché Saint-Pierre to buy something to cover the mattress.

"Out there, you will be known as Demoiselle Janvier," I told her.

"Mademoiselle Janvier? Why?"

"Because you look like the beginning of January, with its cool mornings that prick up the senses. And it's *Demoiselle*, not *Mademoiselle*. That's what we call a young woman in the Antilles who isn't married."

"Well there's no chance of that," she said as she shrugged.

OUR PLAN WORKED as though God himself had ordained it, and I thanked him for his divine mercy. Chantal and I, we got along very well. She was no princess; she didn't care about down pillows or fine china. We ate modest meals on a little table that I had found in the street. Meat and cooked vegetables made on a little portable stove. She left when the sun was high in the sky and I would see her walking slowly in the street. She brought back two or three men per day at the beginning. And then more. It didn't seem to bother her, but when she looked tense or when she seemed tired, I told her to take a break.

We quickly earned a bit of money and the first thing that I did was to send a sum to Man Pilote so that she could fill a shipping container of all the things that I used to buy at the Saint-Antoine market. When I opened the packages, I felt twenty years younger. I was ready to conquer the world once more.

I was nearing my forties. In the street, the men still looked at me as I went by. I paid no mind to the insults that older women or alcoholics spat at me from time to time, "*Sale Nègresse*," and, "Go back to where you came from." I would shop with my basket on rue Ordener or boulevard Ornano, where the Senegalese grocers would sell me the *musculine* that gave Chantal her energy, all with my little beret set on top of my bun that was starting to go silver. *Musculine* was an elixir that was hard to find. You had to either go to an abbey buried in the French countryside, or else find it from the Senegalese, who would hand it over with their blessings. You have to check the label, because sometimes it's fake stuff they're trying to sell you.

Thanks to word of mouth, I started to find the items I was looking for. When I wasn't even expecting it, the doorbell would ring; women from La Pointe or even Haiti would be there to sell me jewelry, bottles, and coffee that they had roasted there. The Senegalese spread out arrays of fine handmade leather shoes before me. Objects that you would still sell today at top dollar.

Later on, a few older residents of the neighborhood started to bring me their trinkets. One woman sold me her collection of corsets and embroidered handkerchiefs. I appraised it all, taking stock, and I offered my price. I was in my element. I made sure that Chantal had a quiet little spot to herself.

We earned our living nicely together. But I never meant it to last. At the first police scare, I ended it all. Besides, my shop was launched; whatever happened, I could survive. Chantal found a lover and told him she worked for me as a salesperson. And would you believe it, now I am her eldest son's godmother.

Lucinde

IT WAS FORTY YEARS AGO, but I still remember it. I still have the scars, thank you very much. Antoine came at me like a cannonball and knocked me right over. At first, I tried to defend myself, and then I rolled into a ball on the floor of her store to protect myself from her blows. Your aunt, she is a real hellcat. I still cannot believe she has uterine cancer. Her uterus was never good for anything, how ironic is that. I prefer laughing about it as you can see; otherwise I'll start crying.

I had shown up one morning in Montmartre to see how she was getting along. There was this girl living with her back then. Stretched out on an old couch they had found somewhere, she was petting two long-haired dogs that started yapping something fierce when they saw me. Can you imagine? Two women and two hysterical dogs in that tiny apartment with no windows at the back of the store. A ghastly smell hit you in the face.

Antoine had just slid the bolt of the door to the shop closed. Through the window, passersby could see the inside, and I can tell you that they stopped mostly out of curiosity about all the dusty things lying around inside: veiled hats, tattered leather gloves . . . I noticed that she had set out a maternity dress to sell that I had given to her years before. A dress that I gave to her, I'm telling you, for her to eventually use, not sell! I had crocheted it in a canary-yellow cotton and the dress was basically new. I made the mistake of mentioning that to her that day. She started laughing, calling me Brigitte Bardot with my fancy ways and the company that I kept, and then she lost it because she thought that I was looking down on her friend, that I was criticizing her dogs and on and on, *nanni nannan.*

Because I wasn't putting up with it, she lunged at me and I ended up on my back. Luckily, the girl pulled us apart because otherwise Antoine would have beaten me to a pulp.

For ten years at least, I almost never saw her. We would call each other from time to time. When she came to see me at work at the Palais de Justice, one out of every three times I would have people tell her I was out. Given the way she looked, my colleagues thought she was coming to ask for legal aid.

After Tatar and I divorced, I lived alone with my daughters. Until they were eighteen, he paid child support more or less when it suited him, that is to say four times a year, just about. And then nothing. He felt it was enough to accompany them to Guadeloupe from time to time. It was still up to me to pay for their plane tickets, and you know how much those cost. He kept the place in Champigny and moved our maid in with him and got her pregnant. The very woman who I was kind enough to bring with me when we left Pointe-à-Pitre. I wasn't mad at her; she had simply always lived off of my leftovers.

SEE, I LOOK BACK AT ALL THIS, our entire history, and I can see clearly that I missed out on something. In the end, I struggled by myself to raise my daughters, and I never found anyone to rebuild my life with. I still sew a bit, but I never did what I had actually wanted to do with my life. It's Papa's fault for not taking care of us. It's your father's fault since we had to raise him without Eulalie. I used to weep in anger over it. Antoine and I were made for glory. What happened?

Antoine kept on like that, coming to see me once in a while. I couldn't begin to tell you how exactly she made a living. She continues to not care about her appearance or what people think of her. At over seventy, she is still beautiful. She's my older sister, and I refuse to watch her go. That cancer of hers, she'll surely wrap it around her little finger and send it packing, you can bet on it.

Petit-Frère

THE FIRST YEARS in Paris, Antoine seemed to take up her old habits. At least from what I could tell from afar, as I didn't go to see her much anymore—it required too much of me. She managed to re-create the same pigsty that she had back in Pointe-à-Pitre. I would barely listen to her far-fetched stories as I looked over her shelves. Fruit liqueurs, neckties, a collection of discount perfumes, exactly the same as what she had sold there, with colorful labels and kitschy names: Follow Me, Open to Love, Guilty Pleasure. It was an entire arsenal—curios and false treasures, an avalanche of amber liquids, a heap of brass trinkets in all shapes and sizes, glossy shells and molded plastic knickknacks, fascinators made of paper, and brooches made of pearly polymer—a disorganized cache that dated further and further back in time, behind which she hid herself away with her dogs and her rigid ideas. At one point, I advised her to buy her store instead of renting it perpetually, and I think that's what she did in the end.

Over time, the customers dropped off and Antoine became a curiosity for the tourists; a creature in her authentic state, a part of "the real Paris" that flaneurs were happy to discover. She had tricks up her sleeve that were more or less profitable. One time she got mixed up with the people at the rum distillery on boulevard Saint-Germain. You can imagine what she would have tried to rope them into. She had a falling-out with the owners and their business relationship didn't last.

She would close the store as she pleased, as soon as she felt the hours were too long or the day too gray. Sometimes she would find a plane ticket to go back to the Antilles and show up at Papa's house. On the phone, he'd tell me that she was worse than all the hurricanes that he'd ever had to endure. Antoine doesn't have any real ties anymore. She is at home in her store, at a church, and with her freedom. Paris or Pointe-à-Pitre, what difference does it make? When she left the island in 1968, she left her store on rue Schoelcher as it was—I don't know if she even locked it when she left. She never went back to see what had become of it.

WHEN I TAKE HER to the hospital for her treatments, I recognize that she is the only one of us who has stayed true to what we were at the beginning. She never diverged. To this day, she remembers the first names of our Ezechiel first cousins many times removed, whose names I had only ever vaguely heard. For her, the past and the present dance in the same golden bubble. Sometimes she catches my arm and says to me with determination, "I have to get my store ready to reopen." I don't know if she's referring to the one in Paris or to back in Pointe-à-Pitre.

For Antoine, it all still exists: Eulalie on Hilaire's arm, the snobby expressions on the faces of the Lebecqs, the baby that was never born but whom she baptized all the same, Man Pilote huddled in the heat of the city center, the *soukounians*, the steer with glowing rays of light, Hilaire all alone, a hundred years old now, sitting on his stool in front of his house, even Armand's pale eyes, even Papa Mischief.

And yet, she will never go back. None of us will. She tells me, "I can't stand the heat anymore. It hurts my head." And I think that she'd yearn for Montmartre, its dirty roads around Château-Landon and the herbs she buys on boulevard Ornano and then forgets at the bottom of a plastic bag.

We did what we could for our children. We left our island and our parents behind. Soon it was no longer a question of going back. The banlieue,* the place that you can't decide if you love or if you hate, that was our home, a place of forgetting one's origins and indifference. A liberating kind of detachment. We agreed to come here. You can say that I left one nowhere for another nowhere, but I've grown used to it.

I walk the length of the man-made lake where joggers pass by in the red sunlight. As I go by, ducks cackle and moorhens hide in the tufts of reeds. In the distance, the buildings turn pink in the shimmering light. Toward Paris, the sky grows heavy with exhaust fumes. I no longer have the body I had as a boy, but I'm not an old man yet. I keep in shape. My running shoes came from the big specialty store next to the tennis courts on the south side of town.

Of course this banlieue is bleak and empty,† with its

* Note from the author: The banlieues are not ghettos, just drab places on the outskirts of Paris, built quickly to be functional housing for lower-middle and middle classes. These are unlike U.S. suburbs where the rich live; they are characterized by dull strip malls and government housing. Antilleans are able to make a life here, but they must forget where they've come from and fall into a kind of anonymity, far from their tropical home culture.

† Note from the author: This feeling of emptiness is because the large buildings are all identical with straight roads and trees set in straight lines, the opposite of the more charming city centers like Paris with twisting roads and well-lived-in houses like in the Sacré-Coeur neigh-

science-fiction landscape, its opaque facades, and all that aluminum endlessly reflecting the cloudy skies for eight months of the year. All this space is what I need to house the tears and blood that I haven't shed, don't shed, will not shed.

I can take the metro to go to the theater. I took you often. I wanted you to know early on what I had to work hard to get, what I had to earn. There are a lot of Antilleans in the city. I helped a few come over; childhood friends looking for a place to land, cousins, Martinican colleagues. I don't see them very often.

At the hospital, the other nurses liked me. I loved standing up for our interests at the ministry and talking about the union, and justice, and improving conditions for the patients. I was noticed, promoted. Those who liked me the least were Antilleans. They would have liked for me to be advocating for them in particular, instead. I didn't agree. It's all of us or none of us. What I wanted was justice. So they said that I was a *négropolitain* and after all I had married a White woman. I didn't care and I was passionate about my work. They thought I was condescending. According to them, I had forgotten where I had come from. In reality, it's just the opposite.

We no longer belong to Guadeloupe, but even so, I bought the plot of land just behind Hilaire's house. I built a little house there, despite the difficulty of all the paperwork at such a huge distance. It took us ten years to do it, your mother and I. So there must be something left of Guadeloupe in the deep recesses of my heart.

---

borhood where Antoine lives. In the banlieues of Paris, there are many people, but there is a feeling of emptiness because there is little social activity since people take the metro to work and return in the evening only to sleep.

*Antoine: Kimbé Red, Pas Moli**

NOW THE EZECHIELS AND LEBECQS ARE SCATTERED between Guadeloupe and the mainland, anchored in Morne-Galant, living in Paris just outside the *périférique*, the outer belt or even farther, in Belgium or elsewhere. That, I know. And I know that Hilaire loved some of his grandchildren and would love the others as well if they hadn't been far-off with names he didn't know. Since the thousands of people left in the 1960s, Antilleans have become as numerous on the mainland as they are on the islands themselves. Some will remain attached to their homeland; others will be like rocks scrubbed by water and salt—no residue at all.

We Antilleans have always known how to adapt, haven't we? From inside the slave quarters all the way up to the public housing, we know what it means to survive. But you won't find a close-knit community among us. Listen, the only people I confide in are the saints who talk to me through the tingling in my fingers. And Lucinde has two women at war inside her head: a fearful *Négresse* who complains about being poor, and a White aristocrat who despises the *Nègres*. I don't know how she deals with it, but it does tire her out. Your father decided

---

* *kimbé red, pas moli*: common Créole expression of encouragement: Stay strong, hang in there.

that the most important thing was the poor at war with the rich. But he certainly knows that the poor are capable of fighting viciously among themselves over the tiniest thing, and it's been that way ever since the rich mastered the trick of pitting us against each other. In Guadeloupe, it was the mulattoes taking the side of the White masters who were against the *Nègres* and the Indians, and then the educated *Nègres* against the *Nègres* in the *faubourgs*, and it goes on and on until the owner of three chickens thinks he is Whiter than someone with only two.

I hear that now many Whites from France are moving to Guadeloupe because they think that their lives will be better in the sun. They might make it, the ones who are clever enough to end up on the side of those in power, instead of the weak ones. The ones who don't will end up on the beach drinking bad rum with their Black brothers. It seems they're even drinking beer there now. Beer! What does your mother have to say about that? I'm not ignorant, I know that where she's from in the North, they brew the best beer in the world. In Guadeloupe, do you think that bargain beer is actually any good, getting warm in that sun? *Awa* . . . Definitely not.

COME CLOSER. Don't worry. For the illness I have, nothing is better than grapefruit. You buy them nice and yellow and almost bitter like *chadeks* from Martinique, not those giant orange balls, too sweet, that come from Florida. You cut off the white pith on the inside and steep it in some water. Maman drank that every Sunday. Don't tell me its cancer, all of that is *bitin à Blancs*, just White people's nonsense. I'm not going to slip away just like that. As soon as I'm better I'm going to open a little store.

So tell me, is it getting clearer for you about us and our lives over there? The true kingdom is in heaven, though; don't laugh—I'll be praying for you, because even if you don't know it, you're a good Christian woman. I make sure of it, with all those masses that I offer for your salvation and for your father's too, and all the other nonbelievers in our family.

Well of course I didn't want to go back to live in Guadeloupe. To do what? I hear that your brother has gone to live there, in Morne-Galant. Well, there you go, that's the cycle starting over again. His son is quite cute. He may have light eyes and blond curls, but he's a real *ti-moun* from Guadeloupe. Just look at the tips of his fingers, where the nail starts. The skin is still a little dark. Same with his little hazelnuts and the crumpled skin around his winkle. A *chabin* baby is always *Nègre* in those places.

And you, my girl, give it some time, God alone knows where your children are going to end up.

I WENT TO SEE ANTOINE at the hospital from time to time, taking turns with Petit-Frère and Lucinde. My father had her list out all the names in the entire family and then the names of their mutual acquaintances, allowing Antoine to revel in her still-excellent memory. Lucinde contributed chocolates and a list of complaints about the showers, the meal trays, the housekeeping—and goodness knows what else—that she submitted in a huff to the nurses' station. It was her way of preparing herself; Antoine had explained to her what color she wanted to be dressed in on the day that she died.

I had long since stopped asking the three of them any questions. I had drunk up their stories and their silences eagerly, as though something important was about to be lost, a mythical time from before I was born. I had mined my notes, constructed a story that held up but felt shaky, and read and reread my work. I still hadn't shown them anything. They knew I was doing research on our family, but they didn't follow up with me after all was said and done, after they had shared everything so openly. It was as though modesty prevented them from asking what I had done with their secrets, or as though having spoken to me at all was more than enough.

I didn't want to see Antoine get worse. The last time that we spoke, she was calm, sitting in her bed, her head resting against two white pillows. Not knowing what to talk about, I sat next to her and went back to my line of questioning from ten years earlier.

"What did you name the baby?"

"Ki ti-moun?"

"The one that Eulalie was carrying when she died."

"I'll tell you the next time you visit. Let's say on Saturday?"

"Why Saturday?"

"Because I'll still be alive next Saturday, and beyond that who knows. I can't go before market day. We'll visit Château-Landon, like the first time you came over, and we'll buy guavas."

"But the doctors won't let you leave to go to the market. I'll bring the guavas."

"And you will plant the seeds where I tell you."

"Those seeds won't grow in Paris."

"Next to Papa's house, there was a giant tree. Lucinde and I would climb to the very top."

"Do you miss the *jardins créoles* you had back then?"

"One always needs a *jardin créole*, my dear! No Antillean standing in front of even a centimeter of earth can just sit there and not plant something. It's our way of *marronner** a little bit over the heads of Whites. But do you know what a *jardin créole* is, exactly?"

I paused before answering. I thought back to the hill where Hilaire dug his sloping furrows into the loamy soil.

---

* *marronner*: Before abolition, *Nègres marrons* was the term used to describe slaves who fled to the hills of the jungle to escape.

"It's a tiny spot where you grow medicinal plants, food to nourish the body, and flowers as a feast for the eyes. You mix the species on purpose to protect them from disease."

Antoine smiled when she heard my description.

"That's right. For island people, it's both a pharmacy and a food safe. But they're not only that. Why do you think that men and women alike all hurry off to spend time in their gardens? Even those who live at the center of town, as soon as they can, they get a hold of a little piece of land outside of the walls where they live. Because in that soil where everything grows so easily, that is where we bury our troubles. Every little worry from the day. And then we talk to our ancestors who dug into the same soil before us. It would be good for you to have a *jardin créole* also."

"I don't know where I could have one, Antoine. We're too far from Morne-Galant."

"Wherever you can manage one."

I looked at the pale sun through her window and I smiled.

"I could have one in my mind. A lovely messy jumble. Like you."

She seemed a little irritated, so I changed my approach.

"Listen," I told her, "you're right. Even now, I could have already created one around me. Where I live is very special. Full of people, all of them different from one another, mixed together. Rich, poor, young, old. That's what you loved about living near Sacré-Coeur, isn't it? It's not really that way up near the basilica anymore, but you see it in other neighborhoods. My neighborhood is still in harmony like that, full of life. I couldn't live anywhere else but in a *jardin créole*. I get that from you. We're freer when we are in the middle of the spectacle of this world."

"The spectacle of this world. That's quite an idea. It is a lovely spectacle. I played my part, then, *petite*. I'm happy. So I'll see you next week?"

"Yes," I said.

And then I stroked her thick, gray hair.

• • • • • • • • • • • • • •

Acknowledgments

FROM THE AUTHOR

Thanks to Liana Levi for her trust and her listening ear.

Thanks to Sandrine Thévenet for her attentiveness, her encouragement, her rereadings, and her unfailing enthusiasm.

Thanks to the women at Liana Levi for their warmth, their energy, and their love of authors.

Thanks to Denis, my abiding sentry, my first reader, my most precious confidant.

FROM THE TRANSLATOR

My thanks go to France's Centre national du livre and the Collège international des traducteurs littéraires. Insights by François-Olivier Chené, Michael D'Arcy, Jennifer Sinnott, Chris Kelly, the FSG editorial team, and Estelle-Sarah Bulle were invaluable as this book was being brought into English.

A Note About the Author

Estelle-Sarah Bulle was born in Créteil, France, in 1974 to a West Indian father and a Belgian mother. She studied in Paris and Lyon and now resides in Val-d'Oise, France. *Where Dogs Bark with Their Tails* is her first novel and was awarded the Prix Stanislas and the Prix Carbet de la Caraïbe et du Tout-Monde.

A Note About the Translator

Julia Grawemeyer is an American educator, translator, and writer whose translations have been published by Schaffner Press and the *Kenyon Review*. She teaches French and intercultural communication to middle school students in Columbus, Ohio.